BLUEHOLE

by
J. D. SHOOK

To Nancie,
Hope You Enjoy.

To L. M. Robbins (Pete), whose edits, rewrites, and lifetime friendship made this book possible.*

Bluehole was our secret place. A place of lore and mystery. Just beyond imagination, it was a lure to every teenage boy who loved to fish. Yet Bluehole was real; one of the larger pools punctuating the sinuous course of Ten Mile Creek. About ten miles long, this waterway erupted from a limestone spring just north of town and, gaining stature, meandered through land bordered by farm and forest until it eventually emptied into a larger creek which merged with the Trinity River some fifty miles south of Dallas. Bluehole lay almost exactly in the middle of its route. Over the years, many had talked about the fabulous body of water. But very few had been there. We knew where it was and tried to keep its secret to ourselves. We simply didn't want others, including our classmates, "muddying" the water. Call it selfish, but then what other characteristic could you so readily attach to teenage boys?

* Of course he's still cattle.

SUMMER BEFORE

It was a strange Texas spring, with dark May mornings and heavy rains. By summer Ten Mile Creek was filled to overflowing...and we knew that somewhere in the murky depths of Bluehole, the Monster awaited...

My feet were stuck. Instinct screamed for me to tear through the undergrowth, up the steep bank and into the adjoining pasture where nothing on two legs, and precious little on four, had a prayer of catching me. Instead, I stood paralyzed, eyes glued on the brushy far side creek bank, desperately trying to identify the thrashing that had sent our pulses racing. A quick glance revealed that Pete too was riveted on the opposite shore.

"What the hell?" He muttered hoarsely.

Sweat was streaming down our bare torsos, soaking cutoff jeans and running into our tennis shoes; two fifteen-year-old boys petrified with fear. Yes, *what the hell? Too large for a bird or squirrel.* That sudden, violent crashing in the brush. *Not noisy enough for a cow.* Whatever it was, it had interrupted an argument began a month before...a fantasy I had nurtured and continued by painting what I hoped was an irresistible picture.

"Think how great it will be floatin' down the cool, green water, fishin' holes we can't get to from the bank. There's no tellin' what we're liable to find."

" 'Bout what we always find."

"We could float all the way down to Bluehole."

"We can walk there now."

I shook my head. "Pete, the way you walk is the problem. You stomp around and scare the fish."

"Horseshit!"

"It's true! Brim are skittish."

"You are so full of it. Since when you a brim expert? An' what about you singin' 'Little White Cloud That Cried' at the top of your lungs?"

"My singin' don't bother the fish."

"Well it bothers me; an' that song. You ever listen to the words? Sounds like a fairy. An' I guarantee you the fish hate it much as me."

"Why do you always call Johnny Ray a fairy? You don't know. Anyway, with a raft we can glide right up to the best spots."

"Glide my ass! Rafts *make* noise bumpin' into stumps 'n things."

"But the brim don't hear it 'cause they're underwater."

"Sound carries underwater, nitwit. An' how we gonna' steer the thing? Goddamn, if you don't win the dummy prize!"

"Would you please stop takin' the Lord's name in vain?"

"It ain't vain, Don, it's on account of your idiot raft idea."

"Pete, we need a raft, and we're gonna' have one!"

"What we're gonna' have is more trouble'n we know…"

"Trouble? What trouble could there be with a raft? Where is your imagination…your sense of…"

Without warning, the crash came. I wheeled toward the far bank, heart thumping in my chest. "Sssshh…" Pete urged with a signal for silence. Momentarily frozen, we scanned the undergrowth…

In the damp stillness there was only the buzz of insects against the current's soft burble. We looked for the telltale shaking of a branch, a thin sapling bending unnaturally, a spastic rustling of leaves. But even our sharp, young eyes revealed only thick, green foliage and thorn bramble.

Awakened from a shaded slumber, our canine buddies stirred, heads lifted, nostrils flared to sift the vagrant air currents. Fuzzy assayed a tentative 'Woof!' and a subterranean rumble issued from Jeff's massive chest. Finally, Pete snorted, "Prob'ly a coyote."

"That was no coyote! Daddy says they only run at night and they're silent as death unless they scare somethin' up and all start yappin'. Anyway, those dogs would *really* be all riled if it was a coyote."

"All right, a cow then."

"Nah…wudn't a cow. They're clumsy. They're…"

"Well, what then? Man with a hook?" He laughed nervously, the attempt at urban legend levity betrayed by his white-fingered grip on a hatchet handle. I knew he was scared, as scared as me. Pete was not that hard to read.

We lived on the edge of town a block apart, separated by a vacant lot. With a helping wind, I could sail a flat rock into his back yard. We became inseparable friends during the winter of seventh grade, soon after my family moved from Dallas. Pete was taller than me and a bit heavier. His dark eyes and generous mouth were accentuated by an olive complexion which made him appear older than his fifteen years. My tanned, "ruddy" skin highlighted bright blue eyes, uncommon in a family tree that bequeathed a swagger to my walk. Brown hair framed our ready smiles and we shared a flair for the dramatic. Our imaginations were rich and fertile, nurtured by an inordinate passion for reading. Jack London was my favorite, he doted on the "Tarzan" tales of Edgar Rice Burroughs.

Every friendship is a partnership of sorts. In ours, I had the grand ideas and they always tended to involve considerable labor…which Pete went to great lengths to avoid. He would have been satisfied to fish until he was tired of it, then daydream on the bank; but once I conjured my vision of floating Ten Mile Creek on a raft, I was determined to build one and would not yield easily.

"You ever build a raft?" he asked, already knowing the answer.

"Nah, but it has to be simple. All we have to do is cut down some trees, trim off the branches, brace 'em up, an' tie 'em together."

"Simple? Brace up what with what?"

"Didn't you ever read Huckleberry Finn?"

"I done forgot more about Huckleberry Finn than you'll ever learn."

"So you know we can do it," I stated, as if I had proven something.

"I know you know as much about buildin' a raft as I know about buildin' an atomic bomb. An' that was the Mississippi River, dummy, not Ten Mile Creek!"

"What's the difference? Water's water an' trees are trees."

He regarded that remarkable logic quizzically, then brightened. "What's wrong with your dad's little boat?"

5

He didn't know it, but I'd already considered Daddy's boat. He had built a small craft that fit on the roof of the car, and I had timorously advanced the idea that Pete and I might use it. The answer had been emphatically negative, extending to questions I should have thought of such as, "How would you get it back to where you started?" That eventuality had not dawned on me, and I elected not to pursue it because it could not be handily resolved; but there would be no admission of such an obvious oversight to Pete.

"Pete, that ol' boat's all rickety, an' it leaks. An' besides," I posited sagely, "how would we ever get it down to the creek?"

"Put some wheels under it and tow it with our bikes?"

"Are you outta' your mind? A raft's the answer. We don't need a motor n' we can steer it with long poles. That's how you steer rafts anyway." He studied me with weary intent, then uttered a long sigh, which I knew signaled acquiescence.

We required tools and Daddy had every tool imaginable, but I wasn't allowed near them unless he was supervising. Even then, he was impatient and unfailingly critical. A man of few words or associates, his tools were friends accumulated throughout his life. He was thoroughly familiar with each and treated them with great respect. After considerable agony and knowing the dangerous ground I was treading, I decided to borrow them without asking. That included the treasured blonde-handled hatchet Pete held as he continued looking over his shoulder across the creek. I deduced that he was still as nervous as I was …

"Well," I said, finally breaking the silence, "It would take a pretty good-sized critter to get through stuff that thick."

"You've heard the stories."

"Beast of Ten Mile?"

"Comes down to water from the cedar breaks."

"Aah… just another cock'n bull story. The only beast down here is the one in Bluehole."

Pete beamed, "Yeah, the King, the Whopper, the Very Brim of Very Brims."

"The Monster!" I almost shouted.

"You reckon he's really big? I never seen a monster brim."

6

"Well, Uncle Johnny said he gutted one once that'd swallowed a half-pound perch."

"Come on, brim got these little bitty mouths."

"Daddy says bluegills can go over three pounds."

"I'll believe that when I see it!"

"Or it could be a warmouth. They have big mouths, like a bass."

"Reckon Uncle Johnny mighta' been into the giggle water? Like I said, I'll believe it when I see it."

"Uncle Johnny don't drink, he's Baptist. An' you'll see it real quick 'cause I'm gonna' catch him soon as we finish this thing 'n get down there." I walked toward a stack of logs I'd set aside to be trimmed. Pete didn't move.

"Hell, Don it's hotter'n a eight page bible. We could be home in the shade, sippin' iced tea."

"Let's just get on with it." I said impatiently, unrolling a length of 3/8 inch rope I'd also helped myself to from Daddy's tool-locker. As usual, I tackled tasks straightaway. Pete, on the other hand, had perfected procrastination. So I wasn't surprised when he plopped down in the shade of a nearby pecan tree.

"Why don't we just go catch some fish?" He grumped. "It's way too hot for this, an' I ain't havin' any fun. You always have to go an' complicate things."

"Come on," I persevered, "let's get back to work."

Just moving was work. There was no breeze and the humidity hung heavy. With the ground still soggy from recent rains, we slopped through mud that sucked at our shoes. To make things worse, we were ravaged by mosquitoes and great clouds of gnats flew up our noses and lodged in the corners of our eyes. I remained nervous about whatever we'd heard and continued to sneak an occasional peek at the far shore. Pete seemed to have forgotten the incident.

"Jeeezus, Don!" his whining litany continuing, "It's hot as a whore's dream down here!"

"Stop with the cussin', damnit!" I snapped, increasingly exasperated. "Why don't you just shut up, and help me tie these together?"

7

"Hot as a fresh fucked duck an' we's choppin' down all these stupid trees. This whole deal is crazy anyways," he muttered as he slapped murderously at the back of his hand, leaving a flattened mosquito and a generous blot of dark blood.

"Pete, don't you know anything worth doin' is worth some effort?"

"Well, that depends on what I'm doin' n' how much effort. An' I dunno' what I'm doin', and the effort it's took already is way too much."

I sighed, "Such a whiner."

Pete flicked away another blood-bloated mosquito. "Honest, whatta' y' reckon made that noise over there?"

"You heard the same stories as me." I answered, visually inspecting the far bank.

"I don't believe everything I hear."

"Yeah, but what if they're true?" I continued, laying out several logs to tie off.

"No way. They're just stories."

"Well, stories or not. Let's get to work. I don't want to be down here too late."

"You scared whatever it is ain't gone, ain't ya?"

"No." I lied, refusing the bait. "I just don't want to be down here at night."

"Yeah, our folks'll really be pissed if we get home after dark."

"So shutup'n' help me finish!" I grabbed the hatchet and walked briskly in the direction of some saplings. I cut down a few while Pete returned half-heartedly to tying off the ones we'd already trimmed. I was finished before he completed two rows.

"Crap!" I yelled, yanking the rope away from him. "Fuzzy 'n Jeff are better help than you, and they're dead to the world. Look at 'em!" Both dogs were stretched out in the shade of the near bank. "There's nothin' more worthless than collies."

"Like tits on a boar." Pete grunted, inspired to finish another limb. Sweat dripped from his forehead like a faucet with a fast leak. "We could trade 'em." He teased.

"For Dalmations maybe?"

8

"Or a couple o' fat little flop-eared Cockers."

"Or chahoowahoowas, like old lady Burbridge's."

"That's cha-wa-wa, idiot!" he chortled, "an' her name is Chiquita, an' if you point your finger at her, she'll squat right there and piss…and that hacks old lady Burbridge off somethin' fearful."

"Yeah," I laughed, "anything but collies!"

The reference to collies was an inside joke. Cindy, our little bitch that threw their litter, was a pedigreed collie, and I'd witnessed her mating with Rudi, a large neighborhood collie that we knew had papers. We assumed that when the pups arrived they'd be pureblood. The joke was on us. Five of the seven were plainly collies, but Fuzzy and Jeff were startling anomalies. Overhearing our attempts to puzzle that out, Pete's dad patiently explained that a litter can have more than one sire, and that Cindy had obviously not held to the mating with Rudi. We considered that weighty information and came to suspect that a huge, free roaming chow was their sire. As they matured, we grew increasingly certain of it.

Pete's pup, who he named Jeff, grew into a big rust-colored dog with a collie's peculiar folding, or "tulip" ears and symmetrical build…only at close to eighty pounds, he was heavier than the biggest collie. It sorely vexed Pete that I refused to name my puppy Mutt.

Fuzzy was perpetually happy and called to mind Jacob's coat of many colors. His ears flopped to either side of his huge head, and his conformation could best be described as "irregular". He was a little heavier than Jeff; a burly mishmash of gray-black-brown-bronze-blonde buffoonery.

Where we went, they went - if they happened to be around - since leash laws were non-existent and most dogs ran loose. If we left without them they usually tracked us down. Pete and I came to understand that dogs intuit remarkably well; and neither of us was surprised that they considered us, our parents, and our siblings a single family unit to whom they felt equally responsible. They snoozed into late afternoon as we finished our craft.

"Looks good to me." Pete said, tying the tools up in a bundle, glad to be finished.

"Good? It looks great! Let's get her launched."

The dogs briefly raised their heads. *Insane!*, they must have thought, before settling back down.

With knotted muscles rolling under slick, sweaty hides, and feet digging for purchase in the slippery slime, we heaved and pulled until our heavier-than-expected craft finally slid to the edge, then eased into the water.

"Hot dog!" I shouted, immediately jumping in, grabbing the raft and stabilizing it against the surprisingly swift current. Near the bank, the water was only waist-deep but it dropped off quickly. I tested the bottom ooze...squishing it through my toes. It was comfortable and cool, but the bubbles that rose to the top carried the stench of ancient rot. Fuzzy and Jeff grew curious about our activity and ambled over toward us.

"Hand me the gear!" I yelled.

Pete handed me two double half-hitch rigged cane poles and a small tackle box.

"Now the tools." I instructed, placing our gear on the raft.

"Well, by your fuckin' leave, sir!" he said, handing me a bundle secured to one corner of the raft while ignoring my usual scowl at his profanity. I placed the bundle on the raft and Pete eased himself into the water.

"Ain't this great?!" I shouted. "How's she look?"

"Like the Queen Mary. Fine, I guess. Let's get on board."

I hesitated. "Where's the bait?"

"Bait?"

"Yeah, the salt pork. We can't catch fish without bait, dummy."

"Well, it was right here...with the...rest of the stuff I handed..."

Staccato barking erupted from the bank.

"Them sonofabitches!" Pete roared, "They must'a et it!"

"Ate our bait? Ate the salt pork?" I moaned. "Why didn't you watch 'em?"

"Me? I got some sort'a patent on dog watchin'? Why didn't *you* watch 'em?"

I sighed heavily, glaring at him. "Well, don't worry about it. We'll just catch some crickets."

10

"Never mind the crickets." He grunted as he struggled to keep his end of the raft from sweeping away with the current. "I'm losin' this thing!"

"Well, let's get on then. But you shoulda' watched the dogs." Pete rolled his eyes.

As we hoisted ourselves onto the raft, it immediately became obvious we had miscalculated. Instead of riding high and handsome on the gently flowing creek, we were barely afloat. In seconds, we weren't even that…the water was up to our shoelaces; and the raft, now fully into the current, was slipping out from under us. The dogs padded up and down the bank barking excitedly.

"We're movin'!" I yelled, as the current grabbed us.

"An' we're sinkin'!" Pete yelled back.

"Watch out! Don't panic!"

"Goddammit!" he roared. "It'd help if you'd do somethin' 'cept holler don't panic!"

"Hey! Watch it!" I yelled again, struggling for balance.

"Watch *what*, Don?" he grunted. "I be damned if you don't screw around and drown us!"

We were both strong swimmers, so we weren't going to drown, but we didn't want to lose the product of all that sweat and mosquito bites. Our shouting increased along with the dogs barking as they ran along the bank paralleling our progress downstream. A word from either of us would have quieted them; but we had our hands full with the sinking raft.

Technically, we were still aboard but in water lapping at our ankles, adjuring and insulting each other; and it was all too much for the dogs. When we looked up again they were swimming determinedly toward us, deadly intent upon confronting the demons we had obviously blundered into. At the same time, I saw another reason to panic. "Save the tools!" I howled.

"Screw them tools." Pete screamed back. "I'm tryin' to save the raft!"

"No, screw the raft! Those are Daddy's…" but before I could finish, the dogs reached the raft and scrambled on board, clawing and scraping for a foothold.

Pete exhorted Jeff, "Stop it, Jeff! Get away!"

"Down, Fuzzy...down, boy!" I shouted, splashing water at him, trying to shove him aside.

"Down? Down on what you idiot?" Pete yelled incredulously. "They're sinkin' us now!"

"You gotta' better idea? Then you do somethin' dammit!"

"Jeff, you get away!"

"Oh, that'll do it. That'll do it all right!"

We quickly descended into tangled, spewing disarray. All the while, the current had carried us farther out and down the creek, and the green saplings were barely capable of supporting even their own weight, much less ours. The raft simply sank. Now the creek-boat captains were reduced to two soggy boys attempting to look after two soggy dogs who were doing their best to protect the two soggy boys. Suddenly the task at hand was to ensure that all hands got back to the bank, now a fair distance away. The raft had vanished.

"Let's get outta here!" I sputtered.

"No shit!" Pete agreed.

We turned and struck out for the bank in slow, rhythmic strokes, Fuzzy and Jeff dutifully paddling after us.

"You n' your stupid raft." Pete gurgled. "I told you somethin' bad would happen".

"Oh shutup!" I retorted, spitting water. "Where is it anyway?"

"Where's what?"

"Where's the raft?"

"Think Titanic!" Pete yelled, changing to a strong side stroke.

Reluctant to completely abandon it, I paused, treading water. Then I ducked under, determined to see if I could save our creation...at least, Daddy's tools. Surprisingly, through the murk, I saw it a few yards away. I let the current carry me back the short distance and managed to gain a handhold. It appeared to be hung up on something, so I got a good grip, flailed my legs, and heaved as mightily as I could, trying to dislodge it...only to be rewarded with a fierce, stabbing pain in my right triceps.

The creek was habitat for a wide variety of animal life, some of it hostile, some of it dangerously venomous...and I feared I'd been stung or bitten by a critter of some kind. Panic seized me. I tried to jerk away and kicked hard for the surface, but the pain intensified so much that I thought maybe I'd been struck by a snake, or that a snapping turtle had locked onto me. A fire burned in my arm, but worse, *whatever* had me was trying to hold me under. I broke the surface in a fit of terror.

"Oh, my God, Pete!" I screamed. He turned and looked back. As I tried to pull toward him, something came up out of the water, followed by another jolt of pain. Blood ran down my arm and I clutched it against my chest, only to be spun around by the current. When I tried to pull away, the pain increased. I began to lose control. Pete realized I was in trouble and quickly stroked back to me.

"Don! Don't move! Be still!" he commanded, holding me up.

"I can't be still! It's killin' me!"

"It's a goddamn hook!" Pete shouted, "Be still damnit!"

"A hook?" I groaned.

"A *big* fish-hook! An' it's tied onto ...*be still, I said!*"

"I can't! It hurts, dammit, it hurts! Get it out! Get this thing outta' me!"

"Don, you're snagged! It's hooked deep! You gotta' hold on a minute!"

Even as a teenager Pete had thick, strong, fingers, but his efforts at removing the hook were accomplishing nothing. It was awkward and clumsy for him since he was treading water only with his feet. Because of the barb, Pete saw that he'd have to work the big hook forward through tight skin and bunched muscle; and the remaining exposed shank gave him precious little with which to work. He pushed the hook forward tentatively and I screamed in agony. "What are you doin'?"

"Be still! I've gotta' work it outta' your arm!"

"You're not helpin'!" I screeched.

With my free arm, I hung onto the tightly strung, heavy cotton line lying just below the surface. I couldn't see it clearly, but it was obvious that whatever had snagged me had also snagged the raft, which surged back and forth with the current. The heavy raft was stretching the line, and the strain threatened to rip the hook through my arm or drag me under. Worse, there were other hooks every few feet, and Pete was being careful to ensure that neither he nor I were snagged by one of them. He finally grabbed the line and took the strain off the embedded hook. At the same time he was desperately treading water to stay afloat and beginning to tire. I went under again, lost contact with him, and knew I was going to drown. *No, no!* I thought, *not today* and fought upward.

Forcing my face above water, I held there briefly; but as I looked around, Pete had disappeared. I felt something bump into me underwater and had jangled thoughts of his drowned body being forced into me by the current. Strangely, fear dissipated to be replaced by comfortable despair. I thought about my family, wondered how they'd deal with losing me. I envisioned my friends and classmates, wondering if they'd even cry. And the team...*Who would play quarterback this fall?*

Then Pete surfaced like a breaching whale. He bellowed, "Hold on!" took three deep breaths, turned turtle and disappeared beneath the surface. Seconds later the pressure lessened. He was doing something; and, if nothing else, Pete was at his most resourceful in the face of a challenge. I clung to the faintest of hopes as the bubbles of his escaping breath appeared in front of me.

Then I was free. The hook was still in my arm, attached to a short piece of cotton line, badly frayed at the other end; but I was free of whatever had been holding me. Then a waterlogged Pete surfaced. "Sonofabitch!" he snarled, spitting bits of frayed line. "It's a trotline!" he yelled, lifting a heavy line out of the water to reveal short, dangling lines with hooks tied every few feet, some baited, some bare.

"A trotline?" I whimpered, pain clouding my ability to think.

"It's my trotline!" a deep voice boomed from the opposite bank. "And you little bastards done fucked it up."

Our heads whipped toward the voice.

"You deaf? I said you done fucked up my trotline!"

Pete and I looked at each other. "Garrison." Pete whispered. My heart sank and fear knotted the pit of my stomach.

Dee Garrison was the stuff of local legend. Rumors of him and his crazy brother had long plagued our imaginations; but in our wildest inventions we never expected to find ourselves in a confrontation with him. Yet there he stood, all one-hundred-ninety pounds, white skin stark against the dark green undergrowth, glowering like a bad dream.

"I'm sorry, we didn't know it was there!" I heard myself say just as the heavy raft snapped the trotline with a muffled "pop", and a long section of it ripped across the water, silver hooks flashing in the sunlight. Garrison reacted like a man possessed.

"There goes my fuckin' trotline!" he screamed, "all that work an' money I done spent!"

We struck out for the far side of the bank.

It was him that made that noise. He was watching us the whole time.

Exhausted, we pulled up onto the near bank, thankful that Garrison was on the other side. We were catching our breath when he roared, "Who's payin' for my goddamn trotline?"

Pete and I looked at each other. Turning to Garrison, his eyes narrowed as he yelled, "We ain't got time for this, Garrison! My buddy's hurt and I gotta' get him to the doctor!"

"Fuck you and your goddamn buddy! Somebody's payin' for my trotline!"

"Well, we ain't got no money and we ain't payin'," Pete dismissed him with, what seemed to me, a gauntlet.

What's he doing?

"By God it's your money or your ass!" Garrison bellowed, splashing through the shallows in our direction. He was a third of the way across before the water deepened to the point he had to swim. He crossed quickly in strong, sweeping strokes. The pain in my arm was replaced by raw fear. For the second time that day, I was ready to run.

"This here's Garrison proppity, y' know. Y'all tresspassin'!" He yelled, standing up in the knee deep shallows on our side. "Now, who's gonna' pay?"

Let it alone! He doesn't mean it. He's just mad about his trotline.

"Garrison, you deaf? You ain't gettin' nothin' from us. What is it you don't unnerstan' about that?" Pete yelled back defiantly.

Oh, crap!

Now, Garrison was beside himself with rage. He was big and threatening and, while Pete would never admit it, I knew he was as scared as I was. But regardless of *our* trepidation, Fuzzy and Jeff were singularly unimpressed. To those two, the equation was very simply balanced. A human threatened their gods...but he was only human, and

15

no match for the slashing savagery they brought to a fight. The only course of action they knew was to attack, and sepulchral warnings issued from two heavily muscled chests as they placed themselves between Garrison and us.

"You do them dogs a big favor t' keep 'em offa' me," Garrison warned, but the words were somehow absent their former conviction.

One- hundred -sixty pounds of unrequited malevolence stiff-legged their way to the water's edge, thick ruffs bristling, ears laid back, lips wrinkled and lifted to reveal gleaming ivory daggers...all amid a hideous duet of rising and falling growls and hoarse, chopping barks.

"I tole you I ain't afraid o' yore fuckin' dogs."

"You better be!" I shouted. "They're trained to kill!"

"Yeah," Pete challenged, reinforcing my bluff. "Since you so brave, jist get all of 'em you think you can handle. They'll tear your throat out!"

The dogs continued their resolute advance toward Garrison, who abruptly backed into deeper water. "I catch you little fuckheads down here agin I'll stomp yall's asses." He turned, stroked quickly across to the far bank. Once on the other side, he stood up and shouted. "You little shits ain't seen the last 'a me!" He turned and disappeared into the brush. We both ushered a sigh of relief.

"Come on", Pete said, "Let's get outta' here."

A wave of nausea swept over me and I remembered the deeply embedded hook. Intense pain returned. Pete regarded me with what might pass for sympathy in a normal human.

"It's gonna' hurt when the doc digs that out."

"Thanks for reminding me, dummy. And what is your problem anyway? Are you crazy? Were you tryin' to start trouble with that guy?"

He shrugged. "Don, *he* was the one lookin' for trouble, not me. An' what was that about Fuzzy 'n Jeff 'trained to kill'?" He laughed.

"I had to come up with something. You were about to get *us* killed." I laughed with him, ignoring the throbbing pain.

"Did you see the look on that bastard's face?" Pete continued, laughing louder.

"Yeah, yeah! He believed it! He believed it! Oh, God my arm hurts!"

16

"I know, I know!" He screamed hoarsely, laughing even harder...

Our laughter grew, turning into guffaws of released tension. Finally, lack of oxygen forced us to stop with exhaustion. Pete, laboring to breathe, reminded me, "Your dad's gonna' be pissed about his tools...an' don't you go tellin' him I'm the one that lost 'em."

All I could do was shake my head and go on hurting. "Pissed" would represent the best possible outcome. We emptied the water from our shoes and Pete wrung out our shirts. My arm was on fire.

"That fucker's crazy." Pete said offhandedly.

"Amen."

"And so are we...floatin' down the cool, green creek..."

"Mighta' made it if *they* hadn't got in the middle." I interrupted, nodding toward Fuzzy and Jeff. Pete snickered, watching the dogs maintain an alert watch down Garrison's direction of retreat.

We didn't tell our parents about Garrison, fearing they'd bar us from our beloved creek. My wounded arm somewhat mitigated Daddy's anger over the lost tools. A few days later we looked for the raft with no success and figured it had washed on down to the Trinity River. After a while, we forgot all about Garrison. There were more important things to consider...after all, it was 1954.

PRELUDE

Our world was exploding with bright prospects. The scar of Korea was fading and the great socio-political upheavals of the sixties lay ahead. But, best of all, I would be sixteen soon...old enough to drive.

In our little North Texas town, life proceeded according to rigid, time- honored patterns. Parents were respected, exercised total authority, and exacted meaningful discipline which, more often than not, featured corporal punishment. Rewards were rare but penalties were unfailing, and the dues of life were always paid. Right was right and wrong was wrong. We had yet to be introduced to the concept of gray areas. With religious principles and moral values serving largely to shield us from reality, we existed and were relatively content within an envelope of common standards. We vaguely understood that the future held complex problems; but we had neither time nor inclination to pursue abstract possibilities. We busied ourselves in simple lives sans computers, video games, drugs, disobedience - civil or otherwise - or more than two hours of television every evening; and then, only when finished with homework and chores.

Racism was nonexistent. Not that we weren't aware of it. It just didn't infringe on our daily routines. The only "Negro" (the term "black" was not yet in vogue) in town did farm work for the father of one of our classmates; and any discussion of him centered around the rumor that, when on his knees, his penis dragged the ground. The high school janitor was a Mexican named Emanuel. He did his job, laughed a lot, and thoroughly enjoyed listening to us massacre the Spanish we'd just been exposed to in Miss Rigor's class. Word circulated that "niggers" were infiltrating a nearby school system. But this didn't directly concern us, so we more or less ignored it.

School dropouts were either male or pregnant, and either from the social strata we called "white trash" or simply heedless of the disgrace they heaped upon their families and themselves. We were capable of reading relatively complex documents, of writing the language understandably, and of adding, subtracting, multiplying and dividing accurately - without pocket calculators. We could place the states on a map and knew their capitols, and we spoke the English language quite well when formal usage was appropriate.

There were inviolable rules. Disrespect of an adult earned a liberally applied belt or paddle. Gross disrespect of, cursing, or actually assaulting a girl assured a remorseless beating ... or worse. Blatant disrespect of a teacher meant permanent expulsion; but very few students were ever lost to that process, and none were diagnosed with "attention deficit disorder", or prescribed mood altering drugs to treat a condition that did not exist then and arguably does not exist now. Nor were classes or curricula set aside for "special education" students. Instead, butts were busted until recalcitrant students willingly and graciously accommodated to the rules, tedium, and rhythm of school life.

Our world may have been simple but it was challenging, and our days were full. We attended to our tasks, worked for wages in whatever jobs we could find, played hard, actively pursued the opposite sex, raised our fists when we had to, and studied hard to make passing - much less decent - grades. Evil was the subject of Sunday Morning sermons and enjoyed little currency in our existence. Crime and corruption were anomalies played out on television or movies. And the idea that we would ever be required to defend our own lives was as remote as the edge of the universe.

PISTIL

During that same summer, Dawn Ferguson burst through pubescence to arrive ahead of schedule at the physical status of womanhood. We noticed the monumental changes when school resumed in early September.

"Lookit that!" I exclaimed, nudging Pete in the adjacent seat. He turned and his jaw dropped.

"Sanctus," he breathed softly as Dawn glided into the classroom and slid into a desk across the aisle from us, "et benedictus est." Pete was fond of abusing Latin.

"My, gosh!" I whispered, remembering the skinny redhead of last spring. Could this even be the same girl? That thought was wasted because, in one second, I fell helplessly and unalterably in love with the fall model. She turned and smiled at Pete.

How pleasant life would be if he would somehow manage to shoot himself ...

She was tall and lissome, and curves and swells had replaced the previous knobs and angles. The bodice of her canary-yellow dress was filled with promise; the knee length hem of her skirt revealed smooth, tapered calves and ankles.

Oh, Dawn of fireburnt hair and alabaster skin... your every gesture's perfection.

My eyes followed her, desire barely disguised. Normally studious, I began to lose all semblance of concentration waiting for her to intentionally drop a pencil, or find some other reason to bend over. If luck was with me, I would observe a generous portion of cleavage...maybe even an almost exposed breast swinging freely in its lacy brassiere.

She assayed this game with the finesse of a femme fatale, not only for me of course, but for every boy upon whose upper lip the first coarse hairs had just emerged. We had absolutely no clue what she was about, but she manipulated us instinctively. After the second bell, she would delay taking her seat long enough for all male eyes to gravitate to her. At the right moment she would flick her hair with knowing indifference, absently adjust clothing around firm flesh and slowly

20

assume her seat, taut buttocks bunching, smiling with casual aplomb, tongue flicking swollen lips…whereupon we spiraled into the stratosphere of lust.

"You see that? You see that? Did… you… see… *that*?" Pete chanted softly, symbolically banging his head against a row of lockers.

"I saw you make a fool of yourself." I feigned indifference.

"She done it on purpose", he responded indignantly, "deliberately rubbed them tits up against me!"

"No she didn't!" I protested.

"Oh yeah, buddy she done it alright!"

"No, you leaned back into her."

Ignoring me, he performed a standing roll along the row of lockers, "By God, she was rootin' them hard little nipples all over me!"

"You're crazy!" I almost shouted, more than a little jealous that at least part of what he was saying was true. "You have no class, you're crude, and you're an idiot!" my rant continued.

"Well, you seen it." He persisted.

"Pete," I argued hotly, "I saw you intentionally jam your typewriter keys so she'd help you. Then she leans over to untangle your keys and you deliberately lean backwards…away from the typewriter. That really makes a lotta' sense."

"No sir! No sirree Bob! She laid 'em up against me on purpose!" And then, with a look of aggrieved innocence, "An' I don't blame her…and you shouldn't either, Don. What girl wouldn't wanta' rub her tits up against somebody as handsome as me?"

"Shut up, Pete!" I muttered balefully.

"An' we both know what comes next…" he continued.

"*Shut up!*" Now, I yelled and other students looked our direction.

"Fact is, buddy, she loved it." He was at his very best now, coolly analytical against my rising anger. "Can you imagine how good it felt to her…to *her,* mind you…to waller them torpedoes up against my muscular back? An' I bet I know what she'd *really* like to rub 'em on."

"*Shut up!*" Now, I was bellowing…quite beside myself.

"You're just jealous!" He mocked dismissively.

"I don't have anything to be jealous about!"

21

"Oh, but you do...an' you are!"

"I'm not tellin' you again, I'm not!" I snarled coldly, and abruptly turned away.

Of course I was jealous. I was more than jealous. In fact, I was furious that, as far as the object of our concentrated passion was concerned, he was one up. However it had happened, Pete had contrived to actually know the feel of her breasts, those magnificent orbs I fantasized kneading like firm baker's dough. If Pete and I had one thing in common...*a fact I remain loathe to admit*...it was that we attended assiduously to identical female types, frequently ending up with terrific crushes on the same girl. My own prurient interests, while utterly rampant, were always in check. I went to great lengths to keep them that way. A hedonist of the purest strain, Pete demonstrated all the restraint of a goat.

Interestingly, we found a remarkable number of shared *amours du jour* in church. We both enjoyed attending; I for at least some of the standard reasons, Pete for others not ordained by the church, parents or a higher power. But we both took great joy in honoring the Sabbath because we knew *girls* would be there to help us do so. Girls with soft, moist, rose painted lips and firm, round haunches...girls in sweaters that proudly advertised swiftly expanding bustlines, girls smelling faintly of lemon and jasmine. They too, honored the Sabbath, especially those of Southern Baptist persuasion.

All the churches in town: Methodist, Baptist, Christian, Assembly of God, Church of Christ, and a few other obscure brands, had pretty girls on their rolls. And, generally speaking, these pristine damsels maintained proper demeanor while attending services. However, as a denomination, Baptists ranked head and shoulders above all the other available sects in providing adolescent females prone to spontaneously expressed religious desire...which we learned was not only possible, but relatively simple to transmute into that of a sexual variety. Coy smiles were traded between invocation and benediction, followed by lascivious kisses stolen in darkened stairwells and pitch black Sunday school rooms, while just around the corner, parents chatted innocently over coffee and cookies. Regular attendance at services assured realization of our more base proclivities. Good bad boys got the bad good girls.

We showed up fully prepared...freshly bathed, a mix of talcum powder and baking soda slapped haphazardly into our armpits, hair slicked back and shining with Brylcreem or Bakers Best. We sang the great hymns of the church with ringing voices. And we prayed. I prayed diligently and earnestly, sticking to traditional subjects of prayer...that the perishing would be rescued or the dying cared for, by way of example. But Pete was as pragmatic in prayer as he was in life. He prayed powerful, complex prayers, and sincerely believed that they would produce results. However, the requests he laid before the throne of grace differed significantly from those of even the nominally faithful...and radically from those who had achieved more advanced levels of sanctification. Pete found it not only logical but efficacious to pray for a skirt raised to reveal bare, lightly freckled thighs...for a plunging décolletage to provide an unencumbered view of the milk-white glories nestled therein. He routinely offered up prayers that he would find himself in deep-breathing embrace with Emily Whitsell, or Alice McDavid....or...*and damn him for it to this very day*...the focus of our shared lust and the single true love of my life, Dawn Ferguson.

A problem we shared in our myopic pursuit of her was that we could find nothing we thought might gain her attention. She had no interest in fishing, dinosaurs would assuredly bore her, and she didn't keep tropical fish. My rendition of Mario Lanza's high C might have impressed her but, as Pete so readily pointed out, such insipient high-notes were akin to the wailings of a castrated capon, and any such impression left on Dawn might negate our expressed objective. And that about exhausted what we had to offer. After intense reflection I hit upon the solution. Dogs. Dogs were neutral. Dogs were harmless. If I approached the issue skillfully, I reasoned, I would be able to proceed from a discussion of dogs to my profound desire to be her exclusive suitor. Importantly, I would be able to freeze Pete out of the situation. In the end, I was right...at least about capturing her attention.

Gradually, I overcame proximity induced lockjaw and told her stories about Fuzzy and Jeff. She listened, mildly amused. I made my tales overly vivid, which wasn't difficult given a vast and complex imagination. I picked the dog ploy because Pete had quite innocently managed to gain Janice Holt's focused interest by happening to have

23

Jeff along. Janice was spectacularly endowed and had either forgotten or, as I later came to realize, deliberately ignored the ritual of placing a hand at the very top of her loose fitting blouse when she bent to pet Jeff, thus allowing Pete a lingering glimpse at the objects of his most intense interest, which were, in Janice's case, the most magnificent examples available. His dark eyes glowed as he whispered the startling result:

"I seen *everything*, Don, even the *nipples!*"

"Baloney." I argued, assuming vast hyperbole.

"She's got tits like a Fort Worth sow!"

"You woulda' had to been underneath her lookin' up to see *Janice's* nipples."

"Well, either her brassiere was too loose or her tits was too heavy, 'cause when she bent over...they just plopped right out there."

"You really saw her nipples?"

"I swear by Lucifer and all his angels and dominions."

"Don't talk like that! You're gonna' get yourself in trouble with that kind of talk an' I'm gonna' get in trouble listenin'. Were they pink or brown?"

"Pink, dummy. They don't turn brown 'til they nurse a baby. An' near 'bout big around as a one o' them demi whatever cups mama's ol' biddy friends drink coffee out of."

"You have all the luck."

"It wasn't luck, Don. That's skill. You hafta' know what you're doin'."

From that incident sprang a grandiose plan. I perfected the preliminary necessities and practiced a technique that would allow me to repeat the process by which Pete had gained visual admittance to the *sanctum sanctorum*... and to do it reliably. Had I understood the subject of my scheming more fully, I would have known that any girl with an appreciable rack was dying for us to see them. It was only later we came to learn that girls are born exhibitionists, genetically wired to effortlessly display their physical endowments to attract males. They uniformly covet the ability to attract male sexual attention...as currently demonstrated by breast enhancement surgery costing thousands of dollars and undergone by hordes of women with breasts they consider small, shapeless, or otherwise unattractive. They coveted that attention then no less than now; and Dawn Ferguson was no exception to that

24

rule. My tales were pure fabrication but she toyed with me, enjoying my juvenile attentiveness. When she finally suggested that *we* bring the dogs by her house, I was overjoyed, in spite of the fact that her invitation *seemed* to include Pete. I quickly convinced myself that she didn't mean it that way and dismissed it out of hand.

Pete was far too direct, I told myself. That was the reason I did not include him in my plan. Success required finesse, a quality completely absent in Pete; and I plotted the timing and circumstances under which I could introduce Dawn to Fuzzy and Jeff. One afternoon, I knew she had an after-school conference scheduled with Mrs. Billings, our English teacher, when no one would be around to witness my rejection or laugh at my ineptitude. I found her frighteningly lovely as always, bent over a water fountain just outside the classroom.

Deep shadows lay across the hall as cloud- shaded light filtered through the windows; but as I walked toward her, the sun emerged and brightly illuminated the scene. It was an omen! Dawn assumed an angelic aura...which I have now come to learn typified an adolescent need I had to legitimize sexual impulses. She wore a snugly fitting red sweater with a very tight skirt. I was mesmerized. *They are torpedoes*, I thought, instantly regretting my regression into crudity and cursing Pete for introducing me to so unromantic an analogy of a shapeliness that rivaled that of the armless Venus. I stuttered several times attempting to frame my thoughts, hoping my timing was right to broach the subject. I stumbled again before finally getting across to her that she might enjoy seeing the dogs I'd told her so much about. Tiny droplets of water clung to the lips of a nymph.

"Why don't you come over tomorrow, Don? After all, it'll be Saturday."

My heart vaulted into my throat. "Really?" I squawked, face flushed and hot, a river of adrenaline coursing through my veins.

"Sure," she said. "You make them sound so funny."

"Well, they're not really funn", I stumbled, swallowing hard enough to bite off the end of my last word. "I mean, they're not exactly 'ha, ha' funny...they...they're just dogs. But they do...they... uh...funn things. They do funny things. That's it. Yes."

She smiled, obviously amused at my bumbling effort. "So just bring them out whenever you're ready. I'll be home all day."

"Bring 'em?"

"Yes, Don. Come out and bring your dogs."

"Great! I'll uh…bring 'em out!"

She reached for the door handle, turned and favored me with the most radiant smile. "And, Don don't forget Pete."

"*Pete?*" I croaked.

"Yes, Don. I believe Jeff is his dog and yours is Fuzzy. Isn't that right?"

"Oh, uh sure."

Crap! How does she know so much about which dog belongs to who anyway? What has he been up to? What has he not told me? Maybe he'll fall and hit his head and they'll take him to the State Hospital in Terrell. I'll bring his Tarzan books when I visit him and he can holler Kreegah! till he's hoarse.

The enchantment of the moment evaporated and the surging torrent of adrenaline withered into a fetid ditch. I felt a sudden lassitude.

Oh well, I'll drag him along if I have to. Maybe he'll forget and holler Kreegah! and I'll act like he must be crazy… and she'll forget all about him.

Dawn swiveled away, her twisting hips bewitchingly sensuous. I was alone with my thoughts. At least, I thought I was.

"Now that there's some prime lookin'piece 'a ass, ain't it?" a voice echoed down the deserted hallway.

"Huh?" I reacted, turning toward its source.

"Yeah! I'm talkin' to you, dipshit. I said ain't that some fine pussy right there."

"Garrison!" I blurted out, recognizing David, Garrison's younger brother.

"You tryin' t' tap you some o' that, boy?"

"What?" I sputtered, weak-kneed and suddenly nauseous.

"Goddamn, you deaf? I said, you tryin' to tap you some o' that?"

Dirty coveralls and a flannel shirt confronted me; and there was a sneer on a face otherwise remarkable only by a surfeit of angry looking acne lumps. Fully expecting him to pull a knife or a gun or simply flail away at me, I was tempted to follow Dawn into Mrs. Billings' classroom.

But how will I look if I do that? What is he doing here? Didn't he flunk out for the third time last year?

"You kin forget that, shithead," he continued, breath reeking of tobacco. "That there's strictly Garrison pussy."

Swallowing hard, I finally found the nerve to speak in sentences. "Where have you been, David? I thought you graduated." Garrison may well have been slow, but he was not without the ability to recognize badly disguised guile.

"Shutup you fuckin' wimp!" he snapped. "What I done ain't none o' your goddamn business!"

Obviously, normal conversation was not an option and I was too frightened to speak anyway. Larger than me and almost as foreboding as his older brother, he was fully grown and came from an unfamiliar, frightening culture. For the moment I was rooted in place, unable to speak, hoping beyond hope that someone or something would happen by to discourage the developing confrontation. I got Buddy Phillips.

Where is Pete when I need him?

"What're you guys doin'?" Buddy chirped cheerily, striding toward us. Buddy was the smallest boy in class and, by some measure, the most affable. He was a substitute halfback on the "B" squad football team and, although tough for his size, he didn't exactly represent what I thought I might require in the way of backup.

"Who the fuck are you?" Garrison snorted.

"Oh, sorry." Buddy replied, undaunted. "I thought you were somebody...else that is." Buddy, for his small size, was no woosie.

David Garrison turned his back on Buddy and squared back around on me. "You wanna' stay healthy," he said coldly, "Don't be messin' aroun' with me and Dee's pussy."

My fear began to evaporate as bitter rage welled up. Whether it was the arrival of an ally or simply my anger over his attitude didn't matter; I was momentarily tempted to rip into him. Buddy probably saved me from myself.

"So what you guys doin' anyway?" he asked.

Garrison muttered something and glared at Buddy. "Fuck you, midget," he spat, then walked away, shooting one last venomous look over his shoulder.

27

"Wow, he's a real winner." Buddy said, watching David walk away.

"Yeah," I agreed, still shaky.

"Wasn't that David Garrison?" Buddy asked.

"Himself." I responded.

"I thought he was in jail."

I shrugged.

"Ain't heard about him or that brother of his in a long time." Buddy continued. "What's he up to anyway?"

"Trouble." I said without thinking.

"Huh?"

"I don't know Buddy. He just showed up." I lied, not wanting to get into specifics.

"That's just poor white trash without the poor. Gives me the willies!" Buddy looked at his watch, yelped, and abruptly changed the subject. "Hey, I'm supposed to meet Kara Lynn at the library. She's helping me with geometry." He started off.

"Maybe she can help me too." I said, deciding to go with him, not because I really needed it; but because I wasn't excited over the prospect of being alone. As we started down the hall, Buddy launched into a nonstop verbal barrage I knew would not stop until he exhausted his subject matter. I was obliged to feign interest, but my mind was elsewhere. I kept expecting Garrison to reappear. Taking some comfort in Buddy's presence, I reviewed the reasons we had officially "cattled" him in the first place.

Being "cattled" wasn't the worst thing in the world. One could land in Joe Luden's algebra class. Other than that, there wasn't a close second. For Pete and me, the world was filled with "cattle" of the human variety who couldn't think or act except in traditionally accepted, unimaginative fashion. Pete and I had long observed such predictable behavior and we found ourselves unable to countenance it in silence. We saw it mainly in our schoolmates, but there were many others, adults included, who fit the bill. We were compelled to strike out against it and did so by "cattling" ...as in officially, formally, "cattling" someone.

It wasn't difficult to achieve cattle status. Ask a redundant or stupid question and you were cattled. Wear a shirt that matched your girl friend's blouse...cattled. Comparing the vocal talent of Elvis

Presley to that of Jussi Bjorling was a first class ticket to the realm of cattledom. Conforming to fads guaranteed permanently cattled status. People did cattle things every day, and we took it as our anointed task to point this out.

We crowned ourselves "King Cattlers." To be sure, there were early attempts to denigrate our efforts, but we knew we'd win. After all, *they* were cattle. And in short order, it came to be that we were not required to explain ourselves. *We* cattled at will, and *they* were required to accept it. We only cattled boys. Girls paid us no attention whatever, other than expressing mild amusement at the eternal maneuvering of cattle designees to gain uncattled status. A game developed among the guys. A finger pointed in warning by either Pete or me and cattle behavior would instantly cease. The recipient would await the verdict, the crowd, anticipating, then clamoring for a cattling declaration.

"Lookit that ducktail," one would hint.

"Yeah, and he's got his collar turned up jist like Elvis."

"That's cattle if I ever seen it."

So emphatic were our pronouncements, so humiliating the process, that individuals like Buddy would beg to be uncattled. But Buddy's transgressions had been especially blatant and his repeated requests were summarily rejected.

Buddy was short, personable, and bright. An eternal smile glistened beneath, mischievous eyes. Buddy was on the "B" football team with Pete and me. Early on, we considered bestowing upon him the title of Honorary Cattler. This would have been no small deed. Indeed, such a position had never been awarded. And he might well have achieved that exalted status had not Cupid twanged his tiny bow and stuck the arrow of love in Buddy...whereupon he became crass, dependent and, worst of all, willingly so. To make matters worse, the object of his affliction was none other than Kara Lynn Carter, a girl of such substantial size that seeing them together provoked stares of disbelief.

We arrived at the library only to see Pete closing the door very quietly and looking behind him to see if his departure had been noticed. "Pete, where you goin?" Buddy called out.

"Be quiet!" Pete whispered hoarsely, "I'm sneakin' detention."

"You can't do that." I declared.

29

"I hate to disappoint you buttbreath, but I already done it."

"You're gonna' get in trouble." Buddy said, looking anxiously at the library door.

"I'm already in trouble you ninny. Why you think I'm hotfootin' it outta' here at four o'clock?"

"What'd you do?" I asked.

"Told Laura Cates to go erp."

"What?"

"Hell, she said I made her sick."

"That's why you got detention?"

"Damn right. She said, 'Pete, you make me sick.' So I said, 'Then, Laura go erp'."

"That's pretty crude, Pete." Buddy said righteously

Bristling, Pete immediately turned on our diminutive friend. "You better be careful, Buddy. Any more comments like that, you'll never get uncattled."

Buddy was unnerved.

"You heard me," Pete said, nodding at me for support. I hated to do it just at that moment, but jumped in anyway.

"You knew the consequences when you got…uh…over romantically involved with Kara Lynn."

"What? Now come on, you guys. What's wrong with Kara Lynn?"

Actually, nothing at all was wrong with her. Kara Lynn Carter was warm, considerate, entirely likeable, very pretty and had a nice figure but, at just under six feet and near 170 pounds, she was very large. She dwarfed Buddy. She had a happy though somewhat "bossy" disposition…but all the girls in our little class were a little bossy.

In those days, the girls kept order…in class, and in general. Perhaps that was a reflection of two parent homes in which mothers reported miscreants to fathers…who solved the vast majority of problems with a belt. "I'm gonna' tell your folks," was a phrase that uniformly terrified us. Since teachers were completely respected but could not be present in class one hundred percent of the time, it was up to the girls to maintain decorum in their absence. They did this by "taking names." If you didn't "settle down" when warned, prompt reportage was assured. There was no thought of ever threatening a girl to ensure her silence. Even had we been so cowardly, the girl would have reported the threat to her father, who would have shown up to visit with the offender's father…and there'd be hell to pay. There were also older brothers with whom it was wise to concern one's self, and you wouldn't have to *wait* for them to pay you a visit.

If girls were bosses, Kara Lynn was the boss of bosses… *capo di tutti capi.* She stood six full inches taller than Buddy and outweighed him forty pounds. She was as big as any boy in the class; and Buddy was smitten with every inch and pound of her. While curious, his infatuation, in and of itself, wasn't abnormal; he simply happened to be attracted to big girls. What was unpardonable was that he openly cavorted with her…and that would not do. Open, cooing displays of adoration, i.e., cavorting, were worthy only of contempt, and we were compelled to warn Buddy that he stood in imminent danger of being "cattled".

Buddy swore to cease and desist, but Pete observed them walking to class holding hands and cattled him on the spot while a huffy Kara Lynn, hands on hips, instructed Buddy to ignore him….an adjuration he observed reluctantly, later begging for absolution. But he had irrevocably crossed the cattle guard…and joined the herd that grazed in the pastures of cattledom.

"But at least lemme' go fishin' with you guys," Buddy squealed. "I ain't never been to Bluehole…shoot, I ain't never even been fishin'…an' you promised you'd take me."

"We don't take no cattle on our fishin' trips, Buddy." Pete dismissed him abruptly.

"But you ain't got good criteria." Buddy protested.

"Criteria?" Pete was shocked. "Where'd you come up with that word?"

I'd heard it on television during "Art Linkletter's House Party" and thought I knew what it meant. But not being certain, I skipped back to the subject at hand. "Look, Buddy," I said, repeating what he'd been told a dozen times. "You let yourself get pressured into doin' somethin' you really didn't wanna' do, and that's the thing about being cattle. You know if you follow the herd, chew your cud, let anyone skin or milk you…you're cattle. It's that simple."

31

Pete added, "And you knowingly defied a King Cattler...which was me...and that's grounds for cattlin' right there!"

"But..."

"No buts! You were warned." I said emphatically. "Buddy, you gotta' squelch your carnal impulses!" Pete almost yelled.

Buddy and I both looked at Pete, who turned sheepish and said, "Well, that's what dad tells me."

"Come on, ya'll," Buddy persisted, "I want to catch the Monster too!"

"Speakin' of which...." Pete warned, as Kara Lynn's bulk rounded the corner to bear down on us. "Quiet!"

Kara was definitely not hard to look at, just large. She'd never had a boy friend and now that she had Buddy, she was going to hang on to him as long as she could.

"Buddy!" she announced imperiously.

"Oh, crap," Pete sighed resignedly.

"Don't you guys say anything!" Buddy warned.

"You better remember what we been tellin' you if you wanna' get uncattled," I whispered.

"I cain't stay bein' a cattle, you guys." Buddy was desperate.

"Well, here's your chance." Pete whispered out the corner of his mouth.

"Hi, ya'll." she greeted us. "And where have you been, Buddy Phillips? You were supposed to meet me in study hall."

"Had some trouble with David Garrison." Buddy said.

"*David* Garrison?" A frown clouded her very regular features. "He's not even supposed to be here."

"How do you know?" I countered.

"I work in the Principal's Office. Him n' Dee tried to get back in school and David got turned down 'cause he's still on probation for stealin' tires."

"What about Dee?" I asked.

"Don't know. Mr. Wayne didn't say anything about him." She replied indifferently, her attention centered on Buddy. "Anyway, why didn't you meet me right after the last bell so you could walk me to study hall?"

32

Pete demonstrated silent sarcasm, ever so cleverly disguised by lifted eyebrows.

Buddy stammered something unintelligible.

"We sidetracked him." I said, hoping to buy him a little room.

"Well," said Kara Lynn, grabbing his hand. "Let's get you back on track, young man."

Pete and I regarded him impassively. All he had to do was refuse courteously. We both hoped he'd suck it up and dismiss her.

"Come on, Buddy," she insisted.

"I'll see you guys later," he replied sheepishly as Kara Lynn led him into the library.

"Definitely cattle," I stated.

"Utter and complete." Pete added.

That night I had a dream about Dawn. In it, she was wearing the same red sweater I'd seen her in earlier. Only she wasn't at the fountain and there was no straight skirt. Half-naked, she was walking down the hall, away from me. I kept running after her and she kept getting farther away...skipping between the shafts of sunlight streaming across the corridor. I called after her, "Dawn, Dawn wait a minute! I want you to meet Fuzzy and Jeff!" But she wouldn't stop and, finally, all I could see was the back of her head and her soft, incredibly lovely red hair.

Then, as if by magic, I was right next to her...close enough to smell her faint perfume. She turned to me and said, "I'm Garrisons' prime piece of ass alright." And I saw her smile, and I saw her hair...but she was no longer half-naked; and I was so confused by her dirty coveralls and flannel shirt.

BRIC DODD

Head football coach Bric Dodd was an elitist who never considered fielding a "B" squad. But since there were enough boys who wanted to play who weren't big or fast enough to make the "A" team but demonstrated reasonable potential, he changed his mind. Pete and I weren't big, but we were hitters; and being a hitter paid big rewards if you wanted to gain Coach Dodd's favor. He rewarded us by starting us on the "B" team.

I was the quarterback, mainly because I was an accurate passer, was the fastest guy in school, and relished being in charge. Pete could run like a deer but couldn't hold onto a football...or any other kind of ball for that matter...and played at guard and tackle.

Hitting was everything if you played for Bric. He, like any coach worth the title, lived to win football games but, even more than that, he loved bruising, hell-for-leather hitting on the field...both in practice and in the game. He dealt with losing, albeit reluctantly, but he went berserk if players wouldn't "find somebody and hit 'em."

"We'll have the 'Tough Twenty," he bellowed to his all male classes in Health Science, the only subject he taught. Dodd used this mixed-grade class to advance his football fantasies. "We'll roll 'em out on the field in a cage-on-wheels. We'll have a Shetland pony pull it and we'll throw 'em bones to gnaw on 'til the game starts." Then he'd laugh outrageously and vigorously rub the side of his head next to his ear, which eased the itch of a fungus he acquired in 1942 as a Marine platoon leader lieutenant in the Pacific.

"Whatta' y' think o' that, Robbins?" He asked, moving to Pete, seated on the front row next to me. Before he could answer, Dodd kicked him in the shin.

Pete groaned and grabbed his leg.

The entire class laughed as Dodd grinned. "That didn't hurt now did it, Robbins?"

"Nossir, Coach." Pete moaned.

Dodd's grin widened. "Then why you rubbin' your leg, Robbins?"

"It hurts, Coach!"

The class roared. He turned to me...

"The Tough Twenty feels no pain. Ain't that right, Shook?"
I had a quick, intelligent answer, "Pain's relative, Coach."
He kicked me too.

He played semi-pro ball in Hawaii before the war and even managed to gain a try-out with the Chicago Bears. According to his newspaper clippings, which we dutifully acclaimed as if every time we viewed them was the first, he was a good player, a halfback who, as was the practice then, also played defensive back. Stocky, solid, outrageously strong, thick black hair covering a big, square head as well as the rest of his body, Bric Dodd cut an intimidating figure, especially when he elected to level his jet-black eyes on boys on the field or in class. And doom on the boy with a smart mouth or one who happened to cross him. His justice was swift and direct: a well placed kick to the shin or a thump on the forehead with a thick middle finger.

Like several of our teachers, Dodd endured a tough war. His began on Guadalcanal and ended as a major on Okinawa, wounded by a Japanese machine gunner. In the nineteen-fifties, long before political correctness reared its snake's head of mendacity, the classroom discipline exacted by those veterans could sometimes extend beyond a paddle or a kick to the shin...or the thump of a finger. I was about to grab my shin when acid filled my esophagus. Dee Garrison lumbered into the room and took a seat in the back.

Dee was past twenty. Nobody really knew exactly how old he was. It was common then to attend school irregularly; work a year, sometimes more...come back to school...work another year. Most were serious students whose family needs required that they work. They eventually graduated, while others amused themselves as long as they could rather than gain an education. Since his family had money, we suspected that Garrison came to school because it provided a ready supply of subjects he could bully. He was a tall, heavily muscled man with advanced acne, bad teeth, stinking breath and a pungent body odor. Most of the teachers avoided him. He had been expelled from school for an altercation with the Agriculture teacher and now, he had shown up in Dodd's Health class...*our* health class. I glanced over my shoulder at him and he looked even bigger than he did that day at Ten Mile Creek.

"Awright," Dodd drawled, furiously rubbing his ear. "This is Health Science, and I'll be covering the ways you boys can achieve and maintain your health." He paused, and his dark eyes locked on Garrison. Dodd was as serious about teaching as he was about coaching. He made a practice of walking up and down the aisles as he lectured. This ensured that no one was reading a comic book or otherwise idling. Seated on the very last row, Garrison had tilted his chair back so he could lean against the wall. Many teachers ignored Garrison. A few made feeble attempts at correction, only to end up ignoring him as well. We knew Bric Dodd would not ignore Garrison. We knew Garrison had no intention of granting Dodd any more respect than teachers he'd managed to intimidate. Taken altogether, the situation meant a confrontation was imminent.

Dodd launched promptly into curriculum but none of us paid attention, riveted instead on the encounter that was sure to occur. None of us doubted that it would. It had to, because Coach Dodd was who and what he was, and Garrison was proud of being a bully. True to form, Dodd proceeded slowly down the aisle. When he got to Garrison's desk, he rubbed his ear, grinned that wicked grin and said mildly, "Sit up in your chair there, Garrison." Garrison grinned back, but made no effort to comply with Dodd's instruction. His broad back remained planted against the wall of the classroom, big feet dangling absurdly below the chair's bottom rung. Dodd paused a long moment but said nothing, and continued his lecture up the next row. Garrison shrugged his shoulders, spread his hands, and turned the corners of his mouth down in silent, contemptuous dismissal. All of us felt a little sick. Dodd took no apparent notice but went on lecturing up and down the rows at the same measured pace. I stole a look at Pete who was scribbling furiously in his notebook. He must have felt me looking at him; we often seemed to connect that way. He shook his head negatively. I wasn't sure what he meant. There was no air conditioning so the windows were open, and I could hear an occasional vehicle trundle down the nearby street.

Would Dodd go back down the rows? The question had to be answered. If he did, that would mean certain confrontation. Or would he stay at the front of the class? That would mean Garrison had won. Eons passed. I wanted class to be over even if it meant our hero caving to a bully. The tension had my stomach churning. Dodd finally finished with the rows. He paused at the teacher's desk and laid his textbook down. Then, he rocked up and down from heel to toes a couple of times, cracked the knuckles of both hands, and started down the first row again. I knew something was going to happen.

Dodd strode quickly to a position just to the side of Garrison. "Garrison," he asked very businesslike, "you good and comfortable there?" Garrison sneered, but didn't move.

It happened with the abruptness of a shark attack. Dodd lifted his knee to his chest and slammed the sole of his shoe into Garrison's side, sending the big boy sprawling heavily out of his chair. Dodd's face was now black with rage and he sprang on Garrison like a big cat. Before Garrison had time to react, Dodd had the fingers of his left hand knotted in his stringy hair. He twisted the angry, pimpled face up, there was a flashing motion, and we all heard the meaty sound of Dodd's thick, flat hand pounding into Garrison's face. The bully threw up an arm and tried to yell, but managed only a strange, strangled sound. Dodd slapped him again, then again, his hand rising and falling like an axe. With his left hand still tangled in Garrison's hair, Dodd reached down and grabbed Garrison's belt, jerked him bodily over the overturned chair and started up the aisle toward the front. Garrison was already bleeding from nose and mouth, and Dodd kept up a grunting, roaring commentary…

"Get up Garrison! Get up! Stand up there, goddamn you!"

Garrison, of course, could do neither. Dodd released Garrison's hair to grab and twist the back of his shirt collar. Now he was jerking Garrison up the aisle by his collar and belt and Garrison's head was making sharp contact with every desk en route. Garrison was babbling. "No, no…come on now, Dodd…lemme' *go!*"

But Dodd didn't hear him over his own raving rant. "Get on up here, Garrison! You wanted this, now you gitcher ass on up here with *me!*"

We were paralyzed, riveted to the altercation unfolding in front of us. Most of us had never seen grown men fight.

When they reached the heavy metal door, Dodd evidently forgot which way it opened, which was to the inside. You had to pull it towards you. Dodd tried ramming Garrison's head into it, whereupon the bully flopped to the floor in a cowering huddle. Dodd jerked the door open and dragged Garrison into the hall. We could hear lockers banging as Dodd slammed him into them, roaring all the while. "You want some more o' *meeee*, Garrison?" we heard him bawl.

The crashing grew fainter as they went down the hall. Eventually, there was silence. I heard Pete's whispered, "Damn!"

The classroom chatter started only to stop suddenly as Garrison limped back in, breathing heavily, blood still trickling from his mouth and nose. He was followed closely by a grim faced Dodd. Garrison went straight...and in complete silence...to his chair. Blanched and sweating, he sat straight up for the duration of class, eyes fixed and glassy. Dodd resumed his lecture as if nothing had happened.

Thirty minutes later the bell rang. "That's it," Dodd said as we sprang up. "Except for you, Garrison. I ain't done with you."

I had left my backpack against the wall near Garrison, and had to go past him to retrieve it. I picked it up quickly but, as I walked past him, he stopped me with a large foot and raised his eyes to mine. "You better be careful you little motherfucker," he hissed. "You and that worm-ass buddy o' yours owe me already; and somebody's sure as hell gonna' pay." I froze, not certain what to say or do. I looked around for Pete but he was leaving the classroom. Dodd cleared his throat loudly. Garrison lowered his eyes, pulled his foot back, and I left hastily, still not sure why he had singled me out. We never saw him in school again.

Pete and I had thoroughly explored Ten Mile's shaded banks and had identified likely fishing spots along the way. During one of those sojourns, we stumbled upon Bluehole.

By land there were only two ways there. One was by way of the big highway bridge along the upper bank. That route was the shortest, but it entailed a slow and very precarious trip along a narrow ledge with a thirty foot drop. The pastures had long been fenced along the creek and trees of every description had grown down the fence lines. Because of their roots, bank erosion had stopped just short of the fences, but even that narrow strip was washed out in several places and trees had fallen in others, creating enormous gaps in the path. We had to negotiate the fences to go around every gap.

The route we generally took was longer but less arduous. It started at the railroad trestle on Old Cedar Road and followed Five Mile Creek to its confluence with Ten Mile, from where it was a short hike to Bluehole. It followed the low bank and sometimes involved wading in waist- deep water in a few places; but that was no great bother. In fact, it was often a soothing relief from the brush and bramble we'd fought through getting there.

BRIM

Bluehole was a prolific producer of brim – oval to almost circular shaped sunfish weighing anywhere from a quarter to a half pound of glimmering, brightly hued scale and tasty flesh. Brim ("bream" in other parts of the country) included fat bluegills and red-belly or long-ear sunfish, which we referred to as "pumpkinseeds", legions of smaller green sunfish, brilliantly striped warmouths, the myriad hybrids we called "goggle-eyes"...and even an occasional, sturdy rock bass. All were "brim" to Pete and me. Along Ten Mile Creek, and especially in Bluehole's shaded depths, they waited motionless, as if suspended by invisible wires, fins slowly fanning the clear, cool depths of their dim sanctuary. And any minnow, crawdad, worm, snail, small crustacean or waterbug that came too close, that skittered, crawled, floated or ventured carelessly toward those murky depths was at risk. In a flashing blur of color, a brim would strike. Then with fins fluttering and gills moving almost motionlessly, it would return to suspended watchful animation.

Bluegills grew to comparatively prodigious size; warmouth and the rare rock bass could go more than a pound. They were tough little fish. We knew from experience that, ounce for ounce, no fish in North Texas waters fought harder than the ubiquitous brim. But it was more than experience that drew us to Bluehole. It was the gut feeling, the awareness that Bluehole held the prize, that somewhere in those blue-black depths was the Monster, the King, the Whopper. I was gonna' catch that big boy. And Pete? Well, he could watch me do it.

After supper (dinner was a noon meal) I usually walked the hundred yards or so down to Pete's house and dug in again with him and his folks. Stuffed near to bursting with flank steak beaten tender, coated in flour and fried, then served with brown gravy accompanied by sautéed onions, mashed potatoes, red beans cooked with slabs of salt pork, turnip greens, sweet cornbread with huge glasses of iced tea, and all that topped off by lemon meringue pie, we'd sit around the table and argue about everything from grasshoppers to Mozart. During the fall, we talked football. When our regular subjects wore out, we inflated the exploits of our dogs; but we saved our most passionate exchanges for who caught the most and biggest fish. Pete's dad immensely enjoyed those arguments. He egged us on, laughing heartily, remarking that he'd heard it all before, which indeed he had. Our script had been conceived over years of camaraderie and rehearsed during hours of endless debates. That we knew our lines well was unremarkable.

From early spring through late fall, the concrete sidewalk in front of Pete's house retained the sun's warmth well into the evening. Later that night, soaking up the warmth while watching a couple of billion stars wheel their immutable paths across the Texas sky, we continued our verbal jousting. We relived the Coach Dodd-Dee Garrison incident. Pete's dad had dismissed Garrison's comeuppance as being long overdue, but I detected a grain of concern in his comments. We finally exhausted that subject and returned to our favorite agenda item…

"Oughta' be down at Bluehole right now." Pete said.

"You're right. We'd be gettin' our arms jerked off." I recognized the error immediately.

"Gettin' *what* jerked off? If I'm getting' jerked off, I'd a damn sight ruther it was somethin' other'n my arm."

I tried to steer things back my direction

"But maybe not. I ain't sure the big ones bite at night."

"They bite when they're hungry."

"When do they sleep?"

"You ever seen eyelids on a fish, dummy? Fish don't sleep."

"Course they do. They gotta' sleep."

"Maybe they can roll their eyes all the way backwards in their heads like Daggie Underwood. I seen him do that lots'a times. Remember back in eighth grade when he done that to Laura Cates an' she fainted?"

"Daggie is a moron."

There was a precious pause.

Where is he headed now?

"Talkin 'bout morons, I got me one o' them. Has one eye and gets all swole up when he's excited."

How did I manage to get here?

"Named him ol' Hector. Likes to be petted. An' I am thinkin'…thinkin' mind you, about precious Dawn pettin' ol' Hector."

I knew what I was being dragged into, but had to respond.

41

"Well, Pete, I suspect Dawn isn't all that fond of petting dwarves. And anyway, let's not talk about her."

"Oh, she'd like ol' Hector."

How is it I know you're gonna' tell me why?

"It come to me in a vision.

"What kind of vision?" I asked without thinking.

"Angel come down and lit on my shoulder an' whispered it in my ear," he intoned solemnly.

"Pete, that kind of talk plays lightly with the affairs of the Lord, and you can go to hell for that!"

"Well now, I ain't said nothin' 'bout the Lord. You done that. And why do you think He's so interested anyways?"

"He's always interested in us."

"Well then He's really interested in you, 'cause you've had the hots for her ever since she drug back to school swingin' them Jayne Mansfield tits ever which-a-way. You're as bad as me, I'm jist honest about it. An' He knows that too, by the way."

"I'm not like you. I don't act like you act and I don't say the things you say."

"You jist think 'em. And thinkin's just as bad as sayin'. 'As a man thinketh in his heart, so is he'. Proverbs twenty three and seven."

"That's gotta' be the only scripture you know, an' you only know that 'cause you feel guilty all the time."

"I learned that in bible memory camp for your information, but if it's pussy we're talkin', I *am* guilty all the time. Anyways, you sound like Mama and them ol' biddy hen friends o' hers over to Miz Harkness' Bible Class."

"Satan has completely inhabited you."

"I hope he has. Sumbitch gets all the pussy he wants."

"You just better shutup! Anyway, I don't think like that. I'd rather think about how nice and sweet she is."

"You are so full of it! You think about tappin' 'er. All you an' ever other guy in school thinks about is those tits a' bouncin' and that ass a' wigglin'. Anyhow, if what you say is right, God must be so busy keepin' up with all that combined thinkin' he ain't got no time to worry about me comin' right out and admittin' it. An' God (looking up), I'm admittin' it. That has got to be some *fiiiine* pussy!"

42

His sacrilege would have continued except for the beatup 39' Chevrolet that churned around the corner and skidded to a stop.

"Hey! Shitheads!" A familiar voice yelled from the passenger-side front seat.

It was full dark, and I couldn't tell who was yelling at us, who was behind the wheel, or who was in the back seat. I yelled back, "What's up, there?"

"You two better watch out" came the disembodied voice.

In the flare of a cigarette lighter, I recognized Carl Walls in the front passenger seat. I could feel Pete's bristling anger as he rose and stepped quickly toward the car.

"You come t' do somethin' besides talk, buttbreath?" The challenge was unmistakable.

Walls turned and spoke to the driver. Inaudible words were exchanged and everyone in the car laughed. I came up beside Pete. "We got better things to do than waste time with this bunch." I said, studying the gaunt face in the half-light of the corner streetlamp.

Walls was a prime example of white trash. He was the type of non-performer that dropped out of school to become a service station attendant. He had a dark complexion, an unruly shock of greasy black hair, and a surly attitude. Incapable of developing a normal range of personal nuance, he had perfected a sneer. When he spoke, which was far more than necessary, it was seldom anything other than disjointed profanity. Usually we just ignored him and he hadn't bothered us…until now. I started to say something else but Walls spoke first.

"Jist remember you been warned!" Another round of muffled laughter erupted inside the vehicle. Words stuck in my throat, and Pete was equally stage struck when they burned off, gravel spraying and the pungent smell of burned rubber filling the sweet night air.

We watched their tail lights disappear up the street. Pete's dad stuck his head out the door.

"Everything all right out there?"

"Yessir." Pete answered.

"Who was that?"

"Just some guys from school."

"Well, somebody needs to teach 'em how to drive."

"Yessir." Pete answered. His father stepped back inside.

43

"Who was drivin'?" I asked.

"I think it was Garrison." Pete said, looking back toward his house.

"No way."

"That's who it was."

"The big one? Dee?"

Pete nodded.

"After today, I'm surprised he's showin' his face."

"I dunno', Don. He tried to trip you up today an' he may have it in for us."

"Why us? Because of that stupid trotline?"

"I guess. What else can you think of?"

I thought it wise not to mention the hall incident with his brother.

"That seems kinda' crazy."

"Maybe so, but it was him drivin'."

"But what kinda' warnin' was that?"

"Well, you heard what he said when you was tryin' to get by him today."

"Ahhh, that was just talk."

"You don't think it was a threat?"

"Do you?"

"I reckon it was."

"I think he was just mad and embarrassed. He had to take it out on somebody. I just happened to be there."

"But what did that jack-off idiot Walls mean just now?"

"Who knows? Him and his bunch and the Garrisons all run together, y' know."

Pete seemed legitimately concerned. Maybe he knew something I didn't. Maybe my suspicions about his dad's earlier comments concerning Dee were more fact than fiction. Suddenly, I began to worry. "It ain't worth worryin' about." I lied, ardently hoping it would all go away.

"You're probably right." Pete replied as we both settled back on the sidewalk. We stared at the stars awhile longer, enjoying the cool, late evening breeze contrasted with the sidewalk's leftover warmth. We found the Big and Little Dippers. We thought we spotted Venus but

44

couldn't be sure. For that very quiet, very short time, there was no need for conversation. Pete broke the silence. He was serious now.

"You keep wantin' to see Dawn as a saint, Don. An' I'm tellin' you right now, I've heard enough to know she ain't no saint."

"What's ya heard?"

"Just stuff. Remember what your ole friend Mark Twain said."

"Yeah, what?"

"Most people are like the moon, never show their dark side."

"Dawn has no dark side."

"Well…"

"Look, I don't really wanta' know. I just wanta' be with her."

I was the ultimate dreamer, Pete the ultimate realist. But realist or not, he always gave me room when I had to have it. Later, at home, lying awake, I returned to the earlier encounter. I really never got to sleep until I channeled my thoughts to Dawn. Drifting off was much easier realizing I'd see her in school the next day…a day that started with Buddy flagging me down in the hall...

"Wait for me! Wait up, you guys!"

"I reckon we have to talk to him." Pete said, stopping and turning to me.

"Be firm."

"Right."

Breathless, Buddy finally caught up with us outside the Science Room. "Hey, you guys gotta' listen." he pleaded.

"We're listenin'." I said.

"How about uncattlin' me? I've done my time."

"It ain't exactly that easy, Buddy," Pete explained. "You violated the code."

"What code?"

"Code of the King Cattlers." Pete continued, never breaking a smile, "which is me and Don…as in *us*," he concluded, nodding at me.

"Awww, guys…"

"Buddy," I added, "you can't act cattlish and avoid being cattled. It's inescapable."

Sounds pretty good.

"Cattlish?"

"Yes, uh, cattlish" Pete verified.

45

"Cattlish?" Obviously, Buddy had to hear it again.

"Goddamn, Buddy! We done told you a hundred times about lettin' Kara Lynn boss you aroun'....an' what is all that hootchy kootchy crud with you an' her?"

Buddy turned crimson. "But we ain't goin' together no longer." He protested. "I swear we ain't. I don't even like her no more. She's...uhhh...way too bossy."

I looked at Pete...who turned to Buddy. "You ain't jist a' shittin' us?"

Buddy paused...looked around...then his hand shot up in three-fingered salute. "Scouts honor!" He beamed.

"When was you ever a boy scout?" Pete snorted. We both knew Buddy was no boy scout.

"Well, I was in cub scouts 'til me an' Eddie Barto's sister got caught in her closet," Buddy responded hopefully.

"Mary Anne?" Pete asked, incredulous at the thought. Mary Anne was two years older than us and stunningly beautiful...last year's "Miss Sparkle". She dated grown men and had to be putting out because grown men wouldn't date girls that didn't. Of that fact we were absolutely certain. She smoked cigarettes as well, which was another sure sign that she engaged in sexual congress.

"Naw...Texie Louise," Buddy corrected.

"Oh. Well, that's more like it." Pete countered. "An' whatta' y' mean 'got caught'?"

"We was playin' husband and wife and I showed her mine and she showed me hers and we rubbed 'em together...but that's all."

"How'd you get caught?" I had to know.

"Eddie was spyin' on us and he told Miz Barto."

Although I found Buddy's story stimulating, I wanted to move on to something else.

"Let us think about this," I suggested.

"Great!" Buddy exulted, greatly relieved. "I don't wanta' stay cattled."

"Buddy, you want to be uncattled...permanently uncattled, that is?" I asked.

Buddy's eyes widened. "Permanent?" he repeated tentatively.

"There might be a way."

46

"What have I gotta' do?" Buddy was eager.

"Well, this is it...and it's not gonna' be easy."

"Tell me about it!"

"You hafta' do something brave and noble."

"Brave'n noble?"

"Right, Pete?" I asked for his agreement.

"I dunno' about noble, but gettin' caught by Eddie Barto rubbin' your tallywhacker on his sister is about as brave as it gets."

"Noble then," Buddy interjected. "Like what?"

Before either of us could manage an invention, the bell sounded, chairs shuffled everywhere, classroom doors flew open, and students burst into the hallway.

"Gotta' go," Pete said. "Gotta' be in English early today...make up for bein' late yesterday."

"What about the noble thing?" Buddy protested.

"When I get time," Pete smiled, "I'll tell you all about bein' noble."

As they vanished among a bevy of students I turned toward the fountain and was immediately mesmerized. An arc of water disappeared between impossibly beautiful lips, and those lips belonged to the most impossibly beautiful girl on the planet. "Dawn!" I blurted, surprised, delighted, and completely unnerved. I was near to passing out from a massive surge of adrenalin and fighting back an almost irresistible urge to try for a kiss.

"You two are so mean," she replied, bending gracefully to the fountain, heavy breasts straining at the light fabric of her summer blouse.

"What?" I managed to stammer.

"You guys been teasin' Buddy an' he's too sweet for ya'll to be so mean to him."

"Oh, I'm gonna'...what I mean is, we're gonna'..." I was losing ground and I knew it. I had to re-group. "We're just kiddin'." I offered lamely, far more aware that I was alone with her than concerned with the status of Buddy's cattledom.

"Yeah?" she responded languidly. "Well, you know he takes that cattle stuff seriously."

"Oh, he just goes along with it."

47

"Really?" She smiled under arched eyebrows.

I broke into a heavy sweat.

"Yes, Don. And I talked to Pete and he said he was gonna' be a *lot* nicer to Buddy."

Oh damn him! Damn him! Why does she have to mention him? How does he manage to invade my most private interludes?

My heart raced until I thought I might have to sit down.

"When were you talkin' to Pete?" I stammered.

Is that too obvious?

"I sit next to him in English. As a matter of fact, I'm going there right now. He's really nice to me."

What would be really nice is if he'd hang himself.

"Nice. Yes, Pete's very nice," I heard myself say.

I hope the sonofabitch climbs onto the gym roof and falls off.

"Anyway Don, you're still bein' mean to me."

"Huh? Why?"

She paused and smiled alluringly, exposing the tip of a most charming pink tongue.

"Because you still ain't come out to see me."

"Oh…" stammering again. "well, you see…"

The bell rang, saving me from ineptitude. There was a muted, shuffling sound as students settled into place throughout the building.

"Well!" Dawn exclaimed, clutching a book to breasts that swelled sideways from being compressed. "Gotta' get to class. See ya later."

She moved away, hips swinging suggestively, an apparition…ephemeral. She paused a few feet away, then turned back to me. My heart rate skyrocketed and my face burned with embarrassment over my inability to converse even halfway intelligently with her. She smiled. I leaned against a locker and tried to form what I thought resembled one of my own. "You might ask Pete how to get to my house," she said casually before disappearing down the hallway.

Pete! That treacherous bastard! How does he know how to get to her house if he hasn't been there already? Traitor! I've suspected him all along! Damn him anyway and down that old well behind Junior Gribble's garage… the one the fire department had to fish old lady Fizenberg's tomcat out of!

48

Several days later I decided to visit Dawn. Of course, I had to take Pete along since she insisted on it and he had figured my plan out anyway. We actually went so far as to ride by her house. It stood along a seldom used back road that branched away from Old Cedar. But there was a problem. On the day we found our courage, we couldn't find our dogs.

"Where the hell are they?" Pete fumed as we straddled our bikes, poised to venture afield. "Did you think to whistle 'em up?"

I shook my head and adjusted my kickstand, frustrated beyond expression. We had searched the neighborhood high and low. "If we didn't want 'em around, we couldn't get rid of 'em." I said.

"Well, what're we gonna' do?" Pete asked flatly.

"Go see her."

"Without the dogs?"

"Yes."

"Won't that seem funny?"

"Why?"

"Your precious plan, dumbass. She thinks we're bringin' 'em out to show 'em to her."

"Well, we'll just have to invent another reason."

"Like what?"

We reviewed the probability that our rationale for biking out to her house without Fuzzy and Jeff might be questioned. But, it was a long way to her place and we managed to concoct an innovative pretext. We had ventured that far *by accident*, we would explain. Of course, she had invited us, she expected us, and we were determined to go…yet so fragile were our egos that we needed the excuse in the event she ignored, or summarily dismissed us. We were apprehensive beyond description as we rounded the long bend that led up to her house.

"Yonder it is!" Pete bawled.

It was a weathered white frame structure surrounded by scrub-oak trees. Three old, obviously broken cars cluttered the yard, uncut grass and weeds growing up past the running boards. Off to the side was a rusted relic of a tractor with great iron lugs in place of tires. A dilapidated mailbox leaned precariously across a drainage ditch choked with weeds. As we drew closer, our hesitation mounted. Dawn sat on a porch swing, observing our approach with bemused interest.

"That's her!" I muttered breathlessly as we almost collided with the mailbox.

Out of the shadow of the porch, a vision in tight white shorts and a halter top glided to the front step and waved gaily. If she'd simply ignored us and gone inside, we would have been disappointed...but enormously relieved. As it was, we were completely unnerved. Faces burning with embarrassment, we goosed our bikes down the road, giggling insanely to relieve the tension of the moment. Half-a-mile later we braked to one side, panting heavily and each vociferously accusing the other of being the first to chicken out.

Courage failed us that day. We could have stopped, apologized for not bringing the dogs, and drooled over her. Instead, we tucked our tails and ran. Continuing around the next bend, we swore solemn vows that the next trip would be different. Next time, we would carry out our mission. We would summon the courage to face the age-old dilemma of male adolescence confronted by female maturity. We would not zip by like seventh graders. Next time, we would act like the men we were. We would bring Fuzzy and Jeff if we had to tie them to our bikes all night. Next time, as things turned out, we managed all that and a good deal more. Next time, we were on our way to Bluehole.

Fat, purplish night crawlers were the best brim bait, but digging them out of the hard, sun-baked ground was sometimes next to impossible. Also, it was not always easy to keep them in the can. And, for some unexplained reason, when staying in the can they seemed to enjoy curling into tangled balls in the bottom. Untangling them was messy. All in all, worms were hard to deal with.

Consequently, salt-pork became our bait of choice. Cut into very small strips for our tiny hooks, it was a tempting morsel for brim prone to attack anything. Even as it hit the water, the recent hatch would swarm up to peck at it. The problem was getting it down to the larger fish. Brim arrange themselves in layers, the larger ones always in deeper, preferably shaded locations. So I quickly learned to add just a little extra weight to my line. This helped get it past the ravenous youngsters. Despite his intelligence, Pete never caught on to this trick. And I wasn't about to enlighten him. As a result, while I constantly caught large fish...Pete rarely did.

THEM

Jimmy Dillard hadn't wanted to find out what the Garrisons had for him. He was on his way to the sno-cone stand for a rasberry. Jimmy loved the cold, syrupy mush. It reminded him that it was summer and there was no school, that he could sleep late, and that a twelve-hour day seemed like a twelve day week because you could wander at leisure, see your friends, and do almost anything you wanted without care, worry, or responsibilities. But this summer day, the sno-cone stand would have to wait, because the Garrisons had cornered him.

"Come on, you guys. The sno-cone stand is about to close." Jimmy lied, trying to pull away from the firm grip on his wrist.

"Don't be stupid, Dillard. Only babies eat that shit."

"Come on, David. I need to go anyways or I'll get in trouble." Jimmy whined.

"We just wanna' show y' somethin'." Dee said, standing to one side, watching his brother torment the much smaller boy.

"I hafta' hurry. We're going to Royce City later." Jimmy protested.

"Fuck Royce City! Who goes to that dump? Whatsa' matter with you, Dillard?"

Unable to pull away and on the verge of tears, Jimmy was still pleading until Dee stopped him. "Look at this Dillard. Looky here." He partially opened his cupped hands.

"What?" Jimmy asked reluctantly.

"This here, Jimmy...what I'm holdin' here. You gonna' like this." His hands parted to reveal a tiny bird.

"That a sparrow?"

"At's right, a sparrow."

"It's just a baby. What about it?"

"You like birds, Jimmy? Don't you like birds?"

"I guess." Jimmy answered, entirely unsure where the exercise was headed.

"You like this one?"

"I guess."

"You want it, Jimmy?"

"Me?"

51

"That's right, Jimmy, you. If you want it, you can have it."

"I can?" Jimmy's face brightened. Maybe they really thought he wanted their fool bird and he could take it and leave.

"You could feed it some of that sno-cone shit!" David offered.

"You can feed it whatever you wanna' feed it." Dee countered.

"I'll feed it bread." Jimmy said tentatively. "My daddy works at Mrs. Bairds."

"Well now, ain't that just wonderful." Dee commented.

Jimmy looked hopefully at him.

"Okay, Dillard, close your eyes and hold out your hands," Dee commanded.

Jimmy complied, squeezing his eyes tightly shut. Then, he heard a noise he couldn't identify. It sounded like a chirp cut short, followed by a soft, popping noise. Then, he felt something warm and very soft in his cupped hands.

"Open your eyes now Jimmy," Dee intoned.

Jimmy regarded the contents of his hands with mounting horror, then screamed and fell to his knees. Blood and excrement dripped from his fingers. He gagged and dropped the tiny bundle of wet feathers, finally vomiting copiously as the Garrisons roared with laughter.

Dee and David Garrison were clever enough to leave few witnesses that weren't so frightened they only wanted to forget whatever injustice they had seen. Even on the few occasions they were called to account, the punishment was minimal.

Their father had accumulated considerable land around the countryside by loaning at usurious rates, then foreclosing. After his death, their mother held onto the fortune by doling it out to her sons in niggling increments. Scions of a wealthy family, the brothers dressed like rag-pickers. What little they managed to pry out of her was quickly squandered on the north side of the Trinity River where it was "wet", meaning liquor was sold legally. The rest of the county, south of the Trinity, was "dry". It wasn't so much that "county" folks weren't drinkers; it was that admitting it was not good form, and there was no arguing with the clergy...who were uniformly against it and extremely vocal.

Most little towns had their "black sheep"; ours were the Garrisons, to which were attributed all manner of vile deeds, at least some, if not most, accurately so. When K.K. Kennemer's cat, which he had patiently trained to yowl to his accompaniment on a harmonica, was found with its head nailed to his front porch, the Garrison boys were the natural suspects. A suspicious fire reduced the Methodist Church recreation room to a hollow cubicle of smoking rubble and deputies were seen transporting the Garrison boys to the Dallas County lockup. Guilty, everybody figured. And they probably were; only it never came to trial. Then, there was the savage beating of old Bub Blaylock.

Bub owned the last pair of working mules in the county and traveled from house to house plowing gardens or grading yards so they'd drain. Evidently, Bub refused to put his team in a ditch when the Garrisons wanted to pass him on a one lane road. They beat him senseless. Dee, the older one, got probation for that one.

They perfected an air of swagger and braggadocio, and seemed to enjoy trying to intimidate folks, leering, swearing and acting tough. The problem was, our town wasn't an accommodating venue for that kind of activity unless, as Pete's dad often said, you "packed enough ass" to back up your act. Chip Locke threw them out of his Western Auto store, all 5 feet 6 inches and 140 pounds of him, soundly whipping David in the street, with Dee unwilling to intervene. Chip was a 25 mission, B-24 pilot during World War II, another veteran who'd been shot at by enemies who had every intention of killing him. There were a lot of men like Chip in our town. They were more than happy to put the war behind them but decidedly disinclined to humor bullies.

Among the boys our age, however, the Garrison brothers managed to gain the reputation of being "bad", which meant tough. To Pete and me they didn't represent much along that line, certainly nothing to worry about, there always being two of us to take on. They were quite a bit older than us, so we didn't accord them much consideration. When they began showing up more often than usual, and in tension-packed situations, they found a place in the back roads of our minds; but being highly glandular teen-agers attentively inclined to trim ankles, slender legs, volley ball buttocks, and other noticeable attributes of the softer gender, we didn't frequent those roads too often. And when we did, it was usually due to some totally unexpected incident.

Saturday morning action was at the Dairy Queen. That's where the players gathered to re-live last night's game. At the DQ, the players bunched around the "hottest" car, talking about who executed the hardest hit, the longest run, or the most spectacular catch...but the answers to that were simple enough. It was you who made that hit or caught that pass, and you longed to receive that recognition unasked. But these discussions inevitably moved on to the infinitely more exciting subject of which girl was reportedly "putting out", and from that point deteriorated into adolescent male drivel-babble. Pete reveled in any attention he could garner at such gatherings. I, naturally, shunned them...unless, of course, I actually had been Friday night's hero. In that case, I soaked it up.

PURSUITS

For two full weeks following our misadventure with Dawn, we tactfully avoided conversation with her. There were perfunctory "hellos" we couldn't avoid, but we couldn't bring ourselves to say much to her, absent enormous embarrassment; so we were reduced to calf-eyed adoration in the halls, lunchroom, and the few classes we shared. She returned our mooning attention with a sly, knowing smile; without doubt laughing as she recalled the mad scramble of our would-be visit. She wasn't going to bring it up if we didn't. Finally, things returned to normal and our relentless pursuit of her dwindled to less ridiculous proportions. This was in no small part due to our obsession with a seasonal pursuit. The annual hunt for the district football title was on, the pack was in full cry, and much of our testosterone transferred to the gridiron.

In small-town Texas, high school football was, and always had been, King. On any Saturday morning, after a Friday night win, old-timers would gather over steaming cups of coffee at Chig's Cafe to rehash the game. They argued over which team was best, the '42 district champions or the one that won the night before. One hooted at the wobble on the quarterback's passes; another advanced pungent commentary as to the difference last year's all-district end would have made had he not managed to knock up the holiness preacher's daughter...a girl with a stripper's body, the brains of a ewe, and the sexual needs of a cat in estrous...thus requiring his hasty transfer from school to work force. It was a matter of routine for the players to show up briefly to collect accolades and listen with seeming earnestness to the old guys' tips, but it was really an opportunity to bask in the glory of being winners.

Football was the mantle of self respect, the icon of pride, and winning was everything. No matter how badly the week had gone in general: water tower springing a leak and drowning Miz Daniels' prize winning Rhode Island Reds, Cab Arneux cutting off the fingers of one hand snubbing a steer to a post, Bradley Bales' new brick archway collapsing on Greg Arnold...or the alleged ill effects of a damned blue moon...it didn't matter. A Friday night win drove morale straight up. Saturdays, steps were lighter and quicker, smiles were wider, and a hundred hardy "howdies!" bellowed from throats hoarse from cheering the night before. Earl Broaddus shaved the price of a haircut, McDougal's Drugstore sold cherry cokes for a nickel, and the younger town boys temporarily refrained from aggravating old Buster Cuze until he'd wave his walking stick, mouth working wordlessly, dire conjurations of his thoroughly addled brain set free in hugely amusing silence.

But losing was emptiness. Players avoided the old-timers, Earl closed shop early, "the game" wasn't discussed...and the town boys returned to baiting old Buster with a vengeance.

The game of football required a team, devoted fans, a myrmidon coaching staff, and one other essential ingredient: cheerleaders. They were, without exception, female, and the sexiest in school; soft and generous of lip, long of leg, round of buttock, and generally prominent of breast. Those were the only requirements; they were otherwise absent any recognizable talent, and had the collective intellectual curiosity of a brick road. They gyrated, but were not acrobats and neither tumbled, twisted, nor flipped...unless by accident. Their dress was abbreviated skirts, bobby socks and saddle oxfords. Cheerleaders were female equivalents of the starting team; and everyone who was, dreamed, or aspired to be "in" worshiped them - girls perversely, boys with urgent visions of rampant physicality in a darkened back seat. Privately, Pete and I had long ago cattled the lot of them; but we were far more interested in finding reasons to be physical with them than in declaring their ascension to the shrine of bovinity.

That fall we were on the "B" Team, but we suited up for "A" team games and, on rare occasions, got in for a few plays. Most of the time we rode the bench, paying lip service to the action on the field; zeroing in instead on the sidelines where our zeal-inspiring lovelies "rah- rahed" the faithful to brilliant victory or crushing defeat. Like most teenage males with overactive glands, one of our primary reasons for playing football was to impress girls, especially the cheerleaders. Forcefully adjured to keep our eyes on the game so we would have some concept of the situation were we sent in, our attention invariably wandered to the sidelines. Getting caught at this inevitably incurred the wrath of the assistant coach. "You two get your heads in the game!" he would roar, or, "Shook! You gonna' look pretty stupid with one hand on the football and the other one on your goddamn dick!"

Dawn was not a cheerleader. She didn't even bother to try out. She was no more inclined to scream cheerful inanities than Pete or me. And as for gyrating, the only article of her person that did that accomplished it effortlessly and to remarkable effect. From the bench, Dawn-watching was as rewarding as cheerleader watching...and vastly more interesting than the game itself. Since the cheerleaders were all older than us, Dawn-watching was our most compelling reason for being on the "B" team.

Dawn followed every game attentively. Always sitting quietly, either alone or with a few girlfriends, she would follow every play, seldom raising her voice above a mild, "Come on, ya'll." When not following the action, my eyes were fastened on her, and sometimes her glance seemed to catch mine, causing my poor heart to pound like a jackhammer. Since I believed that being on the team had to be one of the keys to Dawn's heart, I regularly nurtured a vision of myself as the "A" Team Quarterback…

I fade back, juking deftly away from one tackler, stiff-arming yet another as my arm whips back… then down and through… the ball a tight, humming spiral into the outstretched hands of the right end racing downfield a full fifty yards away. The crowd's thunderous roar hot in my ears, I turn, and am transfixed by her glowing eyes and lovely features, lit by an incandescent smile. For me… me alone..

"Don, she definitely has the hots for me." Pete said, wearing a huge grin and waving toward the stands.

"What?" I demanded crossly. "Who's got the hots for you?"

"Dawn. Lookit 'er wavin' at me."

"She's not waving at *you,* dummy!"

"Oh, but she is. Look! The game's almost over and she's lettin' me know she seen me play. Lookit that!" He said, waving even more vigorously.

I did look, and Dawn was indeed looking our way and waving. The urge to kick him was gloriously rewarding.

57

"You know Maurice King cut that, don't you?" He remarked offhandedly.

"What?" I screamed

I could kick him through the goalposts.

"That's not so. And don't you say it any more!"

"Don't be a dumbass, Don. Everybody knows he cut her. Paid 'er too."

"Well everybody is wrong…that's all! That's just a mean lie."

"Oh for God's sake! I guess you think she's a virgin." Pete responded wearily.

"Why do you always…*always*…have to talk that way?" I thought that might buy me one minute of peace. I missed by fifty-three seconds.

"Well, that's got to be some tight pussy anyways."

"Pete, why don't you just shutup. And for your information, God's keepin' up with everything …everywhere. And He really gets angry when we talk dirty…like you're doin' right now."

"So now God's got somethin' against tight pussy?" he went on in his familiar air of innocence.

"Oh, you….you… *idiot!* You have no respect even for God!"

Pete could make me lose my temper quicker than anyone. He knew this and took advantage of it at every opportunity.

"Well, I ain't never heard Brother Banks preachin' against tight pussy."

"You will answer someday for your sacrilege." I responded, cold as a sepulcher…at least as coldly as I could muster. Pete took no notice.

"But then any pussy I get will be tight."

I whirled toward him, my rage towering and incalculable …

"Shook…you and Robbins," Assistant Coach Rankin thundered. "You stay right where you are and give me ten laps when this game's over!"

"Now see what you done!" I chastised him in a huff, sitting down dejectedly and turning toward the field.

"Me? You're the one with your head stuck up your ass."

Rankin was in our faces immediately. "You know," he screamed, "you two might get *in* the game if you'd keep your minds *on* the game!" I fumed silently. Pete found sudden reason to inspect his shoelaces.

Just before the final gun in a game we never came close to winning, I chanced another look in the stands but Dawn had disappeared. The team members consoled and patted each other, breathing platitudes such as "get'em next week". Everyone except Pete and me trudged toward the locker room; we headed toward the far end of the field to begin our laps. Coach Dodd stopped us on the sidelines.

"You two represent the future, two of my Tough Twenty" he said softly, grinning and rubbing his ear. *"But,"* he exploded, "if you don't shape up, you won't be wearin' football uniforms, you'll be wearin' them fuckin' *cheerleader* outfits!"

"Well," I said after Dodd stormed off, "thanks a lot for that."

"Screw you." Pete countered righteously. "You was the one gawkin' at her all night!"

Never given to accepting reproof graciously, I shook my head. "I don't know why I put up with you." I said, trotting down the chalk line boundary, trying to put distance between us.

"Because you're a jerk!" He yelled, catching up.

"I'm a jerk? You're an idiot!"

"Yeah, well it takes one to know one!"

"Well, believe me I do!"

We finished our laps in silence and rounded the end of the bleachers next to the concession stand where a lone vendor was locking up. The few remaining fans were heading home…car doors slamming, motors turning over, whine of standard transmissions revving through first gear. As we approached the white portable building, a small group of people surrounded a girl. Drawing closer, I saw that it was Dawn. Carl Walls' angry voice cut through the October night. "What makes you think you're so much better'n me?" He shouted.

"Jest leave her alone, Carl!" Sheila Smith, a short, dark-haired sophomore, yelled back.

"You stay outta' this, Sheila. It's none o' your business."

"Jist get outta' our way Carl. We wanta' go home."

"I don't give a shit where you go Sheila, but before she goes anywhere she's gonna' answer me!"

Dawn's voice was steady and calm. "I've answered you already, Carl. Now, let us by."

"You ain't answered shit!" he yelled. "Why in the hell won't you gimme' what I was promised?"

Fighting the knot in my gut, I immediately calculated the odds. There were three against two and we were significantly outweighed. I thought immediately to grab Pete...but it was already too late for that.

"Leave her alone, Walls!" Pete said, walking into the circle.

He's spoiling for one. We don't know what's going on, we don't have to settle it this way, we're outnumbered... and he's gonna' get us into a fight.

Walls and his friends wheeled toward us. "What the fuck you two doin' here?" he snarled.

Pete shrugged, but didn't answer. I slid up next to Dawn. "You okay?" I asked. She nodded, but her apprehension was plain. I turned to Walls. "Look, Carl what's the problem?"

"None o' your fuckin' business wimp!" His violence and use of the pejorative surprised and embarrassed me, but I wasn't prepared to act.

"He wants to take me home." Dawn stated matter-of-factly.

"That what you want?" Pete asked her quietly.

"I ain't lookin' for no trouble with you, Robbins. You need to stay outta' this!" Walls blustered.

Walls' buddies slowly bunched up and moved in our direction. Sensing their salvation, the girls quickly retreated behind Pete and me. Knowing Pete, I dreaded what was sure to happen. I began looking around for something...anything...to use as a weapon. Pete didn't care that we were outnumbered. I did. I quickly settled on a short piece of three-eighths inch steel reinforcing rod. I hated the prospect of having to use it, but found comfort in the fact that, if push came to shove, we'd have a reasonable chance. I didn't think we were going to scare them away. Even in our uniforms, we probably appeared more comical than formidable. But I knew Pete's next move would be anything but funny. So I acted to end it...hopefully.

"What's this all about, Carl? Whatta' you want with Dawn?" I asked, meaning to buy time as well as hold Pete in check.

"Garrison owes him some money and told him Dawn would square things up for him, and he wants to collect!" Sheila said accusingly.

"Shutup you fat bitch!" Walls yelled back. "This ain't none o' your goddamed business. But I am gonna' collect." He said, turning back to us. "So just get the hell outta' here and leave us to our business!" His sycophants laughed.

"Look, Carl," I said, anger rising up in my throat. "We don't want any trouble."

Walls dismissed my platitude with a wave of his hand. I prayed to God Coach Dodd would show up…or anyone in authority who could end this.

Pete turned to me. "Don?" he snorted, as if utterly amazed, "I can't believe you mean we don't want no trouble. That means you think this piece o' shit and his dirtbag buddies are trouble."

Now I knew my efforts to avoid violence would come to naught this night. I stuttered something, trying desperately to catch Dawn's eyes.

"Why don't we just leave it alone", I said, "everything's gonna' be all right. "He doesn't mean anything bad…do you, Carl?"

I kept hoping Dawn and Sheila would slip away, now that Walls and his buddies were focused on us; but the girls stayed put. Worse, I caught Dawn's disapproving eye. *She thinks I'm a coward because I don't want to fight.* I saw her disappointment. I wanted to explain…grab her and say, *Dawn, this is just a way to get you outta' here! You and Sheila get away!*

The cheerleaders appeared around the corner of the concession stand, pom-poms in hand, headed for the gym to console the team. Unsurprisingly, they completely misperceived the situation.

Judy, the curvaceous head cheerleader, greeted us with a bubbly, "What're ya'll doin'?"

Not missing a beat, Dawn grabbed Sheila's hand. "We'll just go with ya'll. Let's go cheer up the boys." The cheerleaders squealed in delightful assent…and left us to our pursuits.

Walls started to speak but, recognizing he was in an untenable position, grunted something unintelligible.

Judy turned to Pete and me. "You guys comin'?"

Pete beat me to the punch. "Nah," he said brusquely, "we got some business here."

Why'd he say that?

61

"Okay," Judy replied, turning to her cohorts. "Let's go girls. The team needs us!"

And we don't?

Leaving, Dawn shot me a withering glance that ripped me to my core. I was sick at heart. I had failed her. I, who desperately wanted to be her hero, had not stood to the challenge. When she needed me the most, I had wilted...chickened out...and although she wouldn't know it now or maybe ever, that was about to change.

As the girls' voices faded, I assessed our dilemma. Walls was enraged by the turn of events and had courage in numbers; three to two represented pretty good odds. His constituents were large, looked able-bodied enough, and seemed ready for a fight. "Come on, Carl," one of them said, louder than necessary, "let's git this over with!"

Walls looked menacingly at us. "Okay, motherfuckers," he growled. "Let's get it on."

I thought it was an excellent time to make a graceful departure, but Pete was unmoved by Walls' bravado. Relishing what he considered an advantage, Walls began psyching himself up.

"You ain't heard I'm a bad motherfucker I guess", he snarled, jerking his jacket off.

Pete spat, but said nothing.

"Bad motherfucker! You ain't heard that?"

"Walls, the only thing bad about you is your fuckin' breath," Pete said and shuffled quickly into him while simultaneously launching a vicious overhand right. There was the flat smack of fist striking face accompanied by a sharp crack. For a moment, Walls looked shocked, then he sighed audibly, his legs buckled, and he dropped to his hands and knees, blood already running from his flattened nose. Immediately, Pete raised his right foot, still in cleats, and stomped down hard on Walls' hand. Walls screamed and instinctively grabbed the injured extremity with his remaining good one, only to collapse with his face in the dirt. Mechanically, I picked up the steel rod knowing that I would almost surely have to use it.

I hated this sort of thing and, if there was a real difference in Pete and me, that was it. I detested unregulated violence and he seemed to thrive on it once it occurred. I couldn't help but feel sorry for Walls. He hadn't really wanted the fight, but he had talked loud and large and couldn't back down in front of his friends. If Pete had been willing to settle for spirited talk, real violence might have been avoided. What Walls didn't understand was that Pete, in his detached way, thought nothing of hurting him...after all, that's what a fight was all about. With Walls down and obviously out of the fight, I hoped that would do it...that we could leave in rightful triumph, that maybe Dawn hadn't really heard me do my best to beg out of a fight. My pounding heart sank when I suddenly realized that was not to be. The biggest of Walls' buddies charged Pete, followed instantly by the other. Pete got in a solid punch in that rocked his antagonist, but the big boy closed with him and the smaller one grabbed him from behind.

"Goddamn Don, there's two of 'em! You gonna' do somethin'?"

I looked at the ground for a long moment, then sucked in a quick, deep breath and swung the rebar at Pete's largest assailant. It seemed like a half-hearted effort...I didn't really want to hurt him, just... maybe...make him leave Pete alone. I aimed at his shoulder. The boy saw the blow coming and got an elbow up to block it, but the reinforcing rod did its work all too efficiently, landing squarely on the ulnar nerve. The boy sank wordlessly to his knees, in such pain that he was unable to catch his breath.

Surely now... surely... this fight will end, the other one will give it up and we can go home and forget all this.

But Pete's second attacker had somehow managed to achieve what might be described as a rear headlock. They were thrashing wildly, Pete to achieve leverage and advantage, his opponent desperately maneuvering to retain what he already possessed. And Pete was tiring. Nothing is more demanding of energy than a hand-to-hand brawl; and Pete was in one now that was closely contested. His opponent was wiry and didn't seem much impressed by Pete's efforts, which were somewhat inhibited by his football garb. Now Pete was sucking air in great sobbing gasps. Without thinking, I swung the rebar a couple of times. The thin rod hissed evilly, and I hoped Pete's assailant would get the idea of what eventually had to happen to him. "Get away!" I yelled, "get away from him!" I desperately did not want to hit him but it didn't work and finally, Pete began the inevitable slide into exhaustion and defeat. I began to position myself for the stroke that would end it, and at the same time, heard a cry of desperation from Pete,

"He's…got me, Don. Got me!"

But I knew Pete better than Pete knew Pete. I roared at the top of my lungs,

"You're better'n that, damn you! You suck it up and get him offa' you right now!"

Again he cried hoarsely, "Dammit Don! I can't do no more!"

But I could see that Pete's opponent was also tiring, so it was strictly a matter of who could hold out the longest. Now, I wasn't sure I had to do anything after all, so I urged Pete on again.

"Quit whinin' and get on him, Pete!" I yelled, at the same time looking for the opening I needed to end it without severely hurting Pete's adversary.

I was hoping Pete would invent something …anything…when his opponent did it for him. The boy somehow caught Pete's chin and was able to pull his head far back. And in so doing, the boy made the mistake that cost him the fight…and most of a finger. His hand slipped off Pete's sweaty chin and Pete's mouth opened reflexively. One of the boy's fingers slipped between Pete's teeth. Pete twisted hard, the finger slipped between his molars, and he bit down savagely. There was a moment of utter stillness while Pete's opponent, who only the moment before was savoring victory, came to the sudden, perverse understanding that defeat was inevitable,

"I give!" he cried out. "Please…please…lemme' go! I give!"

But granting mercy in a fight did not rank high on Pete's list of meritorious attributes. So, abandoning any semblance of Marquess of Queensbury rules, Pete responded to the entreaty by biting down harder. A high, thin, ululating scream ripped across the darkened field, echoed off the buildings, and rang through the chill night air. The two combatants stood unmoving in the dark shadow of the bleachers, Pete flat footed and unyielding, his opponent as far away from him as he could get, finger locked in the ever tightening vice of Pete's vice-like jaws. Now, a steady flow of blood dripped from Pete's chin, and his teeth ground deeper until I heard the chilling grind of tooth against bone and an unmistakable snapping sound as the bone broke. Then, there were the wet, nauseating sounds as Pete continued to savage the mangled finger.

My God! He'll chew it off if I don't stop him!

I dropped the bar and grabbed Pete, trying to tear him away.

"Pete that's enough. Stop it! Stop it damn you! You're gonna' really hurt him! Let him go!"

But Pete was remorseless and the terrified boy began to whimper.

"Please lemme' go! Oh God, lemme' go!" he begged, the words coming with supreme effort. But Pete was in a familiar, but peculiar, state where talking to him accomplished absolutely nothing. I finally doubled my fist and hit him hard, just above his rib pads. He grunted, but let the boy go and stood to one side, gasping, spitting blood and remnants of flesh. Across the way, in wide-eyed disbelief, Walls had finally staggered to his feet and stood shakily against the concession stand, nursing a badly broken nose and eyes that were beginning to swell shut. Next to him, equally horrified, his other buddy cradled an arm that had no feeling.

Pete's opponent crouched, sobbing, cradling his mangled hand against his chest and whimpering, "Oh, God…my hand! My hand! You Bastard! You sonofabitch! You didn't have to do that to me…didn't have to do that!"

Pete regarded him without emotion and shuffled toward me, on the brink of exhaustion.

"Why," he gasped disjointedly, "did you…hafta' go…and…whack me…in the ribs? That fuckin' hurt, Don."

"I had to hit you. You were acting all crazy and you were about to chew his finger off," I responded reprovingly, "and you wouldn't let him go when I told you to. I couldn't let you do that." I suppose he understood. At least, there was nothing more said about it. Pete wanted to leave immediately, but we saw flashing lights and heard the rise and fall of a siren. "We have to stay," I said. Pete only had energy remaining to nod in assent.

A sheriff's deputy unwound his lanky frame from a Ford interceptor and instantly assessed the situation. He nodded to Pete and me. "You two get on down to the gym. I'm sure Coach will have plenty to say about your little deal here." As we departed, I heard fragments of his trenchant comments to Walls and his friends. Obviously, he was familiar with them. Word the next day was that all three required transport to Parkland, the emergency hospital in Dallas.

The next week, Dawn didn't show up at school. Maybe she had the flu, I figured. It was pretty much epidemic. Word got around about our showdown with Walls and his gang, and it mushroomed into something like the O.K. Corral. Reviews were mixed. Some had Pete and me taking the bullies down, but another rumor had us cutting and running. Pete didn't care who believed what and was quick to say, "Why don't you go ask that stupid Walls why he's got that plastic thing strapped over his nose?"

My concern was for Dawn. I knew she thought I'd let her down, and it agonized me. But with her out of school, there was no way I could explain my actions...or absence thereof. In truth, I couldn't explain it to myself. Whereas Pete had seemingly acted courageously, I had done...well, I wasn't sure what I had done, but it sure seemed like nothing. And that gnawed at my gut. I didn't like myself too much. I was used to leading...initiating action, not standing by wishing there wasn't any.

On Thursday of that week we had a "B" game scheduled. Pete and I both started and I earnestly prayed that Dawn would be in school that day. I wanted to clear things up so she would want to watch us play that night. I wanted her to see a game where I handled the ball on practically every down; where I was brave and important and assertive. After all, her presence was a major reason for playing. I know Pete wanted her there too...but knew as well that if he was praying about her, it wasn't that she'd show up at the game.

There were many stray dogs in our town. One was a large black-brown Chow that belonged to no one. He had a surly disposition and cats, other dogs... even humans steered clear of his menacing presence. A loner, he roamed the streets like a Dark Knight. Most of the time, he shunned human contact, exposing his fangs and moving stiffly away if approached. However, when on the trail of a bitch in season, such was not the case. On these occasions, he became the leader of a pack of canine marauders that plundered the neighborhood.

When least expected, and from out of nowhere, the pack would appear, tongues lolling in single-minded, lust-driven idiocy, relentlessly waiting their opportunity to mount the helpless bitch. Curs, half-breeds, mongrels and pedigrees: all of them followed the chow, urinating and defecating in well kept yards and flower beds, killing an occasional pet and generally causing small scale mayhem.

FUZZY AND JEFF

Old Cedar Road twisted its serpentine, tree-lined way between two small semi-rural towns. Both towns started as farming villages, residents gradually increasing as the city expanded in our direction, and the thoroughfare was officially identified as a farm to market road. Pete and I were heavy users of the road, our bicycles humming over the asphalt, only hitting the gravel shoulders to get out of the way of a passing automobile, or when the tar melted during the height of summer and bogged us down to the point we couldn't pedal. Fuzzy and Jeff could usually be seen trotting along beside us.

Road kill was a frequent sight. Armadillos, possums, squirrels, raccoons, coyotes and foxes in various states of necrosis were common. There weren't nearly as many cars then as now, but there were a lot more critters. Pete and I came to know the anatomy of these animals by poking around in the gory remains, ignoring the stench and roiling clots of maggots. Not wanting Fuzzy and Jeff to join their number, we trained them to trot the shoulders and ditches. Often, they would scare up a rabbit or feral cat and be off like flung bolts through a barbed wire fence and across an open field. Fatigue or impenetrable thicket usually ended the chase and they would rejoin us, tongues lolling, ribcages pumping like bellows.

On schooldays, Fuzzy and Jeff spent their time doing what dogs do best - sleeping. Any dark, shady spot was fine for snoozing the day away, although the traits of their lupine ancestors were unmistakably identifiable. Like their wild forbearers, they preferred den-like hides such as a deep hollow scratched out beneath a dense bush. There, they would drift in and out of dog dreams until we got home from school, rousing only to snap at a bothersome biting fly. When we arrived, they would yawn, stretch, and prance out to greet us, offering their ears to be scratched, ready for whatever we had in mind. Fuzzy would retrieve things we threw. Jeff considered that practice an utter waste, but played a mean tug of war, shaking his head and growling fiercely. Come to think of it, Jeff and Pete were a great deal alike. But, like most dogs, when a local bitch was in heat, sleeping was the last thing on their minds. Then they were driven by primordial instincts older even than their species, instincts they had no choice but to follow. On Thursday, while I was fretting over Dawn and the upcoming game, our faithful canine companions were fretting over their own particular set of problems. There would be no sleep for man's best friend when the unmistakable scent of canine estrus wafted its siren song on the late autumn breeze.

Fuzzy and Jeff approached the all male pack of mutts and strays, ranging from a twenty-pound Poodle mix to a sixty-pound, brindle mongrel. The only thoroughbred was the huge black and brown chow. He was the leader, single-mindedly engaged in servicing a brown and white Springer Spaniel bitch. Her pups would be an ungodly sight and somewhere, somebody was going to catch hell for leaving the gate to her yard unlatched. The pack circled the pair, demented with lust and oblivious to the approach of a big red dog and his burly, dark companion.

Fuzzy and Jeff descended upon them, wicked fangs slashing and tearing. The cur stood his ground for a moment, but Fuzzy feinted, then savagely snapped a foreleg. The brindle made screaming, three-legged haste out of harm's way. The rest of the pack scattered, leaving the bitch and the chow locked rear- to- rear in coitus. Temporarily defenseless, the chow growled fiercely, black lips curled and white fangs bared in glittering defiance. Fuzzy and Jeff ignored his warning and closed on him.

Whimpering in terror, the bitch suddenly broke free and ran, leaving Fuzzy and Jeff eyeball to eyeball with the dog that was almost surely their sire. Hackles bristling and frightful growls issuing from three deep chests, they prepared to clash. The chow stood his ground, growling ominously, fully prepared to defend his dominant position against the invaders. The pack began to reassemble, forming a circle around the prospective combatants. But with the departure of the bitch, an important strategic advantage was lost. Additionally, neither Fuzzy nor Jeff had any interest in the chow. They were consumed with satisfying the biological imperative. Before the fight could begin, Fuzzy and Jeff were out of there and hot on the trail of the fleeing bitch. The pack was only a short distance behind, baying, whining, yelping and barking. The doggy parade lasted less than a block. The terrified bitch spotted an open front door at one of the stately old frame homes along Peachtree Street, and immediately bounded up the porch steps and into the house, with Fuzzy and Jeff close in trail.

Frank Walters, who owned the town's Clover Farm franchise, was dutifully watering wife Jessie Maudine's giant zinnias. Mouth gaping in surprise, he observed three dogs burst through the door through which his wife had entered the house only moments before. And he heard, then quickly spotted, the pack close behind and managed to get the door closed before they too could join the rampage. Jessie Maudine was taking violent, high-pitched exception to the trio already inside just as the pack hit the porch full steam in a frenzy of barking, slobbering, and whining.

Mr. Frank…as we knew him…a decorated World War One veteran, proceeded straight to a chifferobe in the parlor that neither he nor Jessie Maudine had found reason to open more than twice in the thirty years they'd lived there, and withdrew a double barreled shotgun. He levered the action open, verified the dull brass gleam of two Winchester Super-X's nestled in twin twelve gauge barrels of gleaming steel, and closed the breech with a solid snap. "Now," he intoned determinedly as he pushed the safety forward. "Now, you sunsabitches!"

He could hear the dogs' incessant whining accompanied by an occasional snarl from the bitch. Mr. Frank snuggled the gun butt firmly against his shoulder and, with the muzzle, slowly pushed open the café doors that opened into the kitchen. A large, shapeless, black and multi-colored dog was attempting to mount a much smaller brown spaniel. Mr. Frank stepped into the kitchen, leveled the shotgun, and steadied himself for the recoil when Jessie Maudine tugged at his sleeve.

"Oh Pumpkin (her pet name for Mr. Frank from the dim past when they had occasionally engaged in behavior not altogether dissimilar to that which they were witnessing), don't shoot! I think that's Henry and Vawtie Rae's little brown dog there! Shoo!" She scolded, "You dogs git on out! Shoo now!"

Evidently, the pair had not yet coupled and immediately disengaged. Neither seemed unfriendly, and Jessie Maudine moved toward the screen door to urge them out into the back yard. Mr. Frank remained cautious, but the situation seemed to be resolving itself. Only he'd distinctly seen three dogs come in. His quandary was brief. Jeff had visited a bedroom, hiked a leg and left his calling card on a treasured crocheted bedspread, and had now come silently up behind Mr. Frank. Determined to leave with Fuzzy and the bitch who were, at that moment, making their exit through the back door, Jeff burst full speed between Mr. Frank's legs, claws scrabbling madly on the heavily waxed linoleum. Mr. Frank lost his footing and fell backwards, landing squarely on his butt.

As Jeff exited the back door to join Fuzzy and the bitch, the dogs were startled by two, thunderous, almost simultaneous explosions from the house. Inside, two large holes, surrounded by a large number of much smaller ones, were evident in the ceiling of Jessie Maudine's formerly pristine kitchen. What was worse, water was gushing through one of the holes onto Mr. Frank…on his butt on the floor… and also on Jessie Maudine who was crouched beside him in utter terror.

The Spaniel bitch found a small opening at the bottom of the backyard fence and squeezed through it. Fuzzy and Jeff tried the same maneuver only to find it far too small to accommodate their considerably larger frames. But this wasn't their first fence; they were frantic with fear from the shotgun blasts, and when an enraged Mr. Frank appeared at the back door roaring profanities, they simply leaped to the top and scrambled over. They undertook a spirited resumption of their earlier efforts but, by then, their enchantress had long since departed the area.

Driven by riveting instinct, the two sniffed the air and ran in ever-widening circles with their noses to the ground. Before the day was over, they would be far afield. They would roam for days, with insects, rodents, and an occasional rabbit or possum for food, and such water as they happened upon in creeks, drainage ditches, or ponds. All their great adventures very likely started for the same reason.

They always returned after a week to a fortnight, looking feral and bedraggled. Gaunt and exhausted, wounds festering from God knows how many fights, they would drag themselves to the water pail, drink their fill, gorge on whatever we put down for them, then sleep and heal for days.

After more than one of their returns, a trip to the vet was required. And it was always Fuzzy. An ugly tear in his hindquarter turned into an eighty-dollar infection. My parents had to make payments when our family doctor bill came to such an amount; so a vet bill that large was outrageous. Daddy said he'd do it once, but it might as well not be expected again. We tried to corral them, but curtailing the wilder and more independent aspects of canines as crafty and mature as those two was simply not possible. They continued to wander, then return to be nursed; and our parents accepted that situation because they found it impossible to deny us our faithful buddies. As events played out, they never had to regret their laissez faire approach

The crowd was screaming, horns were blowing, cowbells clanging. The team was running toward the goal line, deliriously excited. Buddy had just scored!

I was on the ground, the lard-assed lineman on top of me, utterly inert. I wriggled from under him and limped toward my jubilant teammates. I found Pete in the gaggle of players. His lips were moving, but his words were drowned in the roar of the crowd. Looking across the field, I saw an ecstatic Bric Dodd furiously rubbing his ear, grinning wickedly, caught up in visions of a pony pulling a cage full of savages. Then I looked up and was blinded by the lights...

BLINDSIDE

Thursday afternoon arrived with Dawn still absent. I tried to mask my disappointment. She had to be at the game if I was to have a chance to make her understand what had happened. I'd even considered going by her place again…

"Are you nuts?" was Pete's comment

"Why not?"

"Because, number one, you don't have time, number two, you ain't even certain she's there, and number three…oh screw it! One and two are enough."

"Don't you want her at the game?" I asked.

"Does a fat dog fart?"

"I'm worried about her."

"You're worried you won't get through the game without fumblin' and she'll get to see me at my most athletic and heroic best."

"Oh shutup! I got time."

"Don, it's already past three, and Coach Dodd wants us suited up and ready to go by six."

"I know, I know…"

"We still have to go home and eat, and…"

"Oh all right! I know!"

He was right. We had to get ready for the game and although it was just a "B" game, it was our game, and we wanted to win. More desperately, we knew we had to be aggressive. Bric Dodd treasured "hitting" above all, and expected nothing less of his future Tough Twenty. If we lost, we'd probably endure a workout after the game. We had no idea of what to expect if we weren't aggressive and didn't "hit" according to his standards. We feared and respected Coach Dodd; and fear and respect were blood brothers. Our reverence and fear of him were without parallel.

While fixing supper, Clarie mentioned that Fuzzy and Jeff were somewhere at large again. She strongly suggested that we try to whistle them up before they strayed too far. But there wasn't time for a search. Following the meal, we hustled off to the gym, donned our uniforms, and sat through the usual pre-game rituals and pep talk.

Coach Dodd was always inspirational and came across like a revival preacher exhorting the faithful to earn a place in football heaven. Finally, the pre-game warmup was over, the teams took the field, the whistle blew, leather started popping…and for almost four quarters, we achieved nothing athletic. Facing the final gun and a three-point deficit, fortuitous fate reversed her field; we recovered a fumble near their goal line. At last we were in a position to score. A play later we were still *near* their goal line.

I called time out and went to the sideline. "You know what to do…now get out there and do it! And no "T" plays inside the five yard line!" Dodd screamed…his face only inches from mine.

"You wanna' be one o' the Tough Twenty?" I heard him roar as I trotted back onto the field.

"Yessir!" I yelled back.

"Then let's hear some leather poppin' out there! You tell Pete that big tackle is runnin' all over his skinny ass. They're all gettin' run over." I knew only too well that the big tackle was running over Pete, because after he ran over Pete, he ran over me. Time was running out and we were still three points behind.

The team wanted badly to pull this one out. Coach Dodd had loudly predicted we would win this game. He was proud of this team, the Tough Twenty of the future, his handpicked assemblage of young football talent. Now we had to live up to his predictions; and all eyes were on the quarterback…which was me. I was the center of attention, a focus I hugely cherished. I had my game face on now. I'd show 'em who was in charge out here. We were gonna' score…we had to score!

"Pete, since you ain't gonna' block that guy, why don't you just invite him into the huddle with us?"

"Hell, Don!" Pete snapped defensively. "Which one of him you think I should block?"

"That ain't good enough."

"I'm fuckin' tryin'."

"Well, you try a little harder!"

Pete grunted and secured his chinstrap.

"All right," I said, glancing over my shoulder at the 250 lb. lineman who had just pounded me into the dirt. "Thirty-four option on two. Break!"

We moved up to the line. Pete, at 160 lbs., dug in at the right guard position. I barked out the signals and the ball was snapped. Sooner than I could even turn, much less execute the handoff, the big boy steamrolled over Pete and into Jay Oliver, our halfback, who rammed straight into me as well. We all went down for another loss.

It was a time when players did not engage in silly displays of self-congratulation, but there was plenty of gamesmanship. "Had enough, you little fart?" the hulking lineman asked, grinding me into the brown grass and topsoil. I gasped for breath, cradling the ball which had gone, point first, deep into my diaphragm.

"Up yours, you fat moron." I groaned.

His amused grin quickly changed into a wicked leer, and he laid on me even harder as he levered himself up. I wished I had kept my mouth shut. Looking across the field, I saw Coach Dodd. His dark countenance was frightening...and he wasn't smiling.

In the huddle, I singled Pete out again. "That what you call tryin'?"

"Just run it to the other side, Don. That sumbitch is too big."

That was not what I needed to hear. Somewhere in the dim recesses of my battered brain, Rube Goldberg went to work. A cam lobe rotated past top dead center, tripping a switch, starting a conveyor belt that led to a grinder...that emptied into my imagination: *It was simple. It was biblical...David and Goliath. We would use the big boy's strength against him.*

"Everybody listen up! Buddy, we're gonna' run T- 29 reverse. I want you to flanker way out right. Pete, you get in that guy's way just long enough for me to get by you. Everybody else just hit the guy in front of you." Buddy suddenly grinned from ear to ear. He was going to carry the ball.

"Don, that's a "T" play. Coach ain't gonna' like it." Pete offered.

It was my call, not his, and I ignored him. "Pete, you hold him as long as you can, then when I yell *'Blindside'* let him go. He'll see the reverse and go for Buddy. When he does, I'll hit him low from one side 'n you high from the other. He'll never see it comin'. On two! Break!"

In unison, the team shouted, "Hey!"

As we moved up to the line of scrimmage, I was more than a little nervous, realizing that this was probably our last chance, and that the play was risky at best. It could backfire and lose even more yardage. Buddy could fumble. Worse yet, it was a "T" play, which meant that the quarterback took the snap directly under the center, and Bric Dodd would have my ass for calling it. Bric was a single-wing proponent. If the "T" play didn't work…there was always the bench. Still, vengeance was mine and I would repay. *Thus saith Shook*, I thought. And if the play flopped and we lost the game…so be it. But, since Pete couldn't manage it, I'd take fat boy down! And he would be reminded of that every time I got the chance.

"Set!" I yelled…and both teams assumed their stances. I took my position behind the Center, licking my fingertips indicating that I was probably going to pass the ball…hoping that bit of fakery might work. Then I did something I had never done before when on the field; I looked up at the stands where Dawn usually sat. I rubbed my eyes…no, I wasn't seeing things…there she was! She'd come after all! She was watching me play. In that brief moment everything in my brief life came together. We would score. She would recognize my brilliance and bravery in the face of enormous odds. She would…

"Don?" Pete said quizzically, twisting his head to look up at me from his stance just right of the Center.

But I wasn't through looking. Unaccountably, I saw Dee Garrison seated next to Dawn. This was crazy! *What was he doing there?*

"Don!" Pete yelled and I was jerked back into reality.

"One!" I yelled.

Pete tensed, leg quivering, as his feet sought purchase.

"Two!"

I cut my eyes toward Buddy to be sure he was set. He was ready. "Three!" I shouted. The ball was snapped and both teams surged forward; the rippling snap and thud of heavy contact came at me from both sides. Out of the corner of my eye, I saw Pete make contact with the big boy. I wheeled toward Buddy... "Blindside!" I screamed at Pete...

In football, as in life, things seldom happen as expected. Our opponents missed the reverse and Buddy scored untouched. Pete fought the big boy just long enough for me to execute the handoff and turn my head back to them. I went down in front of him, and he fell on top of me, not exactly according to plan. He didn't fall from my hit though. As the big tackle stomped over him, my ever-pragmatic friend grabbed one thick ankle with both hands. That foot was lifting before the other had yet come down. With his great bulk wildly unbalanced, the huge lineman fell over me and headlong onto his chin...knocking himself out as cold as Ole Kelsey's love life. Pete didn't hang around to assess the big guy's condition. He left that for me.

The final gun sounded and the crowd was wild! Amid the back slaps and roaring adulations, I searched the stands; but could not find her. She had disappeared...if indeed she had ever been there. I also dismissed Garrison as being a part of my vivid imagination. No way would she have been with him.

Dodd caught up to me as I was leaving the field, still looking for her. I expected a great grin and congratulations. Instead, frantically rubbing his ear, he roared, "Shook!! NEVER EVER...NEVER...CALL A "T" PLAY INSIDE THE FIVE YARD LINE!" A massive middle finger thumped solidly into my forehead, leaving an angry red welt.

"But Coach, we won!" I protested.

"Remember that next year when you're still on the "B" team!" Then he grinned, and rubbed his ear.

There was a final indignity: "AND BY GOD, PETE FINALLY FIGURED OUT HE COULD HIT SOMEBODY!" Dodd exulted for all to hear. And my friend, basking in the adulation of the team...all except me...walked away with Coach Bric Dodd's massive arm draped around his shoulders. He looked back at me, alone, mentally licking the verbal wounds Dodd had inflicted. He lifted one thumb and smiled knowingly.

I stood in the middle of the field holding my helmet by the chinstrap. Finally, the bleachers emptied, most of the cars pulled away, and the field lights slowly began to dim. I kept hoping I'd hear her voice, perhaps even see her running across the field, magically appearing from around some corner. I waited until the stadium was empty. Buddy, already showered and changed, walked over. "Thanks for callin' my play."

"Thanks for scorin'."

"Yeah." Buddy smiled briefly, but I could tell he had something to say.

"What's up?" I asked.

"Somebody left this on your locker." He said, handing me a folded slip of paper. "I already read it."

I walked over to a single overhead light near a maintenance shed and opened the folds. Scribbled in large, irregular letters was the message: "It's time for you now." A surge of adrenalin shot through me. "Crap!" I said aloud.

"There's some guys in an ole Chevy outside the gym." Buddy said.

That's all I needed. Walls? Garrison? Both? What was going on? Moments ago I was a hero, now I was getting threatening notes. What the devil was going on?

"Whatta' ya gonna' do?" Buddy asked anxiously.

"Pete know about this?"

"Don't think so. Him and the others are still celebratin'."

"Buddy, do me a favor. Go tell him what's goin' on."

"But what're you gonna' do?"

I took a long moment before answering. "I dunno'."

Empathetically, Buddy studied me briefly. "I'll tell Pete. Hey, if Coach Dodd'n the team's still around we can take care of any problems you got with these guys."

I mumbled something as my brain digested the situation. Buddy ran back toward the fieldhouse.

For a moment I watched him, mind racing, heart pounding.

About that time I heard a

distinctive "click" and the last field lights shut off, leaving only a few scattered, distant streetlights for illumination. Now, not only was I alone, I was alone in the dark. But, for the first time in several minutes, I felt safe, safe and secure, hidden by the night. As Pete had absorbed from one of his Tarzan books and was fond of saying in all seriousness, as if he had come to the realization absent outside inspiration: "darkness is your friend". My heartbeat slowed and I began to relax. Then I saw fleeting shadows in the faint light. It was Fuzzy and Jeff racing across the far end of the field. I knew it was them; I would have recognized them anywhere. "Fuzzy, Fuzzy," I shouted, "Jeff... Fuzzy...here boys, c'mere!" Immediately, the moving shadows stopped, turned in my direction and suddenly grew larger as they bounded toward me.

"Hey, you guys. Where you been?"

"Well I be damned!" Pete laughed, stepping out of the dark. I jumped.

"Don't scare me like that!" I remonstrated as we rough-housed with our canine buddies.

"Hey," he said, scratching Jeff's ears, "you know we got company."

"Yeah, glad they're here. Claire told me they were missin'."

"Not them. In the parkin' lot I mean."

"Think it's Garrison?"

"Him'n his idiot brother. I heard they're pissed off about Walls."

"This is getting old. What'd we do to deserve this?"

"For one thing, we beat shit outta' Walls and his bunch. Dad says you don't always get what you deserve any more'n you always deserve what you get."

I might have laughed, but my throat was too dry. "Coach and the others still around?" I asked, hoping he'd say "yes".

"Nope. Just you'n me." Pete squared around. "Well," he said, "whatta' y' wanna do? It's just them two and there's four of us now."

I swallowed hard. "I'm takin' my dog home." I expected an immediate argument. Instead, Pete grabbed Jeff by the collar.

"Let's go then." He said.

"Y' know, they're gonna' think we're chicken."

"Who gives a crap what they think?" Pete replied as we walked across the field, Fuzzy and Jeff at our sides.

Dawn Ferguson didn't return to school the next day. She didn't return the next week or, for that matter, for the rest of the school year. Not seeing her ripped a hole in my heart. Pete pretended he didn't notice. But I knew differently. We didn't hear any more from the Garrisons or their gang. We were busy, and they were quickly forgotten. What we didn't know was that they hadn't forgotten us and, like warts, we weren't rid of them.

PART II

THAT SUMMER

The weather flip-flopped from the previous year. There had been no rain since early spring. Foot wide cracks in the topsoil provided mute evidence of an oppressive and enduring heat wave. Days soared past one-hundred degrees and nights weren't much cooler. Rivers dried into listlessly meandering creeks. Creeks became occasional, stagnating potholes - exposed bottoms parched and cracked. But Bluehole would never go dry.

Over the eons, slippage along the faultline that had caused Bluehole's existence had created a waterfall over twenty feet high, so Bluehole was at least 20 feet deep. Actually, nobody knew for sure how deep it was. And in its dim recesses, shaded by giant trees whose great lower branches joined far overhead; the "brim" waited for two eager, sweating boys armed with ten foot cane poles, corks the size of a thumbnail, tiny hooks and vast imaginations. We knew the fish were holed up, deprived of the normal sustenance carried down to them by the current. They would be hungry and their freedom of movement would be radically reduced. They would be unable to dart into deep water like frightened shadows at our approach, often taking more than an hour to return to their feeding stations. Now, they would hold their places and continue to wait for any passing food object. Our bait would be irresistible and we anticipated heavy stringers.

TOMORROW

"See? Nothing to it." Daddy said, standing in front of the kitchen sink, easing the sharp tip of the hook through the rind, then burying it in the fat part of the salt pork.

"But won't it come off easy?" I asked.

"No, son," he answered, dipping the bait into the water-filled sink. "Works like this." He gently jiggled the bait up and down, and the little strip of pig fat took on the semblance of a wounded water critter trying to swim to the surface.

"Well, I'll be."

"Remember, you have to keep the tip covered."

"That hook looks awful small." I said.

"Boy, you remember that brim have tiny mouths. They can't take a hook any bigger than this."

I nodded.

"You want to catch brim, you listen up."

"He never listens to anything." Clarie interrupted, entering from the next room.

"Do to!" I retorted, but softly, so she wouldn't hear. Daddy grinned.

"Ma, you stay outta this," he mock-grumped. "This here is fishin' talk."

"That's right." I agreed.

"Besides," he continued, "he's got the feelin'."

"Oh, he does, does he?" she countered.

"Yessum, I sure do."

"Well, then," she said, sarcastically, "I guess I better clean out the freezer to make room."

Daddy laughed. "If he has the feelin'…then maybe you oughtta'. They're gonna' get rained out though."

"But, Daddy," I whined, "It ain't rained all summer."

He grinned then stretched luxuriously. "Don't you worry boy, it's gonna' rain alright."

"Ain't neither!" I muttered, again, under my breath.

82

If he heard me, he ignored the comment and turned back to Clarie. "Well, I'm gonna' go sit in my new recliner and see what Dagwood's up to. Wake me up when it's time to go to bed." As he walked out, my stepmother moved to a small table in the kitchen alcove and began scribbling on a notepad. I started out the door...

"Where are you goin' young man?"

"Down to Pete's."

"And you're gonna' park your feet under their table too, aren't you? You go down there, he comes up here. Do you boys ever get enough to eat? You dry those dishes first."

"Aw, Clarie..."

"And I don't mind you goin' fishin' tomorrow, but I want your little butt home in time to get some work done around here."

"Yes ma'am." I said, starting off, knowing full well I really didn't mean it.

I was almost out the door when she stopped me. "The dishes, Donald."

"But why do I always have to do 'em? What about Connie?"

"Your sister washed. And I mean it about tomorrow. The grass needs cuttin'. And you better come home with something besides chiggers."

"Don't worry. I'm gonna' catch the Monster."

Raising an eyebrow, Clarie allowed a narrow grin to cross her face. "The Big one?" she said, "King of Brims? I believe I've heard all that!"

"Yes ma'am." I answered. "Well, you'll see. I'll show you. When I hold up the King on my stringer, the newspapers will come out and take pictures, an' I'll be famous and I won't ever have to mow the grass again."

She waved me away.

"Anyways, the grass is all burned up. There's nothin' to mow!"

"You heard me, young man! Tomorrow, you mow," she said, throwing a dish towel across the room in my direction, "but tonight...you dry!"

I caught it easily and began my anointed task. I could suffer through one more night of being a peon. Tomorrow would be different.

Tomorrow my days of chores would be over. Tomorrow I'd be famous. Tomorrow, I'd catch the Monster!

Besides being the fishiest looking place we'd ever seen, Bluehole was unique for its whirlpool. In the middle, water had percolated through the limestone bottom and on through cracks in the underlying shale into a broad, deep aquifer, hundreds of feet below. It was like a bathtub drain, and there was almost always a whirlpool in the center of Bluehole that was visible when the creek was high.

We almost always filled our stringers at this legendary fishin' spot... at least, I did... so when we weren't in school, working the oat harvest, baling hay, plowing, pulling cotton bolls, or washing cars at Skeeter's service station, we followed our imaginations and spent a lot of time there.

EXPECTATIONS

"Let's go!" Pete urged from the shade of a giant mimosa tree that dominated our front yard. I was trying to penetrate brick-hard ground with a shovel. "I told you so," he continued, moving toward me in blue jeans, a formerly white T-shirt, and black, high-top tennis shoes.

"So?"

"Sometimes you are remarkably stupid, Don. Ground's too hard and the worms are deep."

"Maybe we could hose it down."

"They wouldn't come up till tomorrow mornin' an' besides, we don't need no worms."

"How we gonna' catch fish without bait?"

Pete smiled and triumphantly removed a waxpaper packet from his pocket. "Stole this from the icebox," he beamed.

I threw the shovel down and stepped closer just as he undid the wrapping, revealing strips of saltpork gleaming greasily in the early morning light.

"What?" I exploded. "You an' Daddy. Saltpork ain't as good as worms!"

"Sure it is. Maybe better."

"Didn't you learn anything from the raftin' trip?"

"I learned Fuzyy and Jeff like saltpork. Same as brim."

"Brim like worms. Especially the big'uns."

"Trust me." Pete smiled, re-wrapping the bait.

"Sure. Like I'm still trustin' you for the ten dollars you owe me."

"I said I'd pay y' when my brother gets well." Of course, Pete had no brother.

"I'll hold my breath. Daddy says it's gonna' rain."

"He had to be pullin' your leg. Lookit the sky."

It was cloudless, bright with the promise of vengeful heat, a day far better suited for fishing than for the chores Clarie had in mind. Sweeping the floor, mowing the lawn, and helping with the dishes were not jobs I relished; especially since I considered them the natural province of women. Summer was no time for chores, while anytime was right for fishin'. "Yeah, you're right." I replied. "No rain today."

"Well, come on then, let's go get 'em! Today's the day!"

85

We found our tackle in the garage, carefully laid out according to my father's detailed instructions. We knew the rules. Specified equipment was ours to use, the rest was not to be touched. As long as we obeyed the rules, we had a fairly free hand. We gathered our tackle, scrupulously avoiding my dad's, and mounted our ancient bicycles.

We stopped at the water hose snaking through the brown summer grass of our front yard and filled our canteens. They were World War II army-issue aluminum flasks covered with heavy, faded, olive drab canvas that snapped securely around the silver containers. Daddy had saved them from his time in the Army Air Corps and carrying them always made us feel a little like soldiers. We threaded our belts through the slots in the covers and strapped them on. Sometimes we stuffed them with cracked ice, but that was tedious and the ice melted quickly.

We grabbed our poles; and, in short order, road gravel crunched beneath our tires. "Wonder where they are?" Pete asked, looking around. He posed the same question I had asked myself. Usually Fuzzy and Jeff, would be whining and frisking about, eager to be on the way. But that day they were nowhere in sight; most likely off pursuing another estrus bitch. *Par for the course.*

"Who knows?" I answered. It was not unusual for them to go missing, sometimes for weeks; but this was the day we were taking them to see Dawn. Experience should have taught us that when we needed them most they were not to be found. In my mind, however, having Fuzzy and Jeff with us was not as important as explaining to Dawn what had happened that night at the stadium. I figured she still thought I was "yellow". I was eager to talk to her, although I wasn't sure what I would say. She hadn't returned to school after the incident and, for that matter, we weren't even certain she still lived in the same place. A senior girl said she'd seen her on a Dallas city bus, so it was possible they had moved. I was ruminating on this when Pete brought up a good point...

"At least we'll have enough bait with them not around."

"Yeah," I agreed, half-heartedly, my mind elsewhere.

We hightailed it down the road that ran in front of the First Baptist Church. As we had done countless times before, we made the sweeping turn onto Old Cedar Road, which led toward the trestle. Only this time we planned a detour by the Ferguson place.

"What about the dogs?" Pete yelled.

"What about 'em?"

"We gonna' go by Dawn's without 'em?"

"Why not?"

"Won't that look a little stupid?" he yelled, hair blowing wildly in the hot wind.

"Well, you can always go on down to the creek and I can meet you there after I go by Dawn's."

He shot me the finger.

We pumped hard, gaining momentum. Speeding by the church, I looked up at the triangular tin-steeple aimed straight toward heaven and wondered if some of my fantasies about Dawn might be sinful enough to plunge me into the depths of Hell. I tried to visualize fire 'n brimstone; but it was hard to imagine anything hotter than Texas summer. After awhile, I gave that up in favor of visualizing Dawn's electrifying sensuality…a great deal more satisfying pursuit.

It is first light. We have been together all night, but nothing has happened. She thinks I am still asleep, only I have been awake for some time now. She rises and stands erect… completely naked; her buttocks round and firm.. Her red tresses hang almost to her waist. She turns toward me and her swelling breasts are in full view, the nipples small and pink. She senses that I am awake, smiles, and lays back down beside me…

"Watch it!" Pete hollered, as I almost ran into him. "What the hell you thinkin' about?"

"Just stay outta' the way," I barked back angrily, my daydream of Dawn rudely interrupted. I could be cranky when my beautiful dreams were shattered by reality, especially when my imagination had expanded into the realm of lustful indulgence.

"You dumb jerk. What is it *this* time…she playin' with your pecker?"

"Oh, shut up!" I responded furiously, standing on the pedals to sprint ahead. I hated it when he could practically read my mind.

Pete laughed, came hard after me, and we pumped into the brassy glare of a North Texas morning. Under a high, blue sky we were utterly without apprehension or fear in the spirited, careless frivolity of youth. Chasing down the summer wind of our passions, we were on our way to an adventure we could never – even in our wildest dreams - have imagined.

Five Mile Creek was one of the larger tributaries feeding Ten Mile. Much of it wound through the Ole Bailey Place and, being partially spring-fed, generally had a stream. Numerous deep pools and generous foliage dotted its lazy course, and rummaging along its banks was an ideal pastime for two teenage boys. Pete and I spent many carefree hours winding through the farm, inventing adventures along the banks of that placid little stream. Old Man Bailey didn't mind us using his land as long as we didn't "run" his cattle or do anything destructive, neither of which we ever so much as imagined. The few times he had seen us jumping the creek or climbing a tree, he ignored us.

A railroad track ran along the eastern boundary of the place. It crossed Five Mile Creek over an ancient wooden trestle. From Old Cedar Road, which paralleled the track, if you twisted your mind just right, the trestle stood as kind of a giant gateway to the rustic little farm.

OLD MAN

Each year Old Man Bailey visited his property less often, especially in the heat of summer. There were better things to do, visiting with his few remaining cronies on the bench fronting the general store on Main Street, or retiring into darkened ambience of the domino parlor. He'd long ago given up the rigors of farming for profit, leasing the acreage he still held, but keeping a few range cows on the little property we considered our private reserve. He held a special place in his heart for that particular parcel. It was the first land he'd purchased when he moved to North Texas, back near the turn of the century.

The farm was two-hundred acres of gently rolling meadows punctuated by groves of bois d'arcs, pin oaks, and scattered native pecans. Five Mile Creek twisted its narrow tree-lined course through the farm on its way to the railroad trestle at the property's eastern boundary. The land hadn't been actively worked in years and served primarily as pasturage for the old man's little herd...and playground for Pete and me.

The old man was solitary and taciturn. If one didn't know him, his presence might seem somewhat forbidding. Early on, Pete and I feared him, but later came to know that he was a quiet, very private old man who occasionally showed up to check his NO TRESPASSING signs and look to the needs of a few cows and one surly old bull. The old man went to considerable lengths to ensure proper care of his herd, especially an aged old Guernsey he had milked daily until she finally went dry.

Earlier that morning, the old man planned to visit his sister Jane at her little general merchandise store at a crossroads in what once was another, though much smaller, farming community, but now numbered only a few ramshackle rent houses. She had been puny lately and, although several years her senior, he worried that age was finally catching up to her. She lived alone and the store served fewer customers each year. Jane fumed about the newly constructed shopping center that attracted customers away from her. " People want way too much nowadays," she swore. Normally, he visited on Sundays, but she'd advised him that one of her beverage vendors had delivered the fifth of sour mash bourbon he'd requested; and the old man happily anticipated pouring three thick fingers of the amber liquid into a shot glass before settling into their game. Leaving the shade of his front porch, where they had spent endless hours over checkers, he grabbed the board and placed it beside him in the front seat, figuring a game or two would be excellent tonic for both of them. He hadn't been feeling so "chipper" of late either. As he ambled out to his battered old truck, a mild wave of nausea hit him and he swayed noticeably. He leaned on the fender for a moment, taking slow, deep breaths. In the fifty years he'd farmed in North Texas, he'd never fully acclimated to its brutal summers. *Can't take too much more of this*, he thought idly, brushing his momentary dizziness aside. He cranked the old Studebaker pickup and whined smoothly through the gears. At the edge of his property, just before turning onto the asphalt, he looked out over an adjacent field. The old man looked again to verify what he thought he was seeing, and jerked the pickup to an abrupt stop.

A blast of heat momentarily blurred his vision; still, he knew what it was. Five turkey buzzards were gathered around a brownish heap; more circled overhead. The old man sighed and winced as another buzzard glided in to land a few yards away, quickly folding its wings and rushing over to the larder. The old man shrugged. He'd lost a cow. *Well, it's probably the old one*, he thought. He really hadn't expected her to make it this long anyway. He thought she was finally barren until, sure enough, her flanks swelled with the last calf she'd ever drop. As he neared the carcass, the buzzards flapped clumsily off; and he smelled the sick-sweet odor of decay. Green-black flies buzzed in a cloud around the bloated remains. Their eggs had already hatched and maggots wriggled throughout several, gaping wounds.

He had inspected dead cattle for the better part of sixty-five years now, and apart from a few that had been brought down by dogs or coyotes, he'd never seen a carcass savaged to this extent. The cow appeared to have been bashed several times in the head. One blow had knocked off the top of her skull, exposing the brain, the horn dangling limply at an impossible angle. But it was the numerous slashes that bothered him. The cow had been sliced, deeply and repeatedly, across the centerline of its spine exposing several vertebrae, the message as sadistic as the act. He absently kicked at the remains, then walked over to a nearby dirt mound and sat down, shaking his head in disgust.

For several moments he remained motionless. Finally, he withdrew a large blue and white handkerchief from his pocket, rolled it, and pressed it to the back of his neck. It was all such a waste. The carcass hadn't even been partially butchered. There was only one answer - the Garrisons.

It had to be them. Those two boys weren't hittin' on all their cylinders. There had been bad blood between him and that family ever since a Fourth of July picnic many years ago. Their father had said something to his sister that had made her face go white. When he'd asked her about it, she'd just told him "never mind." So he'd confronted Garrison himself. "Ask 'at bitch ennything I want to," Garrison replied drunkenly. And the old man had promptly knocked him flat.

Only two weeks earlier, he'd had that man's two sons removed from his property for pelting his old bull with rocks. He could still see the hatred in the eyes of the older, bigger one as the deputy walked them through the gate and out to the squad car. The dead cow was obviously their revenge. But there was another chore for him before his day could continue. Checkers would have to wait. There was the dead cow's calf to track down.

He didn't hold out much hope that he'd find it, figuring they'd probably taken it to butcher. But he had to make sure. Anticipating a possible rattlesnake or water moccasin, he returned to the pickup and removed an ancient Smith & Wesson forty-four from the glove compartment. He fumbled open the lock and swung the cylinder out, checked the loads, then snapped it back into place. Shoving it into his coveralls pocket, he started off toward the creek, where he intended to begin his search.

He'd walked less than halfway across the pasture when he recognized a distant, plaintive bawl. Pleasantly surprised, but mindful that he should pace himself, he trudged slowly over a small rise and saw the calf tethered to a stake in the ground beneath a tall hackberry at the creek's edge. He hurried down the slope toward the frightened animal. Moving faster than he should or thought he could, the old man quickly reached the calf and untied the rope. Intending to lead the small creature back to his pickup, he paused to catch his breath...and suddenly realized that something was terribly wrong. He was very dizzy, not even sure he could remain standing. He coughed several times and bent over at the waist clutching his chest. The calf broke free and ran.

"Damn!" he thought aloud, realizing that the momentary hope he might chase it down was foolish. After two halting steps he stopped, seized by a tight, searing pain that raged in his chest and down his arm. He had lived through twenty-nine thousand days and he'd never been affected like this. He staggered to the hackberry, leaning against its sturdy trunk for balance, feeling the rough bark against his back. He knew he needed to rest. His breathing was labored and his skin tingled painfully. He fumbled at the bandana around his neck and wiped ineffectively at a flood of sweat that instantly appeared on his face. It was a struggle to remain erect and the old man closed his eyes, fighting a vast and compelling nausea.

For a few tense moments he tried to regulate his breathing, hoping that might be the problem. But somewhere in the dim recesses of a mind that became fully cognitive well before the dawn of the twentieth century, formed a terrible truth... and that truth was that nothing would ever calm the heart that suddenly beat so painfully... nothing except its final stillness. A sudden breeze stirred brown grasses and last year's fallen leaves, and even though the wind was hot, the old man's frail body was chilled. But slowly, surely, the pain in his chest eased and he grew more comfortable. He opened his eyes, and the light wasn't as blindingly bright, the heat not such an inconvenience. He thought he heard distant voices.

"Where's 'at fuckin' calf you goddamn idiot?" Dee Garrison whacked his brother across the shoulder as they broke into a jog. "Where's it at Goddamnit? I thought I tole you t' stay here, you ignernt piece o' shit!"

"But you said you'd be right back and you been gone more'n a hour!"

The old man was weak but he remained lucid, and the voices were closer now... one commanding, one whining. Through the blur of heat waves, he could see two figures running toward him and he knew they had to be the Garrisons. *They were coming to take his calf all right!* Fierce anger welled up in him and the old man pulled the heavy pistol out of his pocket. He might be dying but he'd always wanted to leave even with his fellow man. He was on terms with every man on earth except the Garrisons...and maybe, just maybe...he had time left to square that account...

Rudi, the big neighborhood collie, inspired Pete and me to race the train. It was his favorite game. At the sound of the whistle, Rudi would be up and off – a whirling blur of sable and white. The engineers knew him well. They'd blast the whistle loud and long to ensure that Rudi knew they were coming. Rudi chased cars as well, and eventually met his maker that way, as do most dogs that flirt at close range with two- ton vehicles doing forty miles an hour. But his consuming passion was the train. In our way, we shared his mania, seeing the iron monster as a challenge. We raced it too, our passion being the use of its enormous power to fortify the self-image of our burgeoning manhood.

THE TRIP

"Worms?" Pete exclaimed, pedaling beside me under a blistering morning sun; bubbles already belching fitfully in the spider web of tar that laced the asphalt of Old Cedar Road.

"That's right." I replied. "It's just a little outta' the way."

"Since when does Jane sell worms?"

"Always has, I guess. Daddy and me got some there once. She grows 'em in a big planter box out back. Feeds 'em old newspapers. It won't take long."

"What's wrong with salt pork?"

"Brim like worms better." I repeated wearily.

"You don't never let up, do y'? You're just like this damn heat, an' we gotta' climb that long hill t' git there."

"Pete, don't cuss so much." I chastised.

"What's cussin' got to do with havin' t' climb that fuckin' hill?"

Admittedly, it was difficult for me to let an idea go. Once a mindset developed, it was next to impossible to deter me. Pragmatist that he was, Pete saw little value in trying. So he sighed, set his jaw, and we pedaled hard, trying to create a little breeze.

We were acclimated to the heat. Air conditioning was a novelty, a luxury in modern, but by no means all, office buildings, most of the theaters, a few large churches in Dallas, and the homes of the wealthy. Evaporative coolers were common, but the noisy contraptions depended on a dry climate to work efficiently, and the climate of North Texas was like a wet sauna. Oscillating fans hummed to provide some relief; but mostly we perspired all day, slept fitfully, and awakened early on sweat dampened sheets. Midday through late afternoon found us moving as little as possible, holed up like the brim we pursued. We complained, but welcomed the heat as a natural occurrence of summer. "Shocking" was done, the oats were drying and ripening in the fields, and "threshing" was yet to come. It was a time for sleeping late, swimming, sno-cones, drive-in movies...and fishin'. Once we had some worms we'd have everything we needed... tackle, bicycles, and

94

bait.   We were missing only one important ingredient...our canine buddies.

"Where the devil are they?" I panted as we coasted toward the trestle. Pete muttered something unintelligible. Maybe the dogs were simply too smart to be lured out into a blast furnace. Even if they'd been there, their tongues would have been dragging the ground. I often wondered why they were so willing to come along with us, only to be tormented by every kind of crawling, flying, biting and stinging critter that inhabited our corner of the world. I came to the conclusion that they preferred being miserable with us to being comfortable left alone...which could be said of very few human companions.

"I ain't sure we oughta' go by Dawn's without 'em," Pete complained again.

"Well, they're not around", I snapped, irked at his ambivalence. "And I told you I'm goin' by with or without you."

"We'll have to make up a story, that's all. You're good at that," Pete snorted as we reached the crest.

We stopped, straddled our bikes and looked down the long grade to the trestle. Old Cedar Road ran alongside the railroad tracks and we often raced the train on our bikes. The line ran through the middle of town and, since the train slowed coming through and didn't crack on steam until it passed the last town crossing, the outcome was never predictable. When the train was short, we generally lost. When it was a long one, we had a chance of winning; which was enhanced by the grade down to Five Mile Creek, which the trestle spanned.

The grade was steep enough for us to achieve considerable speed before we reached the bottom of the long hill. If we were ahead, the engine would be very close to beginning its passage across the trestle to our right. We would then coast, bleeding off speed on the upgrade and pumping an arm up and down at the engineer, who always acknowledged our request with the whistle. The train would rumble on its way, the rhythmic clicking of cars echoing down the shaded creek. The caboose would clatter by then shrink into the distance as the lonesome moan of the whistle gradually faded away.

We were too early for the race that day so we whipped down the hill, creating a refreshing breeze in our faces. Stopping at the bottom, we looked around for brim, crayfish, and creek life. Five Mile was a pleasant little watercourse that wound leisurely through Old Man Bailey's farm. Its shaded meanderings provided a grand sweep of land in which we played out boyhood fantasies. These ranged from fighting imaginary enemies with our Red Ryder BB guns to releasing swarms of newly hatched guppies and black mollies in an attempt to stock the creek with exotic species. Pete's dad found great humor in that plan. "Marine biologists ya'll ain't!" he laughed.

We parked our bikes in a huge, concrete culvert under the roadway through which Five Mile flowed, its walls decorated by innumerable tic-tac-toe games we'd scratched out over the years with chunks of native limestone. Pete was far too impatient to ever be good at games, so I had to allow him an occasional win so he'd continue to play. From the creek, we'd clamber up head-sized chunks of granite rip-rap to the rails, almost five stories above. On top, we'd walk the trestle, sometimes standing on the very edge of the transverse members to look down on the creek.

The trestle had been there a very long time…solid, imposing, unchanging. Holes were bored up to thirty feet deep into the limestone bedrock. Into those holes were cemented foot and a half thick creosoted logs up to eighty feet in length. These were diagonally cross-braced, forming a sturdy base for the upper works of the structure. Near the top, on either side and joined to the supports, were two sets of longitudinal members - tree-sized timbers fish-plated together and running the length of the structure. These timbers were affixed to thick transverse members bolted up to the vertical supports. On top of these there was another set of longitudinal timbers upon which the crossties rested. That left a gap of sorts – a space so narrow it could only be inhabited horizontally. We planned on squeezing into that space while a train crossed the trestle. Below us would be the rocky bottom of the creek bed, while less than three feet above, thousands of tons of train would screech and rumble. It was exciting, if somewhat foolhardy, to play on the trestle. Sometimes we would cross it balancing on the rails, or run across between them, barely missing the gaps between the ties, risking a twisted ankle or worse if we misjudged or slipped. We liked to stand atop the structure surveying trees, meadows and farmhouses in the distance. We were removed from reality there, separated from the rest of humanity, one with birds in flight or clouds gliding over a picture book world. It was a feeling akin to immortality…not at all unusual for teenage boys who had yet to form a solid concept of death.

"I'm gonna' do it." I said impulsively.

"Do what?" Pete questioned absently, stepping carefully on every other cross-tie.

"Race the train."

"Hell, we just climbed up here. We'll come back and race it tomorrow."

"I don't mean on my bike."

Pete stared at me, not comprehending what I meant.

"I'm gonna' race the train across the trestle on foot." I explained. His jaw dropped.

"Are you outta' your mind?"

"No, I mean it. I can do it. I can beat it across the trestle."

"Sure you can. And I can leap tall buildings in a single bound."

"No, I mean it. I'm gonna' stand at the far end there until the train comes. And when he blows the whistle…like he always does…I'm gonna' take off an' race him across the trestle."

"You're crazy! It's fifty - sixty yards across here."

"Well, I'm pretty fast!"

Pete stomped hard on a crosstie. "You're gonna' run across these with a train behind you? If you miss a tie and your foot lands in a gap, there won't be nothin' left."

"But that won't happen." I said. It was easy to say.

"And if it knocks you off the trestle? That's a long drop and you ain't gonna' bounce."

"Won't happen."

Measuring each step, Pete walked back toward me. "Do you see how carefully I'm walkin' across here?"

"Yep."

"Well, you shit sure can't do that when you're runnin'!" he shouted.

"I believe I can."

Having reached my end of the trestle, Pete sat down next to me. "And when do you propose to do this?"

"Train's due anytime now."

"What?"

"Always comes about this time of day."

"You are out of your fuckin' mind, Don. Come on," he said, rising and starting down the incline. "We still gotta' pick up your stupid worms, go by Dawn's, and get on down to Bluehole. I got fish to catch."

"Not 'til I race the train."

Pete glared at me. "Why are you doin' this?"

"Because I want to."

"You know damn well that's not what I mean. What are you tryin' to prove?"

"Nothin'."

"Bullshit!" His unlined face grew solemn and his dark eyes narrowed to slits. "You been pullin' crap like this ever since the fight with Walls and that bunch."

I blushed. "It ain't that."

"That's it, ain't it? Oh, hell yes… that's all it is! Well, you ain't doin' somethin' this stupid on account of that useless-ass Walls! If that's all it is, we'll just go look 'em up an' whip 'em again. I mean that goddamnit! Now come on, let's go."

"I'm doin' it." I answered, implacable now and scared beyond what I was able to describe. I had committed to something and I could not now, under any circumstance, turn back.

Pete shook his head and started to speak...but lapsed into a long silence. I knew he was right, but I also knew that some demon of my being demanded exorcism and was compelling me to take chances in the hope of acting bravely…in this case, foolishly so. This wasn't a first. The month before I tried to start a fight with a senior who everybody figured was the toughest guy in school. Luckily for me, he waved me off, figuring he lost nothing by refusing and knowing few, if any, would have doubted the outcome.

Pete and I had never talked much about the fight with Walls and his sycophants. I felt badly and he knew it, but that's as far as it went. Neither of us would ever embarrass the other by making mention of the subject. He never referred to it, and had someone been foolish enough to criticize my performance, Pete would have seen to it that he got to demonstrate *his* fighting skills. Until today, he hadn't brought it up, and the only reason he did so now was out of extreme concern that I was about to get myself killed. As far as Pete was concerned, we'd whipped the Walls bunch together, my reticence to become fully invested in the action notwithstanding. That was that… and we moved on to important things. But at that moment, racing the train across the trestle had become extremely important.

"It's comin'," Pete said, ear pressed against the rail.

"Okay," I said. We jumped to our feet and trotted to where the trestle began. I was giddy with excitement…and no small measure of the most pure fear I had yet experienced.

"You sure you still wanna' do this?" Pete either laughed off or otherwise dismissed virtually anything and everything he didn't agree with, so his concern only heightened my fear.

"Just shutup and watch me do it!" I snapped. There was nothing left to say.

"I'll get down to where I see everything!" he exclaimed, trying to sound hopeful as I turned and walked toward the point I had selected to begin the race…and face destiny.

"And if you're so bound and determined, don't chicken out and run 'til you see the steam come out of the whistle. It's right on top of the engine. You'll see it before you hear it and that'll give you a couple steps head start," came his disembodied voice, "and don't do nothin' stupid, and keep your eyes on the far end, and don't look at them goddamn crossties."

I turned and faced the curve in the track a few hundred yards south, which straightened at the top of a long incline just before the trestle. I wouldn't actually *see* the locomotive until it was uncomfortably close.

"Don't worry!" I hollered, brave voice belying the pudding that comprised my innards.

There was a distant murmur more felt than heard, then two sharp hoots and a long moan of the whistle as the train approached the crossing at Cemetery Road. After that, it entered a long grade that led up to the turn at the trestle, at which point the engineer opened the throttle to maintain speed. There was a flat crack as additional steam was forced into two huge cylinders that drove pistons a foot in diameter, which forced massive articulating rods around seven foot driving wheels. The labored chuff-chuff–chuff of steam exhausting from the great cylinders grew in volume. It was well into the grade now. I whispered a quick prayer that it was a long, heavy train, locked my eyes on the curve, and shoved extraneous thoughts aside.

"Here she cooooomes!" I shouted.

"Wait 'til he blooooows!" came Pete's returning bellow. His voice was curiously muffled but I couldn't take my eyes off the curve. There was a trace of dark, oily smoke, followed instantly by a billowing cloud of white smoke, and I was staring into the shining Cyclops eye of a great, black, fire-snorting beast. It rose up before me, thunderous of sound and bristling with motion... menacingly unreal through the waves of heat. Sense and reason were replaced by something like a trance-like state. I was standing in the middle of the tracks at the very beginning of the trestle, a monstrous juggernaut a quarter mile away, bearing down on me at forty miles an hour.

What have I gotten myself into? Don't run 'til he blows, my ass.

The monster drew rapidly nearer. Where was that puff of steam? I could clearly see the great locomotive rocking from side to side like some implacable predator keening for a kill. Jets of steam exhausted sideways from the valve boxes and I heard the loud, hoarse coughs and the metallic click of valves opening and closing. The space between us reduced at an alarming rate.

"Blow that whistle! Blow it!" I shouted... but it didn't. It was then I came to an instantaneous realization of what the big black "W" on the white, vertical sign by the tracks two hundred yards short of the trestle meant.

He's not gonna' blow that whistle until he's almost on top of me! I gotta' run now, or forget it.

I took a deep breath... and the engineer must have seen me. A puff of steam erupted. I whirled and reached top speed as I heard a short, sharp blast that I knew was already much too close. The two hundred ton locomotive hissed and rumbled like a living thing. The whistle shrieked again, the engineer holding it down now in a continuous, piercing blast. I had vague thoughts of him, desperate and cursing, knowing he didn't have time to brake... couldn't brake on the trestle anyway. My feet flew across the ties, the spaces blurs, then disjointed flashes as I streaked across three, then four at a time. Fear vanished and all was quiet. The high speed roar of a steam locomotive

100

capable of generating sixty thousand pounds of tractive effort was so loud that I heard nothing at all, not even the whistle. There was only that magnificently malign presence, my pounding heart, and my flying feet. I was almost there… almost across… almost safe. I felt a great blast of hot air, the forty mile per hour compression wave of a blunt nosed steam locomotive, and everything turned black.

That rush of air actually saved my life, blowing me away from the track. I tumbled down the embankment, completing a headlong somersault through head-high Johnson grass. Just above me, but harmless now, the train thundered along its ponderous way, the hot wind of its passage the most comfortable feeling I'd ever experienced. The whistle assailed the heavens long into the distance.

That is one pissed-off engineer.

The train faded into the distance and all was silent save for the buzz of insects and the soft rustle of grasses. I lay in the yellowing weeds bathed in sweat, ribs heaving, slightly nauseated from the massive discharge of adrenaline.

"Never again," I said softly, "never again."

"Boy, that was close," came Pete's somewhat distant voice.

I sat up and looked for him.

"I said, that was close." He was standing at the end of a transverse beam dead in the center of the trestle.

"You see me?" I asked.

"Of course. Didn't you hear me holler when you ran by?"

He stepped up onto the tracks and walked toward me.

"You mean you were out there all the time?"

"Don, I never been so scared in all my life," he said, sliding down the embankment and skidding to a stop beside me in the grass. "It was so close and so *loud*. Godamighty I was scared!"

"You were scared? I barely made it."

Pete carefully extracted a succulent stem of green Johnson grass from its sheath and began chewing it. I followed suit, and we lay there on the embankment beside the trestle. It had been thrilling and we would relive it endlessly; but it was past now and there were brim to catch, and alluring Dawn to gawp over. We caught our breath, shuffled the rest of the way down the embankment, gathered up our bikes, and headed down the road.

We had traveled only a few feet when Pete pulled over to the side and stopped.

"What's the matter?" I asked, crunching the gravel beside him.

He studied me for a long moment and finally said "You didn't chicken out back there."

"I sure wanted to." I replied.

"But you didn't. And that's what counts. "And Don," he paused… "this danger stuff is over now. No more bravery crap."

I knew he meant it.

"What about you?" I said.

"Yeah?"

"I mean laying out there while the train went right over you."

Pete almost blushed. "Well, that was really nuthin'."

"Sure it was," I said. "It was stupid."

He stood up on the pedals and yanked the front wheel up. "Jerk," he snorted and veered away up the hot pavement. I fell in behind him. Mid-morning approached. We still had to swing by Dawn's place on the way to Bluehole. She was waiting. The Whopper was waiting…and I could read Pete's mind.

"We wasted a lotta' time back there while you tried out your version of hari-kari. Let's forget the goddamn worms 'n go straight on out to Dawn's."

"Pete, we already decided that. It's on the way."

"I be damn if 'at's so. *You* decided butthead, an' it's at least a mile outta' the way!"

"I'm not goin' without worms!" I shouted, skidding to a stop.

He immediately pulled over. He'd give in now. I knew it. He seldom called even my most transparent bluffs. There was a long pause, and just when I thought I might have judged him prematurely, he exploded, "Oh, awright for God's sake! Ain't that just like you?! All this screwin' around and that fearful fucking hill to climb for a bunch o' goddamn worms! And we won't catch one more fish than if we just used the salt pork!"

I knew him too well to bother with remonstrating him for profanity and sacrilege. I had reached the limit of his patience.

"We will catch more." I stated with great finality.

Another long silence, then he seemed to brighten. "I tell you what…you go out back with Jane to get the worms and I'll look for where she keeps her stash."

"Stash?"

"Everybody knows she keeps all her money in there somewhere. She's tight as Dick's hatband…don't spend nary a dime. Billy cross eyes told me he was in there once when she was countin' it, and it had to be ten-thousand dollars."

"Ten-thousand? That's more money than Daddy makes all year, and he's a good electrician. Your friend Billy's three bricks short of a load anyway."

"Yeah, I know…an' if turkey was ten cents a pound he couldn't kiss a bluejay's butt."

"He wouldn't know ten-thousand dollars from a hundred dollar bill and a suitcase full of ones. But what if you did find ten-thousand dollars? What would you do with it?"

"Nothin'. I'd just like to see that much in one pile."

"I'll see it soon enough. I'm gonna' be a millionaire before I'm thirty."

"You pull another stunt like back there at the trestle an' you won't make seventeen, much less thirty."

I smiled, swelling with pride inside about my race with the train. I knew it'd been a dumb stunt, but still…

Heat rose in visible waves from pavement too hot to walk on. We pumped our bikes up the hill as far as we could, swung over to the shoulder, dismounted, and pushed up toward the summit. I looked out over parched, yellow-brown fields for Fuzzy and Jeff. For a fleeting second I thought I saw them - even started to whistle them up - but it was only a mirage. We reached the top with the dogs nowhere in sight.

JANE

There was a time when Jane's store filled an important social niche. Rural America depended on general merchandise for survival and, before expansion's crush of chains, malls, and convenience stores rendered it almost obsolete, her quaint establishment served the needs of scores of rural families. Living in town, we seldom ventured that far into the backwoods. But as the town expanded and the small farms and Jane's business shrank, our visits became unique experiences. Jane was a character and we had heard the rumors. Besides, where else could you find pickle barrels, kerosene lamps, and hard-rock candy? For two teenage boys with inquiring minds, Jane's was a Mecca. It was also not that far from where Dawn laid her head at night.

At first, there had been little pain, only a tightness that made breathing difficult. She fought to stay conscious. In the swirling abyss that had suddenly become her world, she heard angry and distorted voices. But those were not the only voices she heard. Clinging to a bare vestige of awareness, she seemed to fuse the voices she was hearing with voices from her distant past. She allowed herself to float into that curious place…

"Git up, Jane. Rise and shine lazy girl!"

It was not yet four-thirty and she wasn't ready to rise and shine. She pulled the covers over her head and snuggled deep under layers of quilts.

"I said, GIT UP!"

Her father's voice cut through her stupor. Ever so slowly she slipped the moorings of sleep. She stretched, yawned, and swung the covers aside, slipping quickly into a pair of store bought slippers. She padded to a blue and white porcelain bowl and splashed icy water over her face, greeting frigid morning with a shiver. It was time for chores. And it was her birthday.

"Feel any older?" Her brother startled her from the doorway with a milk pail in hand, waiting for her.

"Be right there," she whined, fighting off the desire to jump back into bed.

"Never mind. I'll cover for you this morning."

"What?"

"Mama's fixin' you a special breakfast," he grinned.

Jane managed a sleepy smile, delighted at the prospect of not having to face the biting cold of the long walk to the barn.

"Really?"

"Happy Birthday, Sweetie."

Her brother was a constant in her very pedestrian childhood in the Missouri Ozarks. Each day brought the tedium of morning chores, school, evening chores and sleep. She and her brother did their part in carving a meager living from the family's little farm; and they developed a lasting relationship. How sweet of him she thought, slipping into a plain linen dress and following a delightful aroma into the kitchen. Both tending toward taciturn, they found comfort in each other's company; and their bond survived the passage into old age.

Pain made itself known and Jane retreated from dim remembrance of a frigid Missouri morning to hideous Texas present. Blood soaked the front of her dress. She didn't know she was bleeding out and that it was radically affecting her mental processes. Dimly realizing she was laying in a pool of it, she tried to connect the morning's events. It was all a tangled frieze.

She remembered well enough who her attackers were. She had just downed the last slug of strong coffee and remembered unplugging the hotplate. There were yesterday's receipts to be tallied and she walked up front to the cash register. They came at about that time, and they were so…belligerent…

"Where're all yore customers, old woman?" the larger one boomed as he strode into the store, the smaller one sneaking close behind. The voice was rough and deep. This was confusing. There were two of them… But there were two more, and not the same ones that attacked her.

Pain came in waves now, but with it, memory improved.

"How 'bout closin' the door," she replied. Jane knew who they were and knew their reputation, but wasn't impressed.

"Now that there's kinda' rude, ain't it? You ain't got no bizness and here we come to give you some, and all you can do is holler at me to close the door…like I was yore nigger."

105

Waves of pain advanced and faded. *What about them other two boys?* She vaguely remembered something, but it was unclear. She went away again.

"Goodbye, Billy... I wish you could come to Texas."

Something happened and they left.

The two older, cruder ones confronted her. But wait, this was before...before the other two...so confusing...what was it they wanted?

"What can I git for you then?" Jane asked abruptly, the blood rising to her cheeks.

"Don't bother y'self none. We'll git whut we want," the big one dismissed her. Jane watched as they wandered absently up and down the aisles, pretending to inspect the wares. She could hear them talking in the back of the store, but couldn't make out what they were saying. *Oh well, they'll be gone soon enough,* she thought. Eventually, they approached the counter. The older, larger one had a loaf of Wonder Bread; his brother clutched a small bag of Morton's Potato Chips.

"Got whatcha' need there?" Jane asked.

"Well, we'll take this here," the older one said flatly. Then he slapped a meaty hand on the cash register. "An' we gonna' take whatever's in here too." Jane kept her silence while she pondered her best course of action. There were only a few dollars in the register. "And you gonna' show us where you keep the rest. Now open this," he ordered.

Jane had never been robbed, but the years had prepared her for almost any eventuality. Far from surprised, she found herself furious. "You two git outta here!" she snapped.

"Lissen, ol' woman. I tole you t' open this fuckin' thing. Now you open it and gimme' the money!"

"An' I tole you..." Jane bristled as the smaller one moved toward her, brandishing a large hunting knife.

"You ain't tellin' me jack shit, bitch," he interrupted. "An' you gonna' do it ennyway."

The younger one waved the blade threateningly, motioning toward the register.

"You can go to hell," Jane snarled.

The older one slammed his fist down on the keys.

106

"Open this goddamn thing!" He shouted, "Open it, goddamn you!"

"You ain't getting' nothin' from me you simpleminded bastard," Jane snarled, liver-spotted arms folded in defiance.

"You know whut's good for you, you'll open that fuckin' thang!" The younger one snarled.

"You need money you go ask that whore mother o' yours!" Jane roared.

Instantly, five inches of steel entered her midsection, slicing her liver and nicking a large vein. Jane stopped, gasped, and blinked at the face behind the knife. She didn't really understand what was happening but she felt the effects of shock coming on. Her world became hazy and indistinct. *This ain't really happening,* she thought. With great clarity, she saw a large dragonfly hover momentarily in the sunlight streaming through the open door. Everything was normal except this silly thing that was happening to her. Only a small corner of her mind accepted the reality of her situation, but her autonomous process recognized a grievous wound and began the actions that had to occur if life was to be preserved. Unnecessary processes were rapidly shut down, and consciousness was one of them. She knew she was falling and her last remaining fully conscious activity was to grab feebly at the counter.

"What the hell?" came a faraway voice. "Are you crazy?"

"Ain't no bitch callin' Mama no whore!"

"Oh Jeezus! Goddamn you, you fuckin'*idiot!*

Jane heard a meaty thump followed by a grunt before her world turned grey.

"Git aholt to 'er or I'll whop yore ignernt ass again!"

The younger one caught Jane's body. The old woman was surprisingly light. He withdrew the blade and bright red blood gushed from her abdomen.

"Ain't nobody talkin' to me like I'm some fuckin' dog! "

"Shutup an' drag her over yonder," the older one said, motioning to the pickle barrel.

"But what're we gonna' do? She's bleedin' like a stuck hog. We gotta' do somethin' with 'er!"

"Goddamn you, you done this and you askin' me? Now quitcher fuckin' whinin'. I gotta' think!"

107

"How much we git Dee?"

"How the hell should I know?"

As David wiped blood from the blade and slipped it back into its scabbard, Dee struck a key and the cash drawer sprang open. He ruffled quickly through the bills.

"How much?"

"Sixty-four dollars 'n some change."

"But you said she had thousands!"

"It's here somewheres, only now she cain't tell us because you went and done for her, you stupid sonofabitch."

A firestorm raged in Jane's gut and she knew she was badly hurt. Painfully, she pulled herself to a sitting position beside the pickle barrel. The front of her dress was sopped in blood; an expanding pool of it thickened on the floor. Knowing she had to get to her house or die. She had to get to the phone. To call for help. Using the barrel for support, she drew herself to her feet. She clutched at her wound with one hand and staggered to the counter, dizzy and unsteady. *At least, they're gone.* Making her way from the counter to the door was easy compared to stepping into the blinding sunlight. The trip across the dusty road seemed to take forever. She was careful not to trip, knowing that if she fell she'd never be able to get up. She heard faraway cowbells, the twitter of birds, and her own feet scuffing across the road. Everything was quite normal except an old woman in a bloodstained dress.

She collapsed on the front steps of her house as she heard the sound of an approaching car, and the thought came to her that it might be them again. *They couldn't find the money and they're coming back for it now.*

Jane had a cheap but serviceable double-barrel, twenty gauge shotgun. She kept it loaded with high brass fours. If she could just get to it, she'd shoot 'em in the stomach. Her brother told her it made large holes in things at close range. She staggered toward the front porch as the car neared the store. But she never made it onto the porch. With too much of her little remaining strength expended, she fell in a heap beside the porch, in its shade and just out of sight from the road. The car careened past, never slowing, but the fall startled her awake and she drew her legs up. She was growing cold. *That's strange on a day like this.* But there was one last thing she had to do before surrendering to the void. She crawled all the way under the porch. The dirt there was cool and soft; and she took a strange pleasure in its moldy odor. The web of a large wolf spider was only a foot from her eyes, its occupant there somewhere, but hidden. *Like me.* She drifted away again.

"Miz Dockery?" she heard an adolescent voice from the direction of the store. "Miz Dockery, you here?" She stirred to a semblance of wakefulness. That voice. That was *him*...Billy's voice...Billy Ayers, her first beau...so long ago...Billy of Prescot, Missouri... innocent face... innocent boy. The pain came again, almost unbearable now. Jane could barely hear...but they were there...across the road... innocent voices...She tried to call to them but could only manage a rattling wheeze.

"She ain't here, let's go!" another voice replied.

"No, we need them worms. Look in back and I'll see if she's inside somewhere."

"Don, don't be goin' in there if she ain't here!"

"Pete, just go look. It's okay."

Oh, that sweet voice...sweet Billy, so long ago. It was coming clearer now.

Billy smiled, trying to hide the hurt. "I'll miss you so much, Jane. Please don't go to Texas."

And she begged. *"Papa, please don't take us to Texas!"* But his resolve told her it was already settled...

"The box is still there, but the dirt's all dried up. She must not o' had any for awhile."

"Crap! She ain't open either, I guess."

"We got the saltpork. Let's go!"

Jane stirred weakly. She managed a faint whisper, "No, don't...don't go...I'm right here... Look over here!" She gagged from the effort and darkness blissfully descended.

Tears streamed down Billy's face as he trotted after their wagon, "Don't' go, Jane. Don't go."

Neither Pete nor I knew or cared why Bluehole existed. It was sufficient for us to know that it did exist, and that it was - except for us - virgin fishing water. Most everybody in town had heard of Bluehole but it was a very difficult place to find. Johnson Grass grew up to seven feet and if you approached on foot, you had to know exactly which narrow, diverging small game trails led into impassable thorn brambles, and which ones were passable. We figured that we alone knew how to find Bluehole; and we had long ago sworn an oath on the shed skin of a very large water moccasin to never divulge its location.

THE MISTAKE

Dawn sensed something wrong. The front door to the store hung open. There was an uncommon stillness, and even the ever-present, rising and falling murmur of cicadas was absent. Only a muted creak greeted her as the heavy door swung slowly in the faint breeze. Something wasn't right. She hesitated a long moment.

It had been a tedious walk to the store, and while the cotton dress she wore was light, she grew increasingly uncomfortable as the temperature climbed with the sun. Sweat matted her bright auburn hair and streamed down her face. She hadn't wanted to make the trip but a barren pantry forced the issue. She had the strength and resilience of youth though, and walked steadily, one sandaled foot in front of the other, cotton dress clinging to the sweat dampened curves of her preternaturally voluptuous body. Mature oak, elm, pecan, hackberry and cottonwood trees lined the narrow road, and she walked quickly from tree to tree, then loafed through each patch of mottled shade.

She heard the car long before she saw it and got off the road, jumped the drainage ditch and slipped up near the barbed wire fence of the adjacent pasture. They passed going the opposite direction, much faster than it made any sense to push a beat up '39 Chevrolet. She waved away the dust of their passage. Dawn knew them all too well, but she wasn't afraid of them. She could be over the fence and deep into the vast stillness of the cedar breaks before they could even turn around. They would never catch her.

The older one held a debt of her father's and, to pay it off, she had been forced to drop out of school and go to work in an industry that in her wildest girlhood dreams she could not have imagined. She hated him for that, even though her earnings had paid off the debt. And she hated him for putting his hands on her and forcing her to allow men she found detestable to do so as well. But she hated him most because he knew that she had not only taken money for allowing important and powerful men to do much more than put their hands on her, but that she had actually enjoyed it. It was a discovery that had overwhelmed her, but one that surprised him not at all and about which he only grinned sardonically.

111

Because of him, she could never return to school...the same school at least; and she would live the rest of her life trying to hide that dark secret. She had rebuffed every advance he made and had made her feelings plain, but he had persisted and, until now, there hadn't been a lot she could do about it. But he was paid off now; she owed him nothing. And all she wanted was to stay far away from him.

The ancient building finally came in sight. The interior would be cool, with a washtub full of ice and soft drinks. She was thinking about a Barq's Creme Soda, so cold that condensation dripped down the side of the bottle. Before she popped the cap, she would roll the chilled glass over the back of her neck. The store was built of quarried limestone and its thick walls and high vaulted ceiling provided insulation against both heat and cold. It had been a trading post before the last of the horse culture Indians were driven off the North Texas plains. There was a historical marker on the road out front which people occasionally stopped to ask about. A few Confederate hold-outs fought a skirmish with a Yankee patrol there, and the limestone walls were pockmarked by the musket shot and mini-balls of those ancient warriors. Rumor had it that the Yankees hung the few surviving Confederates from a nearby live oak. She almost skipped the final few yards through the shade of that same oak, now grown huge, finally crossing the gravel parking area and climbing the worn steps.

Had she been less preoccupied, she might have accorded more critical review to the door hanging open. Doors to buildings like the store were always kept shut. There was a large glass pane in the upper half, allowing anyone willing to wipe away the dust, a view inside. The legend: DOCKERY was painted on the glass. Beneath that, in smaller letters, appeared Groceries, Tools & General Supplies. The signage was faded, the paint hard, peeling, and interlaced by a web of tiny cracks. During hot months, the bottom half of windows facing the prevailing wind were open; those on the opposite side were open at the top. In cold weather, the openings were reversed and reduced to allow only circulation of fresh air. But the front door was always kept closed. Now, it inexplicably hung open. In the abstract, she realized that an indefinable something was wrong; but she was hot, tired, and more than a little out of sorts.

"Miz Jane," she called out, stepping inside and closing the door behind. "Miz Jane, you here?"

In the unnatural silence, her voice rang like a struck anvil.

"Miz Jane, where are you?"

Apprehensively, she walked further inside. The stillness was broken only by the hum of a refrigerator and the muted cadence of an ancient mantel clock. Just past the entrance, a pickle barrel stood near a heavy three-sided counter. Resting on the maple top of the counter, rubbed to a high luster by decades of human hands, was an antiquated cash register. Kerosene lanterns were precisely positioned to light the room...as they had been since long before rural electrification made them unnecessary. Near a corner, jumbled magazines were stacked next to some large, empty boxes. For a moment, she took it all in, then stepped up to the counter.

"Miz Jane?" she called out again...to be rewarded only with silence. She withdrew the shopping list from the pocket of her dress and began reading. She finished, carefully re-folded it, and slid it back in her pocket. She slipped her right foot out of a sandal and absently traced a large tic-tac-toe figure in the dusty floor with her toe. *If Jane wanted her to, she'd take a dust mop to it.*

She walked back to the front door and waited. Impatience finally seized her and she hurried across the road to Jane's tiny, weathered house. The front door was closed. She opened the screen and tried the knob. The door was unlocked. She opened it and called out...but there was no response. The house was small and she knew Jane would hear her if she was there. Nonetheless, she removed a sandal and pounded on the door frame with its heel. Somewhere in the far distance a dog barked. She waited awhile, then sighed, and walked back to the store.

She paused before entering again. She wanted to leave but she didn't want to make another trip. The interior had the familiar, musty smell of age. For Dawn, it evoked memories... cold drinks when North Texas was an oven, hot chocolate as a cold north wind beat against the sturdy walls. Sometimes she helped Jane stock the shelves. The old lady was approaching eighty and suffered from arthritis.

Jane could've sold out long ago, or just closed the doors. Her family wanted that, but she was of the stubborn mold and steadfastly determined to continue. "Waldo 'n me run this place nigh onto fifty year. He passed away behind this very counter, and me a' standin' right here beside of him. I ain't no better. I have to keep on a' makin' a livin'." She worked each day from dawn to sundown before retiring to her tiny home. She lived alone and seldom strayed. Exceptions were Sundays and holidays when she would take up the checkerboard against her brother, either at her place or his which was close to town. Jane took lunch in her tiny office in the back of the store. Otherwise, she was always out front, ready for customers. But it was not Sunday, it was not a holiday, and it was not lunch time. And Jane was nowhere to be found. Besides, Jane would never have left the door open.

Tentatively, Dawn moved past the counter and immediately saw that the cash register drawer was open…and empty. "What's going on?" she asked aloud, jumping at the hollow sound of her own voice. She jerked around, as if someone was listening. She examined the drawer…hoping to find a reason for the old lady's absence. But she was no cop; she was just a country girl beginning to grow out of adolescence. There was nothing in an empty drawer that meant anything definitive to her. Still, the human brain is a marvelous instrument, not required to function cognitively to resolve a situation. Dawn suddenly tensed…there was a possibility just outside the level of what she was willing to accept. The speeding car that passed her on the road had come from the direction of the store. And she knew those men, the older one…well. They'd spent time in the Dallas County jail. Maybe they had been responsible for…robbery? *My God,* she thought, *is that what happened? Did they rob the store?* "Jane!" she cried urgently, the edge of hysteria coarsening her voice. "Jane, where are you?" Hesitantly, one step at a time, she moved toward the back.

Each step was an eternity. She felt trapped…prey to be sprung upon and devoured. Behind each shelf she expected to see someone leap up with dreadful intent. The narrow passage to the back became a gangplank of demons… pirates of the soul seized her imagination. Primal responses lifted the hair at the nape of her neck and on her arms. Her vision tunneled and the room grew darker. Silence pounded in her head. She heard the whispery scurrying of mice, the soft tap-tap of a dripping faucet. The muffled tick of the clock was now a heavy wooden mallet striking a hard surface. Her voice quavered in fear and indecision, "Jane…Jane…are you here?" The back door was locked.

She pulled at it uselessly before remembering that it was always locked…dead-bolted from both sides, one lock over another. Another of Jane's idiosyncrasies. "Cain't nobody sneak in or out the back way," Jane would explain patiently.

"Jane!" She cried out again, stamping her foot in frustration. In haste she started for the front, but turned a corner too quickly, bumping a shelf and sending a can of peaches to the floor with a sharp, cracking sound. Another can fell, followed by another…and yet another. She shrieked, and cursed her clumsiness as her hands flew to her face. The cans rolled to a stop. She stood very still… heart thumping wildly…madly…and felt the first, hot flush of tears.

The opportunity to do something…anything…was welcome. She retrieved two of the cans; but one had rolled out of view. She tracked down the narrow aisle and saw the dented end of the can near the front counter. It was just as well that she'd dislodged it, she thought, because it was rusty and couldn't be sold. Maybe Jane would let her have it. But when she picked it up, the rust was wet and slick. She was trying to form the thought that the can was leaking…probably went bad and burst… when she saw the source of the contaminant…and knew more certainly than ever that something was very wrong.

At first it looked to be nothing more than a large pool of dark something. But it attached to nothing. It was out of place where it was…didn't belong there. It was a dark crimson liquid forming a pool on the floor close to, but not touching, the pickle barrel. She gingerly tested it with her index finger. She carefully examined it, rubbing her thumb and first two fingers together, feeling the stickiness of it…analyzing. There was a smell that she recognized. It was the same odor she remembered from the time the train killed Jabbo Dugan…

Just a little girl, she had been asleep in the passenger seat of her dad's old Model A truck. He had stopped at the unguarded crossing down by the propane tanks, waiting for an oncoming train. Jabbo, coming from the other side in his ancient International stake-bed truck, had either thought he could beat the train or hadn't seen it through the plywood board he had installed in place of a broken driver's side window. She stirred from sleep at the prolonged steam whistle, fully awakening to the booming sound of the crash and the bedlam of thousands of tons of train screeching, lurching and hissing its way to a stop. The wreckage of Jabbo's truck...a dying Jabbo pinned inside...had come to rest on their side of the tracks. She remembered standing a few feet away from the smoking wreckage as her dad labored with all his strength to free Jabbo's massive body. She remembered the grunting, gurgling sounds Jabbo made as life ebbed away. She remembered her dad cursing... finally yanking the driver's door open. But most of all she remembered the blood pouring out and down onto the running board...a torrent of it spilling into the soil. And she remembered the smell... the thin, coppery smell of Jabbo's blood.

Instinctively, she recoiled, wiping her hand on the edge of the barrel. She gagged and fought off the urge to vomit. She knew the liquid on the floor... the barrel... and her hand...was blood.

Dawn jumped to her feet, covering her mouth with her hand and muffling the scream rising in her throat. Unformed questions made a jumble of her thoughts. Was it Jane's blood? What could have happened? What was going on here? Slowly, she sorted things out. Was Jane hurt? If this was Jane's blood, she had to be hurt. Maybe Jane had cut herself somehow and was bleeding to death in her house across the way. That's why she hadn't answered! But maybe someone had hurt her when she caught them stealing something. She felt compelled to find Jane. Ignoring the fallen cans, she lunged for the door. But she stopped short. Random thoughts raced through her mind as she reached the entrance, but nothing made any sense. If Jane was hurt and bleeding, why didn't a trail of blood lead somewhere? Why were there no signs of a struggle...anything that might show what had happened? Hurriedly, she looked around, searching for a trail of blood. But there was nothing... only the one thickening pool by the pickle barrel. She wondered how Jane could have cut herself so badly to lose that much blood; but nothing made any sense.

Slowly, she concluded that Jane was hurt badly ...stabbed maybe...and carried off somewhere... She broke off in mid-thought, growing agitated at the possibilities. Her heart was pounding, and although it was relatively cool inside, she found herself breaking a sweat. She knew she had to do something...anything. She couldn't just stay here doing nothing. Done! She would go to the McWhorter place. She knew Mrs. McWhorter...her mother had taken in washing from her that winter and it was the closest house around, only a mile or so distant.

But she stopped again, not because of what she was thinking, but because of what she heard. A car was pulling up, its tires crunching the gravel in the parking area.

She tripped and almost fell in her haste to get to the window. Nervously, she licked the heel of her hand and cleared a small circle on the dirty pane. Suddenly she wished she had never come to the old store that day, or that she had listened more carefully to her instincts when she found the door standing open and the store deserted. She wished she had run down the burning road, slender legs pumping, hair flying...away from this place. She wished she was anywhere but alone in this ancient building with its locked back door, its empty cash register, and an unexplained pool of blood. She backed quickly away from the window. It was all coming together now. Suddenly everything made sense: why the door had been left open, the cash register empty, why Jane was gone, and why there was a pool of blood. A wave of terror rolled over her. *They* were back...and *they* were coming inside. Only this time they weren't coming for money. They were coming for her.

FEAR

She had never experienced this kind of fear. The only fear she'd ever known was imaginary - childhood "boogeymen" - fairy tale fear. But she'd fought her fear so far...and had not yet lost. So there was hope. She tried to reign in her thoughts. Jane was missing - perhaps hurt or dying. Worse yet, maybe she was dead. And they were the logical culprits. She had seen them speeding down the road – racing away from the store - and they had glared at her with open hostility. She'd found the door open, the cash register open and empty - and Jane nowhere around. Why hadn't she been a little quicker mentally and immediately gotten out of there? Too late now for questions. And too late for answers...

Dawn heard a car door slam...then another. The voices were muffled, indistinct, but she knew it was them. She had momentarily experienced the slight hope that maybe it was someone else...but that was wishful thinking. They were there. Now. And they were coming in!

Seized by a nameless and unreasoning fear, she whimpered softly, trying to collect herself...to think. At first, she only managed the thought that she was about to die. But at least, that was something. Now! She couldn't run out the back door; it was locked. The window openings were too narrow. Where to hide? And there was no time...no time left for her. She had to hurry! Then came a deep voice, "Git that tarp!"

She scurried, rat-like, hoping to find a window she had never noticed, a door that hadn't been there, a room or closet that might lock from the inside. Nothing. No place to hide. She was naked. Heavy feet scuffled and tramped on the wooden entry. Utterly desperate now, she ducked behind the counter and squatted in a corner under the cash register. She tried to make a ball, knees raised, feet tucked. She uttered a quick, soundless prayer that they hadn't really seen her, didn't know she was there. She forced herself to take deep slow breaths, and found her breathing so loud that she knew they'd find her instantly. Dawn had done everything she could do, including pressing hard against the wooden counter wall, making herself as compact as possible. All she could do now…was wait.

The front door clattered open and the room brightened immediately. Ever so slowly, she lifted her head and, through a crack in the counter top, saw ceiling beams. Tiny motes of dust swirled in the bright shaft of sunlight streaming through the open door. A disturbed moth circled erratically. She closed her eyes, squeezing them tightly shut, and pressed even harder against the thick oak-planked wall of the counter.

Dawn imagined that she was trembling. In fact, she was very still, the paralyzed stillness of a hiding fawn. The hardwood floor creaked with heavy footfalls.

"Well, where is she?" the first voice asked, cold and flat.

"Ahh…bitch is in here. We'll find 'er."

Footsteps coming toward her now…She couldn't have screamed if she had tried. Her heart was pounding more loudly in her ears than the heavy footsteps. Closer. Louder. Closer. They stopped.

First voice again: "Check 'at back door."

"She keeps it locked."

"Get back 'ere an' check it anyway!"

"Awright, but while you're not doin' nothin', you need to look behin' 'at fuckin' counter."

Her heart made three great thumps…and quit beating. A buzzing sound filled her ears, and her constricted world suddenly grew dark. She almost blacked out, on the verge of tottering into absolute hysteria.

A pair of steps moved away. She felt the entire counter move, ancient wood moaning in protest. Someone was right above her, peering directly into her hiding place. Her mouth opened in a silent scream; but her eyes remained screwed shut in fear that she would be staring into the evil hovering above.

The countertop thumped back down, small puffs of dust billowing up. She exhaled cautiously.

Dawn couldn't believe she hadn't been seen. Looking up, she saw the bottom of the cash register drawer, still open, obviously concealing her presence. Somehow she had wriggled into a space that just happened to place the drawer between her and the searching eyes. She remained completely still.

Voice from rear of store: "It's locked, like I fuckin' said."

"Enny other way out?"

"No. She's in here. Fuckin' bitch!"

There was a thump, followed by a loud groan.

A voice laughed, "Kick somethin' else you stupid shit."

"Fuck You!"

Footsteps moved away from the counter.

"We got enough problems aw'ready without you startin' shit," boomed the first voice.

There were footsteps all over the store now. Slow, evenly paced steps. They were methodically searching for her.

"Where are you, Missy?" a voice sang, as if the exercise was a game of hide-'n -seek.

She pressed her ear against the wood, listening carefully, attempting to visualize their positions in the store. If she had the chance, she thought…if she could just make it out the front door, she could be across the road and into the cedar breaks. And there, her speed and endurance was more than a match for theirs. But one set of footsteps was always too close.

Her thoughts were jarred by the sound of a loud crash. Then another. They were looking for her behind the shelves…by simply dumping them.

"Wal, wherever 'at bitch is, she ain't here. Ya think a' lookin' in the ole gal's house?"

The first voice: "Well fuck! Where's the old lady?"

"She was right here where…" Multiple steps shuffled away at the same time.

Voices running together:

"Why don't you…Left 'er right where she…I told you…Fuck!…outta' the goddamm way! But she was…shutup!...I tell ya…"

First voice - overriding, strident, angry:

"Shut the fuck UP, I said!"

Dawn heard what she took to be four feet plodding to the door…and then… one set of feet crunching away in the gravel. One must be going to check out Jane's house. Then a rasping sound, followed by that of paper being wadded into a ball. Then there was... what? Yes, the smell of smoke. My God, was he going to set the place on fire? She tensed. Another aroma reached her. It was the smell of burning tobacco. Someone was smoking a cigarette. Short-lived relief. One outside, one standing near the doorway, smoking. But what to do? What was there she could do?

Ever so slowly, courage of youth climbing a mountain of fear, she found the nerve to unfold her legs. She had to move. She just couldn't remain in the same place until they eventually found her. Tentatively, she lowered her hands until she could crawl. With each silent motion, she feared he would hear her and charge back into the room. She imagined him jerking her up by her hair - her mother's hair - the beautiful auburn hair she thought Don and Pete were always admiring. She generally ignored them; but she desperately wished they were here right now! Her two schoolmates were silly, like most boys their age, but they also had a reputation. They would not be bullied.

Still, the last time she had seen them...how long ago was that now? Oh, yes, after the football game when Carl Walls had cornered her...back last fall. Pete and Don had come along and she and Sheila, her friend, had managed to escape with the cheerleaders. But something had happened...that's right, Don had seemed hesitant, unsure, unlike what she'd expected. Trying not to show her disappointment, she had whisked away with those silly girls, catching Don's eyes, seeing his reluctance to fight, the uncertainty in his attitude. She hadn't understood that. She had always heard about his willingness to stand up to people like Walls. He and Pete had reputations...

Both were wire-rope hard... long days on the business end of a pitchfork or a hay hook hard, And they were as tough minded as they were physically strong. Still, they were boys. These were grown men so maybe they wouldn't win, but at least they'd buy her time to escape...like that night after the game. How she wished they were with her now...showing off for her...turning crimson at her slightest response to their lusty, addled worship. She closed her eyes and forced that happy thought away. Don and Pete weren't there. She hadn't seen them since that night because the next week she'd been yanked out of school and forced to go to... Because of what she did, she hadn't wanted to show her face or tell anyone, especially Pete and Don. If they knew the terrible danger she was in now…they would be here for her…But they didn't know. They weren't coming. Nobody was there for her. Nobody would be there for her. She had to face this trial…alone.

It took a lifetime for her to reach the edge of the counter. Now, she could see into the room; but she couldn't see the one guarding the door. Now what? She found herself sweating…and hoping it didn't drip off her face to puddle in the dust on the floor. Her eyes darted right, then left…searching for anything that would help, some means of escape, a more secure hide. Suddenly, she saw it.

Dawn instantly knew that what she discovered was better than anything she could have hoped for. It was a place they would never look…never even imagine. It was a large, empty cardboard box. And if she was very nimble, very quick, and very lucky, she could just fit into it.

First voice, yelling:

"Whut?"

A muffled reply.

She knew she had to make a decision.

"Then git on back over here!" came the bellowed response.

She knew she had only seconds in which to decide, make her move, and return to absolute stillness. She made her decision. Scuttling silently across the splintered floor to the box, she imagined footsteps racing toward her, powerful hands reaching for her. The box was on its side, open end facing her. She pulled it upright, then down and over her, coiling herself tightly inside.

It was dark, almost peaceful. Light intruded only where the floor was irregular, or where the box was slightly out of square. Tiny slivers of light in the otherwise absolute blackness. The smell of cardboard stirred her memory. Dawn and her brothers had played house in empty cardboard boxes. She had made beds and set tables for her raggedy dolls…and still had room for her playmates. Now, there was only sufficient room for her to be fully enclosed. She huddled in the dark…sweating, suffocating, waiting…and completely alone.

They were certainly in no hurry. What had actually taken only a few minutes seemed like hours to her. Something banged into something else and the light at the bottom of the box brightened noticeably.

First voice:

"Git over here and hep' me pick 'is fuckin' counter up."

In spite of her peril, she still managed a wan smile. She was right to have abandoned that hideout. They were close to her now. She was only about a dozen feet from the counter. There were other steps, going the other direction.

There was a crash so loud that she trembled, sticking her fist in her mouth to keep from screaming. They had raised the massive old counter, then dropped it back to the floor.

First voice again:

"She ain't fuckin' here!"

"Bitch ain't back here neither," the voice from the rear shouted above even louder crashes, the old floor jumping and vibrating with each one.

First voice, roaring in anger:

"Awright now Missy! I ain't playin' yore fuckin' game no longer! You better bring your little ass up here where I can see you!"

She held tightly to her hopes. She prayed silently, "Oh Dear Heavenly Father, may they not find my hiding place." As an afterthought she added the ritual, "In Jesus' name, Amen."

Maybe, she thought, her prayer was already being answered. Surely, they'd have to leave soon. Somebody would be coming. After all, it was a store, and Jane did business there every day.

There were footsteps, quick footsteps now, moving in her direction. She held her breath, felt the blood pounding in her temples.

The footsteps stopped. They were standing over the box. They must have guessed.

She extended her elbows and knees ever so slightly, pushing against the sides, hoping that she could somehow stay inside, undiscovered, hidden. Then she felt the kick.

The blow landed painfully against her elbow, but did not budge the box. Her elbow first went numb, then the pain grew until it was almost unbearable. But she didn't scream; the pain blotted out her fear. Maybe they'd think the box was full. Maybe they kicked it to confirm that. Maybe they kicked it out of rage and frustration.

The footsteps moved slowly away. Her elbow was throbbing now, but still, she didn't move.

A voice resounded through the room, "Bitch is in here somewheres, I'm tellin' you."

"Goddam! We've tore this fuckin' place all to shit and we still cain't find her. You think she's fuckin' invisible or somethin'?"

There was a shuffling of several feet. She couldn't tell how many, but the sound was receding. She allowed herself to exhale very slowly, almost a sigh. Voices rose and fell, but the box muffled them. She could no longer identify individuals. They continually interrupted each other; and she could hear only bits and snatches of what they were saying.

"I'm for shittin' and gittin'…But what if she seen…Fuck, who cares. It ain't her we got to worry… But I want me some o' that pussy!"

Dawn heard the last comment clearly enough, and shuddered at the thought. They were still arguing, the voices fading. *They must be standing just outside*, she thought. She heard mumbling from inside; but she hadn't heard them leave. She remained still - listening, waiting…

First voice: "Well, let's git. Bitch musta' gone somewheres, 'cause she shit sure ain't here." The voice was terse, irritated.

"Fuck it, let's go then!" another voice responded. *Something peculiar in its tone.*

She was beginning to cramp badly when the front door slammed shut…then she heard many footsteps on wood… then no more footsteps on wood, but the faint crunching of gravel underfoot. Then a silence hung so vast that the sound of her shallow breathing was distinct and clear.

She heard the car door slam. An anxious moment or two…then the rattling thump of another door slammed. All was silent in the stifling darkness. Then a starter grinding, and the wonderful roar of a six cylinder engine springing to life. Her tears came when the sound of the vehicle faded down the road. But still, she waited.

She waited a full ten minutes before emerging from her dark, cramped position. She had sweated through her dress and even the ambient air was refreshing. She shivered and hugged herself, blowing the damp hair away from her forehead. Then she moved to the counter and, laying her hands on top, stretched, catlike. She had won. But she needed to report what she had witnessed. Jane was still missing, there was blood all over the floor, and Jane's store was a complete shambles. They would pay for this, she thought. Jane had a phone in her house. It was a three-party line, and somebody was always on there. She'd just interrupt…and if she had to call somebody, she'd dial zero and someone would answer.

Turning from the counter, she started for the door, stepping gingerly through the mess. Then, her heart froze as she passed the window. Her world turned upside down when she saw, on the other side of the glass, an acne-scarred face pressed against the window.

ESCAPE

For as long as he could remember, he had loved to frighten people – animals – anything that could be frightened. At six, he had slowly and methodically taken a pocket-knife and gutted a helpless hamster, watching in delight as the blood drained from his horrified cousin's face. He remembered the time he had beaten old Buzz Cuse until the mentally deficient old man pleaded for mercy. He remembered patiently waiting for him to regain strength between attacks, just enough to beg. He remembered old Buzz's desperate attempt at prayer. "Ohhhh, Jesus save me!" the old man had blubbered. But best of all, he savored his response. "Jeezus ain't a' gonna' hep' you," he'd snarled, breathless with excitement. "You need to pray to me!"

She was terrified. Terrified, and he loved it. Through the window he could see the animal fear in her eyes. Dawn was going nowhere and what made it so delicious was that she fully understood. Her mouth opened and he relished the horror in the scream that reached him through the thick walls. Had he been in the room with her, he could have smelled her terror. He could almost taste the sweet, slick tears that coursed down her cheeks. He anticipated drawing her close, feeling the rise and fall of her firm breasts as she collapsed against him in great, wracking sobs. And she had been so sure they were gone! Like all the rest, she thought they were stupid, treated them like niggers. *Shit, niggers got treated better.* The girl's panic also inspired another emotion, a familiar and very satisfying emotion. He was suddenly sexually excited. He touched himself and found the sensation extraordinarily gratifying.

He remembered the feeling...almost the same as when he'd beaten old Buzz. Oh, he'd been caught, but he'd spent only four months at the county prison farm. His mother had money and therefore influence, and assault and battery had been easier to prove than attempted murder. Four months was nothing. Even with the prison beatings, it had been worth it. Nothing he'd ever do would be as satisfying as watching old Buzz on his hands and knees, blood streaming from his scalp and face mixing with the mucous and saliva that bubbled from his nose and mouth. Nothing, that is, except this girl, maybe. And he had plans for her. *Oh yes! He had him some plans for her.* There was no pity, no remorse; only an enormous, visceral satisfaction at being in control, able to inflict fear and pain at will, and absent constraint. That feeling rose up in him as he watched her dart from the window...rose up thick, dark and powerful...a feeling of pure malevolence. He was running on straight adrenalin now. Cornering her in the large room would be easy. He would be too quick for her...and far too clever.

"Where are you, Beauty?" he sang out, covering the few feet through the door in long, heavy strides, pausing to scan the room. He would have been disappointed to find her cowering, resigned and submissive. The thrill of the hunt made everything more enjoyable. His excitement mounted. He needed to take this thing slowly because there was much to enjoy. And when it came to cruelty, he was of unflagging patience. The more time the better, the greater the fear...He was fully erect now.

He began his search methodically. There were a limited number of places she could hide, including the cardboard box under which she'd taken refuge. Had she really thought she'd fooled him? Shit! He'd felt her with his kick. He'd known she was there, but he had opted to let her feel safe. He'd allowed her to think they'd driven away, but he had remained...knowing she'd eventually emerge from the store...knowing how a cat toys with a terrified, paralyzed mouse before ripping it apart.

"I know you're here, little girl. I seen you from the winder. Remember? You ain't a' goin' nowheres!" He taunted.

He sensed her presence, cowered behind a shelf or crouched in some hidden corner. He closed the door and moved deeper into the store, patiently surveying each possible hide. She wasn't behind the counter, or at the back door; and in the shadows, the corners all looked empty.

"May jist as well git y' little ass out here, bitch. Harder you make 'is on me, the harder I make thangs on you." His sexual excitement increased. "An' I got somethin' hard for you, Missy," he

127

added, laughing. He was barely able to contain his excitement, the pleasurable throbbing in his crotch. He grasped his penis and began rubbing himself, but stopped abruptly...too soon for that. There would be plenty of time for that, he thought. Right now, he needed to find her.

His eyes came to rest on the cardboard box she'd hidden under and he moved quickly to it, driving the point of his heavy work boot into the box so hard that his foot ripped through and became entangled. "Damn!" he swore. He kicked again, trying to free his foot and, at the same moment, Dawn swung down from a ceiling beam and broke for the door. She was quick, little more than a flickering shadow, but he caught the movement... saw her swing and dart away. Instantly, he turned and kicked again, sending the box flying toward the fleeing girl.

"You fuckin' bitch!" He lunged at her.

She would have made it but for the box, which landed between her and the door. In the time it took her to throw it out of the way, he was on her. She screamed, but he caught her and wrapped his arms around her torso.

"C'mere, goddam you!" He grunted softly, "C'mere to me!"

"Stop it, Dee!" Dawn struggled but remained pressed fast against him.

And he felt his excitement mount to fever pitch. "I tole ya' we were gonna' get this over with someday, baby!" He backed her into the wall, pinned her arms to her sides, and began rhythmically rubbing his groin against her.

"You lied to me! I hate you. Stop it!" She spit in his face. He immediately slaped her hard, knocking her head against the wall. Dawn blacked out. Garrison smelled her cologne mingled with the fear sweat. He heard her moan, felt her body spasm and jerk...then relax as she passed out. He cupped her buttocks and she slumped against him as his hips pumped madly against her, grinding out his passion. His breathing was ragged and irregular now; and he turned his head from side to side as an overpowering orgasm built to the flash point, then roared his pleasure at its release. Bright pinpricks of light exploded behind his tightly closed eyelids and he felt a slick wetness in his groin. He shuddered violently and released the girl to slide down his body and lay inert and silent. He towered over her, legs spread above her, his grin the leer of a demon sated.

Gaining consciousness, she looked up at him and in his beady, glowering eyes recognized the personification of evil. Dawn shuddered. She opened her mouth to speak; but decided it was useless and said nothing.

The door opened and light flooded the room.

"By God if you wuddn' right. She was here all along."

"Whut about the ole lady?"

"Cain't find 'er."

"You stupid fuck! Y' unnerstan' whut y' done?"

"C'mon', Dee I didn't mean ta'…"

"Jest shutup! Jest shut the fuck up. Go in back and find me some rope."

"Whut?"

"You fuckin' deaf? I said…find some rope…'n find her another dress or somethin'!"

"What the fuck for?"

"Well for one thing, this one's soiled…and for another thing, I wanta' see her nekkid agin'." And with a poisonous smile, he bent over the girl and ripped the dress from her body. His breath was so foul that she gagged. She tried to scream, but all that came out was a whimper.

IMAGERY

There was no phone in the store. Phones rang when there was no time to talk. Old Jane ordered her goods face-to-face from the few vendor reps that still bothered to attend to her requirements. She had a phone at her little cottage across the road that she'd never grown comfortable with. It was a three party line and somebody could be listening to her business. The thought of that was intolerable.

Under the porch, Jane regained consciousness. *How long had she been there?* She opened her eyes and looked out between the steps at the store. There was a car parked in front. One of them sat on a fender, fooling with a shirt button, and she thought he was the one that stabbed her. The other one was nowhere to be seen. *Must be in the store, looking for me.* She knew she had to be quiet, but even if they found her she might have to surrender. *Surrender would be easy right now...* but the dark came back before she could give surrender much thought.

At one point she thought she heard steps creak above her head, but she was too weak to turn her head to look. Had she been able, she would have seen the younger one on his way into her little cottage...so intent on his mission that he failed to notice the crumpled figure beneath the porch. On his way back to the store he stopped briefly. She could smell the onion odor of his unwashed body. Hear the movement of the old wooden steps. Finally, she heard him tromp across the road... and darkness descended yet again.

Later, she awoke. Time seemed to have been distorted somehow. She saw them hustling a disheveled young girl, whom she recognized, out of the store and into the car. Her vision was blurred...her recollection murky...but the big one was treating the girl roughly and shouting at the smaller one. Jane didn't understand what they were saying, but the unfolding events aroused her fury. Summoning her strength, she tried to move. The engine started and the car pulled out of the driveway, disappearing from sight down the dusty

130

road. Jane tried again to get up, but the effort was more than she could bear.

Only a short while later, the other two appeared. She wanted to call out to them…to tell them what had happened…but it was too hard, and everything was becoming so confusing.

She must have stayed unconscious quite awhile, because when she awoke, she felt a little stronger. *Maybe she could get those last two boys to help her stop the ones who had attacked her.* She struggled from under the porch and crawled up the steps and into her shack. Shortly, she made it through the door, shotgun in hand, and limped carefully down the steps. But that was all she had. As she reached the road she crumbled to the ground…too late and too weak to help anyone.

A half-mile down the road two boys rode their bikes into the summer heat. Bluehole beckoned…another glorious day stretched out before them…and all the world seemed right.

Fuzzy and Jeff had been running all night and into late morning with a single purpose. It was time to come home. They had wandered far afield and, for awhile, home had been little more than a dim remembrance. Then sore footpads, tangled coats, and a variety of cuts and gouges reminded them of the many luxuries that were their birthright, so they returned. They padded eagerly to the back of the house where a full water bucket awaited . They drank with abandon, nearly bloating themselves before collapsing in the shade of a big willow. Falling into an almost trancelike sleep, they awakened only to the fierce bite of pesky horseflies. Secure in the arms of Morpheus, images materialized, kaleidoscoped, and de-materialized, and the dogs growled, whined, and snapped fitfully in their sleep.

LEFT BEHIND

Until mid-afternoon, both dogs slept beneath the willow tree. Fuzzy stirred first, aroused by the constant buzzing of flies around his open wounds. He rose, stretched mightily, shook himself, then yawned. With a few snaps at the bothersome flies, he stalked stiffly to the water bucket and again drank his fill. The blazing sun had reached mid-morning madness and Fuzzy seemed worried about something. He whined at Jeff, even sat on his haunches and barked at his companion. But the big red dog was comfortable in the shade, totally lost in slumber. Sensing the futility of his efforts and drawn by a dog's strange sixth sense, Fuzzy whined again, cast about for the scent he wanted, and followed until it hit the asphalt of Old Cedar Road. Then, he struck off toward the creek.

The big red dog dreamed on. It had been an eventful trip, inspired, as usual, by the scent of a bitch in season. Jeff had picked it up and immediately, nose to the ground, taken off in hot pursuit. Fuzzy was close behind. They followed the enticing scent, only to find that it led to the door of a small house not far from Old Man Brandenburg's Farm. They nosed about actively, whining in anticipation. Their whines were answered by barking from within the house. Both dogs recognized the barks as that of a female and loosed their own thunderous volleys in excited reply. From inside came an incessant whining. Their excitement mounted even more as they heard the bitch scratching furiously at the door. Fuzzy and Jeff scratched from the other side. Suddenly, the door flew open.

"Get the hell outta here!" Spinster Ida Love, in robe and curlers, hollered, flailing a broom at the surprised mutts. They easily avoided her and retreated to the less confining expanse of the front yard. But the barking from inside continued; and Ida was soon back outside, this time determinedly stalking after them with the broom. Fuzzy and Jeff scurried out onto the dirt road, but the lady had no sooner gone back inside than they were back in the yard, then up on the porch again. The whining and scratching from inside resumed with even greater intensity. They heard Ida's heavy steps long before she flung open the door for the third time, and they retreated to a far corner of the yard. The door opened and this time she wasn't carrying a broom. She raised something long and slender to her shoulder. There was an unfamiliar noise, rather like a dull "ping", and Jeff felt a sharp stinging on his flank. The sound came again and Fuzzy yelped and jumped as a hot pellet struck him on the shoulder.

Jeff twitched vigorously and whined. Then, black nose between outstretched paws, dreamed on...

The telling shots from the pellet gun sent the amorous dogs scooting out of the front yard and down the road. Fifty yards away, they stopped and looked back, hoping their amour of the moment might be close behind. Instead, they saw Ida Love, standing at the edge of the yard, waving the long thing that hurt threateningly. "And stay the hell outta' here y' dumb mutts!" They were mutts all right; but they were anything but dumb, and both of them knew it was time to abandon this particular, passionate pursuit. There were other interesting scents to pursue.

Chasing down stray pheromones proved to be hot, exhausting work and they headed for one of the few remaining pools on Five Mile Creek that transited Bailey's Farm. The trees that lined its banks were no more than a couple of hundred yards away, across a lush meadow now gone brown with the drought. They slithered through a barbed wire fence and headed straight for a small herd of range cows that happened to be in their path. The cattle were at rest, lazily chewing their cuds and occasionally flapping an ear to ward off biting flies. As the dogs approached, an old Guernsey, with an udder full to bursting, hustled to her feet and bawled out a warning. A three day old calf instantly nosed vigorously at a swollen teat. Fuzzy and Jeff returned the cow's threat display with half-hearted barks, ran a few feet toward the herd, then stopped just short. The old brood cow bolted and galumphed off a few yards, followed closely by her calf. She turned, bawled again, and hooked her horns menacingly at the amused dogs. The dogs enjoyed the brief moment, but shortly tired of it, and resumed their sideways trot toward the creek.

As these images flickered through Jeff's brain, he rolled onto his back and his feet moved in spasmodic jerks and twitches.

The water was tepid but refreshing; and the dogs lay for a time in the little pool, having first drunk their fill of water green with algae. The familiar shade of a large bankside pecan was inviting and the dogs shook violently, then stretched before settling down for a nap. It was good, sleeping in the shade of the great tree, and very soon they were as oblivious to the world around them as sleeping dogs ever allow themselves to become…

They had been snoozing for an hour when the cows moved in for their afternoon drink. The dogs awoke briefly but otherwise took little notice. They'd been together here with the cows many times. As for the cows, it was their watering time and they paid no notice to the peacefully slumbering dogs. When they were finished, all but one of the bovines wound their unhurried way back to the pasture. Up to its knees in mud, a sole animal remained, its nose raised, searching the minute air currents to home in on a vaguely lupine scent it had just identified. Fuzzy and Jeff took no notice as the big animal splashed heavily through the little pool; but their delightful naps came to very abrupt ends at the great bull's first, enraged bellow.

The bull lowered his head, snorted, and charged up the bank toward the dogs, the ground quivering beneath his ton and change of bulk. He would tolerate neither intrusion upon his territory nor threat to his harem. To the bull, Fuzzy and Jeff were wolves. Descended from uncounted generations of wild cattle, the dogs' lupine odor occasioned a compelling response that originated deep in his genes. Wolves would not be tolerated, and he attacked immediately. He moved very quickly for such a large animal and was almost upon the dogs before they scrambled out of the way. The bull skidded to a halt, trumpeting defiant outrage as Fuzzy and Jeff disappeared over a ridge near the edge of the farm.

Jeff continued to snooze…but his slumber became increasingly disturbed. Something was terribly wrong…

DETOUR

We saw them from the crest of the long hill we had climbed on the way to Jane's store. They were at the bottom, on the side of the road, changing a flat. One side of their old junker was jacked-up. David was holding the spare upright, watching his brother loosen the lug nuts.

"Lookit those jerks," Pete said, eyes dancing deviously. "Takes two of 'em to change a damn flat. What the hell's that?"

"That's a problem." I responded.

"Why?"

"There's no other way to get to Dawn's from here."

"So?"

"We have to ride by them."

"Easy. They ain't even seen us, and we'll be flyin' like the wind."

"I don't like it."

"For God's sake, Don! We'll be by 'em before they ever see us."

"Whatta' y' think they're doin' out here anyway?"

"Their place ain't all that far from here, I think. Anyways, who cares? C'mon, let's go!"

"Wait a minute!"

"Why?"

"Let's plan this out."

"What is there to plan? Anyway, if we stay here much longer they may invite us to tea."

"I guess you're right."

"So, what're we gonna' do?"

I wanted to avoid an encounter with the Garrisons but that didn't seem possible unless we abandoned our plan to go by Dawn's. And we had to do that. We were at a crossroads with that issue and I was dying to see her. I had a knot in my stomach. We could turn around and take the highway route to Ten Mile and forget seeing Dawn… or ride on and risk an unpleasant incident. *What should we do… whatever should we do?*

"Oh Goddamn, Don!" Pete said impatiently.

Hell, I'd just raced the train across the trestle!

135

"Let's go!" I yelled and pushed off down the hill. Pete laughed his approval and pumped hard after me.

We hugged the side of the road so that high weeds would provide cover until the last second. The first third of the way we pumped hard to gain speed quickly. Pete caught up to me and we were quickly flying over the hot asphalt. The Garrisons loomed up larger and larger as we sped closer. We closed on them in near silence while they were absorbed in changing the tire. As we sped past at top speed and very close, we screamed at the top of our lungs. They yelled and jumped. David let go of the spare which rolled into the side of the car. It wasn't much of an impact but they'd taken no care to ensure the junker's stability and it slowly leaned, then collapsed, over the jack.

David's head jerked from side to side and he pointed in our direction. Dee scrambled to get away from a car which was on the brink of losing its contest with gravity. The flat tire now stuck out at a crazy angle, hanging on the tip of a wheel lug. Dee had yet to make the connection that Pete and I had caused the crash, and began slapping David repeatedly. David pushed him away, Dee stumbled over the spare and landed flat on his butt in the middle of the hot asphalt. The flat chose that moment to lose its grip on the lug, and the old car yielded to gravity and collapsed onto the ground with a solid thud and a small cloud of dust.

We expected them to charge after us; but they knew they'd never catch us. By then we were fifty yards down the road, so they contented themselves with yelling threats and raised fists. We were pedaling hard and laughing heartily at their predicament, but something bothered me... something I'd noticed as we rocketed by them. Pete validated my fleeting concern. "You see somebody in the back seat?" he asked. *That was it*, I thought. I'd seen something, maybe *someone*. Pete noticed something as well. But my concern evaporated as we found ourselves at the narrow crossroad leading to Dawn's place.

In no time we would find ourselves engrossed in the living, breathing wonder that was Dawn Ferguson in a pair of tight short shorts. I felt the excitement rise as we entered the long curve that began a half mile from her drive.

We pedaled the last few yards in slow motion. Then, magically, we were there. We stopped. This was hallowed ground. It was the same small, weathered, frame farmhouse with a few droopy, volunteer cottonwoods shading its faded appearance; but to me, it took on the grandeur of an English Manor, framed by a canopy of giant oaks. It was a montage as distinct and undeniable as my fantasies. How often I had envisioned cruising casually up to that beat-up old house for a tryst with the girl of my dreams... my *one true love... now and forever...Oh, Dawn*...

Fading light melds into a cool, late evening. Long shadows merge into twilight and fireflies herald the approach of night, lighting a path to Dawn.... in emerald green halter top and tight white shorts. She smiles knowingly, slips her soft, delicate hand into mine, and whispers, "I've waited so long."

Pete skidded to a stop. "What's the matter?" I mumbled, consumed in my fantasy... which was developing beautifully. Someone was in the front yard.

"I ain't sure that's Dawn," Pete said, staring intently.

"It's her!" I insisted breathlessly...

"And I've waited forever," I whisper, overcome with the velvet texture of her skin. The aroma of peach blossoms lingers on the night air as she smiles radiantly in the fading light. I move to her, forgetting to breathe. My fingertips trace her face with a touch as light as the soft, cool breeze that gently stirs her lustrous hair. I feel the warmth of her body against my quivering frame. She sighs, her hands find the back of my neck, and our lips meet. Her groin tightens against me ...then releases...only to tighten again. She is questioning me, her body questioning mine. I respond slowly, surely. I move against her, with her, myself against her... faster...harder. I reach for the top of her halter. She moans softly, and pulls it down to her waist, her eyes never leaving mine. She smiles knowingly as my hands find her firm breasts. Her head falls back, exposing the perfection of her bare throat. I kiss it greedily and she moans...a throaty, satisfied sound. She can bear it no longer. She moans deeply...a beautiful, guttural sound...and, with eyes closed and mouth agape, pulls my face into the depths of her cleavage. I consume her breasts, my mouth seeking and finding each pink temple of arousal. I am lost in the overwhelming ecstasy of this wild thing, this passion beyond my ken. "Dawn," I moan, "Oh...Dawn!"

"It ain't Dawn, dummy! It's her mother."

"What?" I sputtered, my reverie shattered.

"What part of 'ain't' Dawn' don't you unnerstan'? It's... her...mother," Pete repeated slowly and distinctly, looking at me askance.

And indeed it was her mother, waddling in our direction. I felt very silly.

The woman stopped a few feet away, across a rusted cattle guard.

"You boys lost or somethin'?"

"No, ma'am," Pete answered. She moved closer to us, squat and plain, with hard, almost flinty, features.

Dawn must have taken after her father's side of the family.

"Well, 'what ya'll want then?"

"Is, is...is Dawn here ma'am?" I stuttered.

"Whatta' ya'll want with her?"

I was speechless and this woman was intimidating. Pete spoke up. "We came to see her 'cause she wanted to meet Fuzzy 'n Jeff."

For God's sake, Pete, what are you telling this person?

"Fuzzy 'n Jeff? That'd be ya'll I s'pose?"

"No ma'am. Our dogs,"

"Don't see no dogs."

Pete found something in the dirt that interested him. It was up to me to bail us out.

"Oh, they're back down the road. They treed a squirrel."

Dawn's mother cocked her head quizzically.

"Well, she ain't here. She went to the store. Thought she'd be back by now, but she ain't."

"Oh," *And what do I say now?*

Pete chimed in, "Umm...which way'd she go?"

The woman turned away and started toward the house. Without looking back she said, "What difference 'at make? She ain't here." She reached the steps, heaved her bulk up them, and disappeared inside.

"So that's beautiful Dawn's mother."

"Reckon so." I responded.

"Well, so much for the old man's heredity theory."

I could hear his dad's oft stated reminder: "Boys, before you whip your wires outta' your pants, take a real good look at mama. Because that's what you're gonna' end up lookin' at."

"Maybe she's adopted." I said.

Pete looked at me incredulously. I shrugged.

"Well, that's that," Pete said casually as we pumped up to a steady cruise.

"That's what?"

"The deal with Dawn."

I sighed deeply, still unwilling to give up the chance to see her.

"Which way's the store?" I asked.

"What store?"

I was already tired of this conversation. "Do you want to see Dawn or not?"

"I didn't know there was any store out here 'cept for Jane's. And we done been by there."

"Forget it," I said, disgustedly, "let's get on down to Bluehole."

We backtracked through the road dust thinking, no hoping, we might see Dawn around every bend; but it became increasingly obvious we had struck out.

But that's not so bad. I could leave Pete at home and come in secret. How can I be sure she wouldn't like him better than me anyway? No...impossible. But if he's not here...Yes, that's it. I'll come by myself.

We needed to concentrate on fishin' anyway. Maybe Bluehole would be more productive than our non-visit with Dawn.

Leaving our disappointment behind, we rode on through a continuing line of trees overhanging the road. We knew those huge oak, elm, pecan and hackberry trees had been planted by birds that lined the fences that sprang up along the roads as they were built. Moving beneath them, we passed through patterns of sun and shade. After a time our pedaling became rhythmically ethereal and my thoughts wandered again. I couldn't get her out of my mind. Not that I wanted to...

A full moon is rising. There is a soft, diffused glow to our world. It is night...but moonlight illuminates a tiny birthmark in the hollow of her shoulder. I kiss it adoringly. All is quiet, save for our labored breathing, her muffled moans of pleasure, and the background of night sounds that caress our senses even as our souls inflame. Her passion climbs toward the zenith. 'You are my goddess of the night', I breathe softly in her ear. We are entwined in the fullness of our love, spiraling skyward on the wings of Eros, rising ever nearer to the full release of our...

"Where the hell you goin' now?" Pete yelled. I jerked back into reality and slid to a halt on the loose dirt.

"Why're you yellin' at me?" I yelped defensively.

"How 'bout pullin' your head outta' your ass?" he fumed.

I had gone thirty yards past the turnoff to Bluehole. I had to get my mind off Dawn, and on the serious business of fishin'.

"An' what's with this 'goddess of the night' horseshit you was carryin' on about?"

I turned scarlet, ignored his scathing commentary, and pedaled brusquely past him.

On the way back to Old Cedar Road we noted that the Garrisons had apparently repaired their flat. The car was gone and only scarred earth and trampled weeds testified to our earlier entertainment.

"They gotta' be some kinda' pissed," Pete remarked.

"Who cares?" I responded, wiping the remnants of a bug from my eye. "They're not worth worryin' about."

We turned onto the big road and started down the long, winding incline to Ten Mile. I couldn't help but notice the empty fields stretching away as far as we could see. We had worked those same fields for one of the local farmers. Only a month before, while we were harvesting the oat crop, there had been a beehive of activity out there. Now, there was only barren ground, which we'd plow in early fall. We'd worked twelve long hours a day under a blistering sun bringing in that crop, and we'd been paid exactly six dollars for those twelve hours. Now, scattered shards of golden brown attested to the countless gallons of sweat we'd expended. Pete pointed silently. Far across the field a large dust devil whirled madly. Otherwise, all was still and silent. *A still life of no life...and yet, filled with life.*

I'd invented a quandary and, as I pondered it, I sensed, more than heard, a faint, deep rumble, like distant artillery. I ignored it and we rode on. I wished we were already there. I couldn't chase thoughts of an ethereal Dawn, naked and glowing in pale moonlight.

ANATHEMA

Accelerated heart rates characterized our fishing trips because Pete and I always "snuck in." Getting caught had never been an issue; but the idea that we were trespassing seemed to heighten our sense of adventure.   Landowners didn't care...as long as we didn't chase livestock or leave a mess.   But not picking up after ourselves, leaving bottles, cans, or paper waste was unthinkable.   If we used a place, we left it as we found it except, of course, for the fish we hauled away.

Garrison Hole was almost a mile upstream of Bluehole at a natural meander where the current had undercut the twenty foot bank to gouge out a sizable hole which, over the years, widened and deepened into a sizable pond.   The land surrounding the pond belonged to the widow Garrison. Although her range cows occasionally watered there, it was otherwise left to wild critters. Coyotes, wildcats, raccoons, opossum, beaver, cotton tails, squirrels, a myriad variety of waterfowl, and an oft rumored, but never seen, cougar frequented Garrison Hole. The widow Garrison's boys occasionally found its isolation useful.

Dee Garrison steered with one hand and used the other to unscrew the cap from the whisky bottle, holding it in his rotting molars. "You jist don't think." He harangued his brother. "You jist like that fuckin' drunk what knocked mama up with you! You ain't never thought about nothin'! You a goddamn congestical idiot from a long line o' congestical idiots!" He spat the cap out the window.

"You just pissed off on account of I cut that old woman. Well fuck her! She had it comin'."

"You know whut y' got us into?"

"Us? Who's gonna' know it was us? 'At bitch has gotta' be dead, so how's she gonna' tell anybody?"

"Goddamn, she better be dead!" Dee roared. His adam's apple bobbed and he coughed at the bite of raw whiskey. His brother eyed the bottle enviously.

"Shit!   Bleedin' like that an' she ain't dead?   Gimme a fuckin'drink, Dee."

"Fuckin' brother'a hers didn't bleed much. Reckon he's dead by now."

"Whew, Dee. Some day, huh? We fuckin' took care'a that family."

"Yeah, reckon Pap'd be proud."

"What about, Ma?"

"Shit, better hope she don't find out. Better hope nobody do."

"And whut about that bitch in the back seat? What're we gonna' do with her anyways?"

Dee looked briefly over his right shoulder. He took another stiff swig and coughed again. "What're *we* gonna' do with her? Well, *you* ain't gonna' do a fuckin' thing, but *I'm* gonna' do whatever I fuckin' want... an' that means some serious fuckin'."

David Garrison grinned vacantly at his brother, then turned to peer at the figure huddled in the back seat. "Hey you... sweet thang...you a' kickin' back 'ere?" A sudden jolt rocked them both.

"Hey! You fuckin' up my drivin' bitch!" Dee shouted. The whiskey was taking effect and Dee laughed far too uproariously at his own twisted humor. He took another snort and absently handed the bottle to David.

In the back seat, Dawn gathered her feet under her and lashed out again, rocking the front seat with a powerful thrust. "That's enough!" Dee yelled, reaching back to slap her feet and legs. "Goddamn 'at slut's strong." He grunted. David attempted a long pull but almost threw up from the bite of straight bourbon. Dee snatched the bottle from him and swigged heavily.

Dawn stifled the urge to vomit, knowing she'd choke on it if she did. She was gagged with a dirty handkerchief, blindfolded with another, and her hands were secured tightly behind her back with rope that cut into her wrists. The dress they had found for her was at least two sizes too large. Dawn was miserable and frightened. She was also very angry.

Consumed by lust, Dee Garrison seemed to have forgotten his business history with her. Instrumental in her truancy, he was also directly responsible for her entry into a darker side of life. She resented, no...hated him for what he had done, was threatening to do. Yet, until he and his worthless brother had made their appearance earlier on the

143

road to Jane's store, she had more or less shelved relevant thoughts of that interlude; assuming he had done likewise. After all, she had not worked for several months and seemed to have made a clean break. Fortunately, he hadn't bothered her. But then, on the road and in the store...rather than treating her as a former financial asset, he had assumed a predatory role toward her...a role that involved a direct assault and kidnapping.

"Dee, I wanta' have me a little fun with 'er. How 'bout I crawl back an' me an' her get with it?"

"You leave 'er the hell alone. There'll be plenty o' time for all that later."

"Then I'm gonna' crawl back there so me an' her can jist get acquainted."

David turned to climb into the back seat only to be caught by Dawn's blind kick. This one drove him back against the dasboard. He cursed, clambered up and again started over the seat. He grabbed at her feet and finally got her under control.

"Hold still you goddamn slut!" he grunted.

Dawn tried to cry out, but managed only a muffled shriek. But her efforts didn't go unnoticed. Dee backhanded his brother and braked hard, stopping the car. He got out and raced around to the passenger side, flung open the door, and jerked a now frightened David out and down into the roadside weeds, where he beat him senseless, first with an open hand, then with closed fists delivered at full force. David lay in the weeds stunned and bloodied.

"Goddamn, Dee...whut 'd I do?" he finally whimpered, spitting a wad of thick mucous and blood.

"I tole you," Dee gasped between deep breaths, "t' leave her alone. But you don't never fuckin' listen. You fuck up everything I try t' do. You jist like a dog...what y' can't eat, y' shit on. I swear, if you was worth killin', I'd do it right now. But you ain't worth it, you goddamned idiot. Now you lissen t' me. I got plans for me an' her, and they'll make a lotta' money for us. But you can't be gettin' with her anytime you get a hard on or you'll fuck up my plans. So anythin' else I tell you, you better do it, an' you better do it jist like I tell you. An' if you fuck up one more goddamn time, I swear I am gonna' bury your useless ass somewheres."

"I won't do nothin' more." David moaned. "Please don't hit me no more Dee. I ain't gonna do nothin' else to 'er. Nothin!"

"Shut up and get back in the car. We almost there."

Dee coaxed the vehicle forward and turned off into a pair of wheel ruts that cut through a green curtain of ten foot high sunflowers.

"Shit, Dee how you find this place anyways?" David ventured, hopeful that interest in anything besides the girl might repair the schism with his brother.

"You so fuckin' stupid! We on the west side of our propitty, and this is the old road they used to bring the binders and the thresher in when Pap let it out to grow oats on."

"I don't remember none o'that," David replied.

"Course you don't," Dee explained, "cause Pap was awready dead when that town guy knocked Mama up with you."

David was silent.

"Aah, it don't make no difference …. 'cept you a goddamn idiot on account o' he was."

David was silent while Dee worked to keep the car squarely in the ruts. He knew very well that he was illegitimate, but it didn't bother him so much any more, and he'd long ago grown accustomed to Dee's abuse. Since confrontation was not a possibility with Dee, he learned to play the fawning fool with reasonable skill.

"How'd you learn all the shit you know?" David asked ingratiatingly.

"I guess I jist gotta' kinda' sense for things."

Blindfolded, Dawn could only guess at what they might be driving through. Sunflowers slapped against the old car's windshield and body with a sound like muffled shots. Finally, she discerned a changing topography. The slapping sounds stopped, and branches of an occasional mesquite screeched down the sides of the car. She was in a nightmare that was all too real. It was obvious they weren't going to let her go; she knew too much. From what she'd heard, Jane was dead and the Garrisons had killed her. A chill took her as she realized that she could very likely die at their hands as well. Dee finally brought the car to a stop.

"We're here."

145

Clarie and Daddy met in her hometown of Newburgh, New York, where he was stationed at the close of World War II. It was a short romance. Both were reeling from broken marriages; both recognized rocklike steadiness in the other, and Clarie shortly found herself in a Quonset hut suburb in Dallas called La Reunion, raising two small children from his first marriage. A year later, another girl came along. They were frugal, saved conscientiously, and in 1952, found the house of their dreams in a nearby rural town . A city girl, Clarie came to enjoy the wide open feel of North Texas and such simple outdoor tasks as tending the flowerbed under a high, blue sky. Liking things neat, orderly, and attractive, she refused to tolerate weeds in her flowerbeds.

THE PACK

Clarie had intended getting to the circular bed around the birdbath for several days, but things kept coming up. She took every responsibility she assumed seriously. Family came first; everything else in descending order, but she would get to every task she'd charted for herself, because that was her way. Even though the temperature was creeping past the century mark, she was determined to do battle with alien life forms most people dismissed as weeds.

Johnson Grass was the primary culprit. It was incredibly hardy, rooted deeply, and was pure hell to dig up. You had to get all the roots or it would reappear in a few days, upsetting the perfectly manicured, *Better Homes And Gardens* look Clarie relentlessly sought. It seemed indestructible, thriving where lesser plants couldn't even live, much less propagate. It grew out of cracks in the sidewalk, between stones on a rock pile, in the middle of an asphalt-covered outdoor basketball court and, of course, in the circular flowerbed around the birdbath.

The birdbath became an obsession. She discovered that constant vigilance was necessary to maintain a pristine appearance, and the flowerbed always required attention. If children and animals weren't tramping through it, then weeds - especially the noxious Johnson Grass- were laying claim to a homestead. Clarie spent a lot of time and effort at the birdbath.

She found the hoe in its designated place in the garage. It was there because Daddy would have a fit if it was found anywhere else, other than in someone's hands. She donned light cotton gloves, grabbed the hoe, and set out to eradicate the archenemy weed. Exiting the garage was like stepping into a furnace. Clarie was from upstate New York, where it never got Texas hot, but she was tough and fully acclimated now. The heat was no excuse, and she resolved that today was the day the war on any and all encroaching flora would start. She entertained no doubts as to who would emerge victorious.

Bermuda Grass had infiltrated the bed from the yard and she attacked that first. After a few minutes tearing at the stubborn stuff, she paused briefly to dab sweat out of her eyes. She was about to resume when she was brought up short by a disturbance a few houses up the block. It was the dog pack again. She inspected them individually to see if Fuzzy was in the group. He hadn't been around the night before and, while that wasn't rare, she always worried about him. She did notice a very large, black, shaggy dog that resembled Fuzzy, but she wasn't convinced it was him.

A car turned the corner in front of the house, honking a greeting that she returned with a wave, scarcely looking up. Somewhere in the vast expanse of Texas sky, an airplane droned its way to a distant destination. Absently, she wondered if it might be headed for New York. It was a nostalgic thought. Her aging parents still lived there, and she missed them. She also missed the cooler, greener summers of her youth. Thoughts came in myriad, fleeting fashion. She was concentrating on the weeds; the others were idle musings…almost like dreaming. Lost in her work, Clarie didn't hear the pack until it was almost upon her.

She wondered how they'd gotten there so quickly. The pack was less than thirty feet away. More surprised than fearful, she yelled at them instinctively.

"Hey…you dogs get out of here! Get away!"

One dog, even two, would have scurried away, but the pack was going nowhere. Paying no mind to Clarie's angry posturing, they followed a bitch that was obviously in season. The dogs panted and sniffed in a very dedicated path across the grass toward the flowerbed. Annoyed at their persistence, Clarie yelled at them again. "You dogs get away from here!"

This time, a single dog looked up. A huge black and brown chow glared at her - a human neither large nor imposing - and considered any threat she might pose minimal. Long black tongue lolling between ivory fangs, the big dog lowered his head to the ground and continued his pursuit of the bitch. The others followed close behind him. Had the chow known Clarie better, he might have taken greater care. Dismissing this frail human was easy enough until he felt the first sharp blow. He snarled savagely and whirled to confront his attacker.

But no other dog was attacking. Only the frail human threatened. The human was obviously the source of his pain, the challenger of his right to pursue the most basic of all instincts. Instantly, the big dog changed from hopeful suitor to ravening engine of destruction. He bristled, bared his fangs and with a growl that rumbled from some hellish depth of his fury, the big chow charged Clarie, the pack closing on her with him.

Meanwhile, Jeff dreamed on...

The sun rolled slowly across the mid-day sky, finding a hole in the willow tree that shaded the big red dog. A burning ray crept onto a paw, then up to his sensitive nose. Jeff shifted unconsciously. A nearby voice penetrated the first layer of consciousness, but it was familiar and only scolded...no alarm there, certainly nothing to wake up for. He knew the voice. It belonged to a person that should be here, a part of his extended family. The voice came again. He almost roused from pleasant remembrance into full consciousness; but sleep was so pleasant he heaved a deep sigh and rolled onto his back.

Jeff whined softly as he dreamed. The voice came again, but this time, something had changed. Jeff transformed from deep sleep into instant, questioning wakefulness. His senses flashed to the alert. Something was terribly wrong and he went from wakefulness to dead run in an instant. He tore around the side of the house and bounded, bristling with building rage, into the yard. Instantly, his keen senses surveyed and analyzed what he saw. There were strange dogs here... in *his* territory. That would not be tolerated.

Clarie recognized her mistake the moment she threw the rock. She really hadn't meant to hit anything. She had picked up the fist-size stone from the flowerbed and flung it across the yard, hoping to scare the dogs away. As luck would have it, the stone landed flush on the side of the chow's head. Only seconds before, the chow's demeanor sent the clear and foreboding message: "Don't get in my way." But things happened all too quickly, and Clarie had a problem. Though increasingly frightened, and utterly alone, she was not one to cut and run. She knelt quickly, frantically running her fingers through the loose dirt, searching for another stone. She heard the prehistoric growl of the big chow, and looked up to see him coming, head low, ears laid back, black mane bristling. Behind him, like wolves closing on a wounded deer, the rest of the pack surged forward.

Clarie abandoned the search for another rock and jumped to her feet. She screamed, beating the air between her and the onrushing pack with the hoe. "Get back!" she yelled. "Get away from me!" Still they came, ignoring her futile attempts to frighten them. She backed up, raising the hoe above her head, stomping her petunias flat, almost falling over the birdbath. "Get back. Get back!" Her voice was now the high-pitched wail of a terrified woman who knew she was defenseless. Growling and yelping in insane fury, a snarling wave of savagery swept down on her. Clarie was desperate now. Her last rational thought was the hope that she would go quickly, not feel the fangs that would rend and tear at her. The huge chow lunged for her throat...

Instinctively, Claire brought the hoe down, trying to strike the big dog. It never landed. In midair, the huge animal caught the handle in his jaws and snapped it as if it was a twig. The speed of his bulk carried him forward, but the distraction of the hoe diverted him from his intended prey. The slashing teeth missed Clarie, and the chow landed to one side of the birdbath. Instantaneously, he spun and renewed his attack. Clarie fell back against the birdbath, holding the broken handle in one hand, the other thrown up over her face as a shield from the fury of her attackers. She waited, but the chow's savage jaws never found her.

Something flew over her shoulder, something big, red, and roaring like a demented demon. A red blur hit the big chow with such force that it knocked him into the pack, scattering lesser dogs in all directions. Jeff had immediately sized up the situation and flung his eighty-odd pounds of deadly fighting skill into the fray. Clarie watched, still terrified but somewhat buoyed, as Jeff worked long fangs through thick fur and into the chow's throat, yanking vigorously from side to side to exacerbate the wounds. The chow fell on his back with Jeff on top of him, jaws still locked in what had become a death grip. The other dogs skittered about as they watched their leader fall to the red stranger. Petunias and iris were flattened as the combatants thrashed from side to side in the flower bed, the chow struggling to escape the red devil that had him pinned and helpless. But Jeff had tasted his sire's blood and sensed his fear. A roar of anguish erupted from the chow to combine with Jeff's deep growls in a hellish symphony. Clarie was petrified by the violence unfolding before her. She could do nothing to help Jeff. But one of the pack undertook to support his leader.

The Terrier-Poodle mix found heart far beyond his size and rushed to the aid of the embattled chow. Maneuvering behind Jeff, he drove his eyeteeth deep into his hindquarter. At first, Jeff didn't notice his efforts; but the terrier improved his bite and caught Jeff higher on the flank, hanging on as the larger combatants carried him along. The terrier, like a tin can strung behind a newlywed's car, was bounced and battered in the violence. Other dogs, inspired by the courage of the terrier, moved closer. There was only the one adversary, and he was outnumbered and taxed to his limit.

But it wasn't Jeff's first death battle. There had been any number of those, and he was still alive and obviously, very healthy. Jeff sensed the threat of the pack, released his grip on the chow and whirled to attack the terrier. He seized the smaller dog by the genitals and ripped them from him, disemboweling him in the process. The terrier, screaming in pure terror and the sure knowledge that he was mortally wounded, scrambled away, pinkish gray loops of intestines dragging behind him. Without hesitation, Jeff flew into the other dogs with such single minded intent and savage fury that they lost heart and scattered in all directions. Jeff turned to finish the chow.

An enormously relieved Clarie had no desire to witness a fight between two large dogs, one of whom she cared for deeply. "Here, Jeff. Good boy. Come here, Jeff."

He stood by her, rumbling fiercely, his full attention still focused on the chow. The defeated dog faced him, rumpled and disoriented, coat streaked with blood from deep wounds to his throat and neck. He was not accustomed to the receiving end of a thrashing and, although he still growled threateningly, he made no overt move. It was obvious he would like nothing better than a quick escape from the fate that faced him. He watched Jeff intently, anticipating his next move. Jeff bristled and snarled, exposing long, white fangs

"Easy, Jeff, easy boy," Clarie spoke softly, soothingly, as she moved next to him, knelt, and placed her hand on his shoulder. "It's alright. Good, boy. Goooood, boy, Jeff."

Jeff licked her face and whined softly before taking two stiff steps toward the chow. "No, Jeff, no! no!" Clarie cried, grabbing a fistful of neck fur. He turned and licked her again, reassuring her that she was in control. "Good, dog," she murmured, "Good, dog." She stroked his head and patted him. The chow saw an opportunity and sprinted, tail curled firmly between his legs, through the yard and up the street. Jeff barked a final challenge as the chow raced out of sight. He whimpered softy and nuzzled Clarie's hand as if searching for a treat. She put her arms around him and squeezed him tightly. "What a good boy. What a good, Jeff," she repeated. What she needed most right then was a good, private cry. She bent to him once more, and Jeff licked her face. Clarie turned and went quickly inside. Jeff trotted to the water tub, took a long, luxurious drink, and began casting about for his brother's scent. It took only a few moments before the big red dog was hot on Fuzzy's trail.

Time was running out and the team was about to score. She saw Don turn and look into the stands. She was sure he was looking for her and she waved at him... and that was when Dee Garrison startled her by sliding into the adjacent seat and throwing his arm around her as if they were a loving couple.

She hadn't wanted to leave, but he insisted. The look in his eyes told her she had better not argue. As they made their way out of the stadium, the roar of the crowd told her that something very positive had happened on the field. She wondered if the same could be said for the situation she found herself in, and the plan Dee had begun to explain as they wound their way past the jubilant fans.

INCARNATE

Memories of that night returned as Dawn lay on her side under a washed out ledge in the limestone creek bank. She remembered all that and groaned at the brilliant sunlight reflecting off the white creek bottom just outside her cave-like confinement. The gag and blindfold were gone, so she could breathe freely, but the light was blinding and she blinked repeatedly. Her hands remained tied behind her and her feet were still bound. Had the gag not been removed, she would have been miserable to the point of madness. As it was, she briefly felt something akin to gratefulness.

Still, she couldn't remember exactly how she had gotten into her current predicament. Most of her recall was a blur, jumbled fragments defying definition or logical order. Yet some were as lucid as the blaring sunlight just beyond her reach. Dee had pulled her away at the football game to advise her of a deal her father had made; of a loan he'd begged from Garrison and later secured with the promise that Dawn would pay it off when he couldn't.

Doyle Ferguson was something of a rough-work handyman. He could do a little framing and he occasionally labored as a mason's helper; but mostly, he dug…ditches, postholes, plumbing trenches and the like, scratching through the thin, bare topsoil, then chiseling deep into the limestone bedrock that lay only a few inches beneath; and did it all with hand tools. There was generally enough work for him to provide a fair share of his family's support. With his perpetually exhausted wife, who cleaned houses and took in laundry, Doyle was raising six children in a dilapidated rent property five miles from town.

While the town's first housing addition since 1930 was in its infant stages, there was enough work promised to him that Ferguson seized upon the idea of buying a ditching machine. Since he had no credit and nothing to offer in the way of collateral, he was reduced to approaching his landlord, one Mrs. Walter Garrison, for a loan. Mrs. Garrison sought to involve her eldest son, Dee, in the rudiments of business and finance, and she assigned him to handle the transaction.

Despite Ferguson's hopes, it didn't take long for things to go sour. The promoters wrongly assumed that people would be willing to spend a great deal more for houses than they could actually afford. In

153

the end, they sold the models at cost, paid off the few contractors who held shop or construction liens, defaulted on the rest, declared bankruptcy and went back to Chicago. Doyle Ferguson only knew enough about liens to know he didn't hold one. But that wasn't Ferguson's most serious problem. Dee Garrison held the note on his ditching machine. And Garrison didn't want the machine, he only wanted money...principal and twenty percent interest, a sum Ferguson neither possessed nor had any reasonable hope of obtaining. And Dee Garrison was no man with whom to be late on a note...much less one to abide default. Ferguson did, however, have one resource he'd never thought of, even in his wildest dreams. It was Garrison who explained it all to him, and it sounded reasonable enough...if Ferguson didn't look at things too closely.

Dawn remembered the pathetic look on her father's face when he admitted that he'd promised her services to settle his debt. Her long-suffering mother cried inside, but moved quickly to bolster her daughter's resolve to get through it. It came down to occasionally making her nude body available for viewing by groups of men she didn't know and would hopefully never see again, some of them much older than she.

The first time, encouraged by a fellow "performer" named Mary Lou, three bourbon straights, and a threatening boss, she actually stumbled into the lap of a customer who helped her up with hands exploring every curvaceous inch of her body. Managing to pull away, she staggered into the alley behind the club and threw up.

"You all right, Honey?" Mary Lou said, bending at the waist, one hand on Dawn's bare shoulder.

Dawn spit, sending remnants of her last meal spewing across the pavement, glancing through blurry eyes at the bulbous breasts swaying above her head. It was high summer, but the concrete felt cold. "Huh?"

"You gonna' be all right?" Mary Lou repeated, helping Dawn to her feet.

For a few seconds, Dawn stared at the slightly-pudgy, mostly-naked stripper offering her assistance. *What was she doing here? What was going on?* "Oh, sure," she said, absently wiping saliva from her chin. "I'm fine. Just kind of sick."

"Oh, baby...you jest too green for this sort'a thing. Why ain't you home mindin' little sister?"

"What?" Dawn was still queezy and more than a little confused.

Gently, Mary Lou led her over to a wooden bench drenched in the glare of an overhead light. "How old you, honey? Eighteen?"

"Sixteen." Dawn replied, sitting.

"Sonofabitch!"

"I'm old enough!"

"For what...kindeegarten? You're illegal and you sure ain't cut out for this. Dee ought'a have his pecker cut off!"

"I really need to get back inside." Dawn rose abruptly, but immediately swayed, grasped Mary Lou's arm and sat back down. "Maybe in jest a minute."

"I'm puttin' a end to yore career, honey!" Mary Lou roared, turning toward the door to the nightclub. She stopped as Dawn grabbed the waist strap on her g-string.

"Please, please," Dawn pleaded. "I gotta do this."

The older woman stared pathetically down at her.

"Please?"

"But..."

"I'll get the hang of it...I promise. I won't get sick no more...I promise"

Mary Lou sighed and slowly shook her head.

Soon, however, Dawn did get the *hang of it* and the term "party girl" took on a new meaning. There was actually a part of her that enjoyed the lustful attention. It was exciting and, somehow, it felt natural. And she made more in one night, serving drinks naked, allowing her firm breasts and buttocks to occasionally be fondled, than her parents made in a week of brutally hard labor. At the same time, she despised what she was doing, feeling dirty and disgusted, beset by an ambivalence threatening to gnaw through her psychic core.

After her father's note was satisfied, she began saying no to the parties. Encouraged to explore other revenue opportunities promising more money than she'd dreamed was possible, she was tempted. "All you have to do is close your mind to what's happening," she was advised. "It's nothing more than the natural thing that happens when a girl is naked with a man." Assured that she wasn't expected to kiss them... *"Save that for Mr. Wonderful.";* and that it would be almost impossible for anyone at school to ever find out what she was doing, she almost relented. But then, to really no one's surprise, she quit. Abandoning g-string, pasties and prying hands, she returned to the life of innocent country girl; investing a surplus of her earnings in several Mary Lou–advised financial ventures. Everything was going well until Dee Garrison discovered her enterprise and quickly set out to square things with a girl he had come to regard as a privately held asset.

"You cain't quit, bitch!"

"I have, Dee."

"You'll regret it."

"I doubt it."

"You owe me."

"Not any more."

"Oh, fuck you. Who gives a shit?"

In her heart, she knew *he* did.

Suddenly sounds, voices, footsteps …just beyond her place of confinement:

"Just git down there and check it out. They was carryin' fishin' poles."

"So?"

"So 'at means they may be fishin', don't it?"

"The creek's dry."

"Quit thinkin' 'n get yore ass down there like I said!"

"Why I always gott'a do shit like this?"

"'Cause you're you an' I'm me… an' I tole you. Now go do it."

"That ain't fair."

A meaty, slapping sound.

"I'll do it! I'll do it, Dee! Don't… don't hit me no more!"

"Stop by the place first. Look under the back porch an' bring 'at fifth I got hid under there. The box with the green end."

"Awright. Awright."

Receding footsteps …

"If y' see 'em, come back 'n git me. An' look out for two big dogs they may have with 'em. They're mean as hell, so don't go doin' nothin' stupid!"

Then silence, disturbed only by the excited cawing of a solitary crow.

She closed her eyes to let memory sort itself out. When she finally felt like she had the events that had brought her there in the right order, she managed to bring herself upright... shoulders propped against the rock wall. She blew matted hair from her eyes and blinked against the blinding glare. Now...to get away...

Fifty feet removed, Dee Garrison paced nervously and smoked. "Too damned hot," he growled aloud, "it's too damned hot." He treasured the dark coolness of the strip clubs he frequented. He'd grown accustomed to the excitement of the night, the noisy, smoky haze...places where reality was something you left at the door. He'd had enough of rural America. Dee fancied the nightlife genre and longed to be accepted as a part of it. He had come to see his future in entertainment of a very special nature. That's what he was all about now. He was going to put an act together that would attract old guys, the ones with fat wallets and permanently limp dicks. *Since they can't do nothin' nomore, they can watch somebody doin' it for 'em. I'll keep things very private, and they'll pay one helluva' cover. A hunnert dollars apiece won't be too much for what they're gonna' see. There'll be more'n enough for the club owners n' performers, an' I'll get the rest. An' that's where she comes in. Since none o' my customers could get it up for Marilyn Monroe, they can watch the finest lookin' hide they'll ever lay eyes on take it from studs that can. It'll be staged jist right, they'll be playin' the same kinda' music the strippers dance to. Hell, I'll make her rich. She oughta' be grateful.*

He deserved this chance. It wasn't his fault he was a misfit. *I done everythin' they asked me to do; hustled up the girl an' made the loan good plus a bunch extra. I been doin' everythin'.... everythin' they want, and they still treat me like shit.*

"Well fuck 'em!", he roared at the top of his lungs, "Fuck 'em all!"

Startled, the crow flapped away, raucous cries diminishing in the distance. Dee dropped his cigarette butt and ground it out. Under the ledge, Dawn jumped at the violence in his voice. She'd felt a jagged edge of rock at her back and had begun slowly rubbing the rope against it. But even if she freed herself, how could she escape?

"My, my, my…ain't we busy in here."

It was noticeably darker in Dee's shadow. He squatted in front of her.

"Yeah, Missy, you real fuckin' busy there, ain'tcha'?"

He jerked her around by one arm and dragged her out into the open.

"Lemme' go, Dee! What's the matter with you anyway?" she snarled at him.

Dee pulled her up, spun her around and inspected the rope around her wrists.

"No harm done. You be rubbin' on that rope next week and still be tied up."

"What is it Dee? Whatta' you want?" she repeated. "I told you I was through. Is that it, Dee? You mad 'cause I quit and you never could fuck me? 'Cause if that's all it is, why don't you just try it now and let's get it over with."

"Shutup!" he answered, and cuffed her with enough force to make her stumble.

She saw bright lights, but held on to consciousness.

"Turn around," he ordered.

She complied meekly and he untied her. Dawn stretched her arms to relieve the cramp in her shoulders.

"Now you can untie y' feet." he ordered, whipping the bitter end into a loop with a simple slip knot.

Dawn bent and untied her feet. She took the obvious chance and pivoted to run, but Garrison slipped the noose over her head and she stopped as quickly as she'd started, gagging as he pulled her back.

"You think I'm stupid, don't y'?"

Her shoulders slumped as her fingers gingerly explored the rope burn on her throat.

"I want you t' listen while I tell you how we gonna' get rich, you an' me."

"Just don't hurt me no more."

"Hurt you? Naw, Missy I ain't gonna' hurt you. In fact, you gonna' like it."

.

158

In the more than one thousand centuries that Ten Mile Creek had existed, there had been countless floods – many of epic proportions. Rushing torrents cut deep banks through the limestone bedrock and, in places, well into the slate- blue, underlying shale pools. Bluehole was the largest of these pools that punctuated the serpentine path of Ten Mile Creek. It got its name because its color was the deep blue of the shale bottom. Its reputation was earned from the mysteries it evoked...including the one about the monster fish that lurked within its seemingly bottomless depths.

THE MONSTER

"Maybe we should try Garrison Hole."

Pete jumped up onto the support, grabbing an overhead beam to steady himself. "Last time we snuck in there, it was full'a turtles."

We had coasted down the final grade to the big bridge over Ten Mile Creek. The design was Warren Truss with verticals - simple and sturdy. The road seemed to run through it more than over it.

The trees that lined the creek were old and large, and road crews hadn't trimmed them back in years. Half the bridge was in the shade most of the time; and it was welcome relief as we eased our bikes off to the side, engaged our kickstands, and hurried out onto the structure.

We peered over the railing down into the creek. In the shade, light didn't penetrate well enough to actually see fish in the depths. We had to stand on the sunny side and wait for our eyes to adjust. This took patience, in short supply with us, so we squinted, gradually adjusting to the glare off the limestone bottom. With no rain for months, the water level in the creek was down so far that long stretches of it lay completely dry. An occasional seedling willow and stands of yellow Johnson Grass sprouted from cracks. We'd fished this creek in early spring and it hadn't appeared nearly so desolate. Now it looked almost hostile. Summer was sucking the life out of Ten Mile Creek.

"You say turtles?" I asked.

"Yeah," Pete answered. "Anyways, it ain't near as deep as Bluehole."

Garrison Hole was only a short distance upstream from the bridge. Bluehole lay much farther away in the opposite direction. It would be easier to sneak into Garrison Hole, only we'd been warned to stay out of there, and we took that warning seriously.

"It's probably dry anyway," I said finally. "If we're gonna have any luck, it'll be at Bluehole."

We lifted the bikes over the fence we had to cross and laid them down, out of sight in the high weeds that grew in the shadow of the bridge. We knew they'd be safe enough, so we didn't really need to hide them. If they were stolen, they'd be discovered very quickly in such a small town. And stealing anything but an ear or two of field corn would get your butt whipped.

"Let's go get 'em!" I said breathlessly, placing a foot on the lowest of three strands of barbed wire, lifting the middle one with my free hand for Pete to crawl through.

"Hurry up, I got the feelin'," he responded, repeating the courtesy and poking fun at me.

I crawled through and we scrambled down the steep dirt embankment, which was no easy task. Most of the time, we made two trips; one with our poles, the other with the rest of our gear. We had to negotiate a steep slope studded with granite rip-rap that was either treacherously slick because it was muddy, or treacherously slick because it was baked to the consistency of powder and gave way easily. We kept our weight on our heels. That way, if we lost our balance, we'd end up skidding at least part of the way on our butts instead of our faces.

I went first with only my pole and managed to balance gravity with momentum. Pete had both hands full, a typical "lazy man's load". He intended to make only one trip. It was no surprise when I heard him yell, then watched him bounce down butt first and finally lay sprawling in deep Johnson Grass. I didn't even try not to laugh at him and finally had to sit down and catch my breath as he blistered the heavens with a brief, but forceful, string of expletives.

"Real cute little move," I offered.

"Screw you very deeply and sincerely," he replied with apparent grace.

I quickly completed my second trip and we made short work of inspecting our tackle. We heard the distant whine of tires and ducked, reflexively, into the tall grass. The whine grew louder until it was drowned in the roar of a pickup crossing the bridge. There was no reason for our secretiveness but, for reasons we couldn't have explained, we didn't want to be seen. As the pickup's rattling passage faded into the distance, we looped under the bridge and headed downstream. Somewhere nearby, but unseen, a band of crows cawed insistently. We knew if we found them, we'd likely find an owl they were tormenting. There was the ever present, rising and falling buzz of cicadas and, from far overhead, the drone of a massive, six-engine B-36 climbing out of Carswell Air Force Base some sixty miles to the west. The air was still and heavy; but as we moved forward our excitement cut through that stifling blanket. We'd walked perhaps one hundred yards when Pete stopped.

"What's the problem?" I asked.

"I had my stringer, didn't I?"

"I guess."

"Well, I musta' dropped it back there."

"When you fell on your butt. What a waste o' time!" I snorted in disgust.

Pete was forever losing, forgetting, ignoring, or dismissing. And while most people would regard those traits as failures, he refused to even recognize them; viewing life as a continuing string of unforeseen variables. That some might be occasioned by flawed actions, or failure to act, he considered an inconsequential component of the variable itself. Were the regrettable homily "shit happens" have then been in common use, it would have been Pete's defining mantra. I, on the other hand, demanded order in the universe and rarely forgave violation of same, in others or myself.

"I need to go back and get it." He said, disregarding my irritation.

"Well, I'm not waitin'!" I barked, thoroughly aggravated.

"Why're you gettin' all pissed off?"

"And you aren't usin' mine!" I said, starting downstream.

"Why not? You won't need it."

I waved dismissively and kept walking.

"Wait up for me at that first hole we have to wade!" He yelled hopefully.

Ten Mile was very different from the previous year, when this part of the creek was just under flood stage. At the first place we would normally expect to wade, I avoided thick mud and thigh-high slime by walking nearly sideways on the side of the steep bank while hanging onto exposed tree roots for support. After that point, the creek channel narrowed. The lower branches of giant creek side trees interlaced overhead and I found myself in complete shade. It was appreciably cooler. I eased across to the far bank where, to my considerable surprise, a small stream of water trickled out of a crevice and down a limestone abutment. I'd never seen this natural spring before because it had always been underwater. Algae had already begun to coat the wet limestone. This was fascinating…unexpected. I tested the rivulet with my finger and found the water surprisingly cool.

It was pleasant being completely alone in such a beautiful setting. *The only thing that would improve it would be if Dawn was here and Pete was home with the mumps.* I had been walking a primarily dry creek bed, but shortly after passing the natural spring I began to notice a shallow flow. *Maybe some other springs feedin' in? Must be. It's lookin' more like a creek the closer I get, so maybe Bluehole's still in good shape.* Then I heard the first muted cadence of water going over the falls and into Bluehole. Immediately, my spirits lifted.

A refreshing breeze blew into my face. *One more bend, then past a dry draw that merges into the channel and I'll be at the waterfall. Yes!* The channel widened above the falls. The water was getting deeper and moving at a brisk pace. My footsteps became careful and measured. Since creek brim "spook" so easily, I wanted my approach to be as stealthy as possible. As I neared the falls I could see sparkling reflections at the far end of Bluehole. *There's plenty of water!* Here and there, sunlight lanced through the thick overhead foliage to form shimmering prisms in wisps of spray thrown up by the falls. On the right, where the fall of water was heaviest, I saw a tiny rainbow. All was silent save for the whisper of the little waterfall. Layers of limestone rose to form the steep sides of a wide, tranquil basin. The water was clear and reflected sunlight slipping through breaks in the overhead trees.

I made my way down to the water's edge. *I know you're here… and I know you're hungry… and I know you're very, very careful.* Somewhere in those violet depths my monster lurked. I knew that catching him would require my total concentration. First, I arranged my tackle. Then I impaled a small strip of salt pork on a hook no wider than a quarter of a thumbnail from shank to barb. A mockingbird glided from a branch and alighted nearby. Upon discovering me, it cocked its head critically and focused its black eye upon what was probably the first human it had ever seen. I held my breath as it finished its business, launched itself into the air and, with effortless grace, disappeared into a tree on the far side of the blue-black pool. The time had come for some serious fishin'. From the far distance came a faint, deep rumble. I ignored it.

I twisted a thin sliver of "wraparound" weight around my line about six inches above the hook. As with everything involved in brim fishin', the weight required to sink the bait has to be miniaturized. We had found the perfect material in the lead and tin alloy that seals wine bottles, and found the bottles by prowling ditches. From the tip of the pole, I unwound an amount of line exactly matching the length of my pole, about ten feet, then tied it off at the tip with a double half-hitch. To "cast" with a cane pole requires holding the line just above the bait with one hand, lifting and extending the pole with the other, then releasing the bait which causes it to fall away, swing up and out, then gently settle into the water…the result of a smooth underhand motion. The best chance of attracting a big brim is with the first couple of presentations. After that, they quickly become suspicious.

I was all business now. I targeted a dark pocket of still water fifteen feet to my right and was about to make my first presentation when a dirt-dauber wasp made the mistake of landing on the placid surface. The Monster struck immediately, the stillness interrupted by a wet, slapping explosion. Ripples spread outward in expanding circles from the strike. *Has to be the Monster! He's there! And he's feeding!* My heart raced and I tasted electricity.

I let the ripples subside and waited a full two minutes before creeping, heel then toe, down the bank to where I could make a presentation at the point of the strike. From the far bank came the mewing of a gray catbird. An emerald dragonfly landed on a nearby reed. I waved off a swarm of gnats attracted by my sweat. The moment was perfect. In one unbroken motion I raised my pole, released the bait, and pushed the pole forward. It was a perfect presentation -as mine usually were- compared to Pete's spastic attempts. Boy, was I glad he'd misplaced that stringer! He'd have whooped and clumped right over to the splash, ruining any chance of catching anything. The light nylon line played out as my bait reached the apex of its trajectory, hung for a moment …then feathered to the surface and settled gently into the water. I waited as the white glob of pork fat sank slowly.

My stomach churned and my grip tightened around the butt of my pole as the bait disappeared into the depths. Nothing. The line began straightening, coming back toward me to where it would ultimately hang vertically from the tip of my pole. My heart was thumping wildly. Still, I waited. Nothing. No nibble, no electric jolt. Nothing.

Another zephyr made its way up the creek sending dry leaves fluttering across the water. Their motion reminded me of Daddy's sink demonstration. His point had been *brim tend to strike at moving targets*. My bait was inert, nine feet below the surface. *Of course, Dummy*. I'd have to retrieve and check my bait to see if it was long enough to wiggle. I pulled back on my pole...and the Monster struck. There was the familiar initial jolt as the big fish hit the bait, then a continuous throbbing as the brim fought violently for deeper water. The line straightened and the pole bent. I had a real fish on! "Oh, yeah!" I yelled.

The Monster fought fiercely. I flicked my wrist to set the hook. Pete would've jerked it through the brim's lips or straightened the barb if it was hooked in the bony palate. Unconsciously balancing my weight, I tightened my grip on the pole.

It's an indescribable thrill to feel an unseen, but very much alive, creature of the depths desperately struggling to escape. The fish's fierce strength bent my rod tip to the water. My line cut through the surface erratically as I maintained steady pressure. I moved with him, then against him, always keeping the pressure constant and playing the fish adroitly. After a minute or so, I realized that there was no doubt about the outcome. The Monster was mine. He wouldn't be getting away.

Calm settled over me. I began to think about what he might be, probably a big bluegill by Daddy's comparisons of size. He had to be two pounds...maybe three...maybe a world record! My picture would probably be in Field & Stream. I visualized holding him up, gripping his lower lip with thumb and forefinger, scales glittering in a riot of color, a fat, slick, gleaming trophy landed through my skill and determination. The throbbing pressure eased. The fish was almost played out. I didn't exactly relax; but I began to exult. I was talking to him now, "Come on, big boy. Come to papa. Come on..." Then, I heard something I didn't want to hear. "Pete!" I yelled reflexively.

I knew my friend well, every quirk of his personality. I could interpret the most minor permutations of his voice. And what I heard was Pete screaming, screaming loudly, very obviously in trouble. His strident voice ricocheted off the steep limestone banks and down the creek. The first booming effort was followed by another, and then another. He was broadcasting my name from the better part of a quarter mile away, and still I heard his clear baritone plainly, "DONNNNNNN!" he yelled.

Pete wasn't one to cry wolf. His instincts were to tackle a problem straight on, asking for help only when he'd exhausted every possibility. For everything I could not know about his current situation, I knew he was in trouble that forced him to command my immediate presence. Pete had gotten himself into a fearful pickle.

I dropped the pole and took off upstream at a dead run. As I ran, my imagination went into overtime. Something was hugely wrong. Possibilities tore through my brain as I blasted ahead hurdling rocks I'd crawled carefully over on the way down. *He's desperate, and that's bad! Quicksand we never knew about? Pack of dogs? Something wild from the cedar breaks? Snake! That's it! Has to be a snake bit him!* That was just the worst possible scenario…but it almost had to be what had happened with water moccasins almost everywhere and rattlesnakes where they weren't. *How far do I have to carry him and where's the nearest phone?* My legs were crying out for oxygen and my heart was racing madly to supply it. For all that, I jacked the throttle up a notch. I flattened weeds and wrist-thick willow saplings, concerned only on getting to Pete. A hundred yards from the bridge now and he bellowed again. I managed just enough breath to yell back, "COMMIIINNN'!"

I redoubled my efforts, ripping through creek side brush, splashing through mud holes to save time, crawling up and down steep banks to get around them. Everything was becoming gray. My desperate body screamed at my lungs. I tripped and sprawled over a fallen trunk, made it back onto my feet and kept on running. The final bend was in sight now. Staggering around it and smashing through a curtain of willows, I found the answer to my questions.

Pete was in the middle of the creek bed, straddling a supine figure. I pulled up short, hands on knees, agonized breaths coming in great, strangled sobs. "What's…what's going…on?" I finally managed to gasp. "What…the hell…happened?" Pete looked up, using his knees to keep his adversary's arms pinned to the ground. I blanched upon recognizing him. *Good Grief, it's David Garrison!*

'Bout time." Pete said. I noticed a large hunting knife lying on the ground nearby.

"What happened?" I replied, winded and bewildered.

"This jerk tried to knife me. Sonofabitch come outta' nowhere an' jumped me, then tried to stick me with that knife."

"Motherfucker!" David gurgled through bloody lips. Pete rewarded his outburst with a resounding slap. The man tried to squirm loose; but Pete held him down firmly, bouncing his knees against his arms.

"Shutup!" Pete yelled, spraying spittle on the man's face.

"Fuck you!" Garrison gasped.

Pete slapped him twice, blood erupting from the impact of both blows.

Garrison finally got the idea and kept his mouth shut.

I hadn't recovered sufficiently to consider the entirety of the problem we probably faced. But the Garrison boys were a lot like us in a way, and one thing was certain: Where you saw one, the other had to be nearby. I was shaky to the point of nausea, but I stood up and walked over to the knife. I picked it up. "See the other one?" I asked, realizing that was probably not one of Pete's major concerns at the moment.

"Nope," Pete replied. "What're we gonna' do with this one?"

"Let him up."

Pete shot me a hard, questioning glance, then ground his knees into the man's arms again and abruptly stood to tower over him, glowering.

"Had t' stop him, Don, but it woulda' been a lot worse if you hadn't made it here."

"I can see he's bleedin'," I responded, "but we got a problem. We don't know where the big one is, or if there's anyone else with 'em."

David rose slowly, staggering and spitting blood.

"Gonna' get your ass for this," he snarled. Pete would've hit him again, but I grabbed him. "He's finished," I said, "Let's get outta' here."

David's face was swollen and bruised...more so, I thought, than it should be from Pete's blows, and he swayed in the heat. His hair was tangled and matted with both crusted and fresh blood. He exhaled heavily, then fell back into something of a sitting position. The fight was out of him. He looked pitiful there on the baking limestone. He certainly seemed smaller than the bully I remembered from the incident at school. *Not much to fear from him.* Still, he was a grownup and, despite the relative tactical positions we occupied, grownups could cause two teenage boys loads of trouble; and I was thinking about that. In contrast to contemporary ethics, we lived during a time and in a place where boys didn't challenge, much less physically confront, grown men...without paying a fearful price. I figured that somewhere down the road, Pete and I were in for an uncomfortable ride.

"Come on, let's get outta' here." I urged   Pete's questioning look lasted only a moment.

We were headed toward our bikes when Garrison yelled at us.

"I want my goddamn knife back!"

There was no chance I was gonna' be that generous *or* foolish. I gripped the handle and threw the thing as far as I could. I had a good arm and it must have traveled at least forty yards, clearing the creek and a stand of willows before landing with a distinct "clink" on the limestone of the opposite bank.

"Shit!" he yelled in a high pitched voice...like a woman's.

Pete and I were both more than a little shaken. We went quickly under the shadow of the bridge toward our hidden bikes. Garrison remained where we left him, spitting blood and swearing incoherently. In the distance, the rumbling I'd been hearing all morning seemed louder.

We started up the bank, thinking only of getting out of there, when a horned- toad darted from beneath a rock in front of us, scampering under our feet. Startled, we jumped back, collided, lost our balance, and fell in a tangled heap. We sat for a long moment, stunned at our own clumsiness. Then, in much needed catharsis, we lapsed into chuckles that grew into hoots of laughter, which proceed into side-splitting guffaws. We rolled on the ground uncontrollably, at least momentarily purging our young psyches of the unwanted violence that had been forced on us. We laughed in the joy that it had been overcome. But most of all, we laughed in acknowledgement of a camaraderie and friendship that transcended violence and most other things we could think of. Finally, after minutes of near delirium, we lay on our backs unmoving. No breeze stirred. No strange sounds were heard. We were suspended in time and place. *Like brim in their murky haunts. Brim? Good Grief, I forgot all about the Monster! The one on my line back at Bluehole!*

"Get up," I yelled and jumped to my feet!

"What?" Pete jumped up because I had.

"I caught him! The Monster! He's hooked on my line at Bluehole!"

Pete's eyes widened, "You're kiddin'?"

"Come on," I yelled, "We gotta' hurry!"

We had taken perhaps three steps when the unmistakable flat crack of a gunshot stopped us dead in our tracks. On top of the bank stood Dee Garrison, in his hand… a black pistol.

"Where ya'll hurryin', shitheads?" He asked casually.

I was paralyzed with fear. I looked at Pete. He was ashen. Dee kept the gun pointed directly at us as he grunted his way down the embankment.

"We gonna' git some shit straight here," he said viciously. "You pretty smart back 'ere on the road. Near 'bout killed me an' m' brother."

"Oh."

"Oh? That all?" Garrison continued.

"Look, we didn't mean anything, and we didn't really even come close…."

"Yeah, we just happened to be ridin' fast right by you guys." Pete jumped in.

"Ya' see, you on Garrison proppity." Dee continued, disinterested in anything we had to say.

"But we…"

"You trespassin' agin. Ain't nobody give you no p'mission to be down here. I warned y' before, an' now I got ever right to kill y' both."

Surely, he's joking. Only, he isn't funny.

169

Dee Garrison was rancid. He appeared to have worn the same clothes for days, even weeks maybe. The whole situation seemed like a bad dream, but the pistol he held on us was very real. If this was some kind of joke, it was time to end it.

My voice shook as badly as my knees. "Dee, this is gettin' a little crazy. What's the matter with you anyway?"

"We fish Bluehole all the time." Pete chimed in.

"Yeah, and we were headed there right now."

He cleared his throat and spat, "Y'all happen t' see my brother anywheres?"

"I'm right over here," David answered, walking up. Sunlight reflected off the knife he had obviously recovered. *Great! I should'a buried the sucker.*

Dee looked inquiringly at his brother.

"I know I slapped y' around some, but you didn't look all 'at bad when y' went to find 'ese sumbitches. What happened?"

"These little turds here jumped me," David answered deprecatingly. "So I had to whup up on 'em…and they run off up here. I'll take care of 'em now, though," he added, glowering.

Pete and I exchanged glances. *This can't be happening to us. It makes no sense.*

"Don't get me started again you stupid fuck." Dee growled. "I got plans for 'em.

Now move!" he ordered, pointing upstream with the gun.

"What?" I asked, realizing he was talking to us and still unwilling to believe the turn of events.

He motioned to David who was standing slightly to one side and behind me. I started to speak when something crashed into my ear and I went to my knees. Faintly I heard: "Go ahead and make your move shithook. I'd jist as soon shoot as look at y." Despite the dull pain raging through my head, I got up as quickly as I could, fearful that Pete might just rise to the bait.

"Gimme' 'em canteens first!" We unsnapped and handed them over. " *MOVE!* " he barked again focusing on me, "or I'm gonna' shoot *you first!* "

That I understood. Pete must've understood it too because we turned in unison and started walking. The Garrisons fell in behind us.

The sun beat down harder than ever. I could smell something wild, feral, and unfamiliar. I recognized it as fear, either my own or Pete's. Maybe both. And I was scared. It wasn't so much the Garrisons themselves. We might have been able to handle them, or at least outrun them. But we had enough sense to be afraid of guns. I'd never been shot at before, never been put in a life-threatening situation. I felt trapped and impotent, bewildered and terrified. But I was not alone. Pete was beside me; and I could see that he was as pale as the chalk-white creekbed.

GARRISON HOLE

The water in Ten Mile Creek was publicly owned; but the creekbed and banks were part of the surrounding farmland, which was owned by individuals. There were public easements, such as railroad and public right-of-way; but access to, and use of, the creek could become a problem. In the past, adults had held creek-side parties, leaving rubbish and disorder in their wake. Landowners had responded by tacking up "No Trespassing" signs. But two boys intent solely upon reducing the brim population were unlikely to ever become a problem. Besides, almost no one ever even knew we were there...

I figured we'd walked for about twenty minutes. We did it in silence except for the crunch of eight feet in the flaking limestone of the dry bed. My heart pounded erratically and I had problems breathing. On top of that, David's blow to my ear had jarred something and I felt dizzy and nauseous, experiencing difficulty concentrating on an exit strategy. Pete was distracted as well. The Garrisons were close behind us and we could hear David talking to himself. If that was strange, their stench was overwhelming; a noisome, dirty-clothes smell that made me wonder if they had ever bathed. Pete edged close and whispered. "Whata' ya' think?"

A sideways glance was my tacit response. I didn't know what to think. I knew where we were, though. We'd been there often enough. We were perhaps half-a-mile upstream from the Ten Mile Creek bridge; significant only in that I knew how infrequently anyone ever ventured this way. And that was about all I knew. I did think that I was about to be sick as we reached an exposed sandbar where the creek emptied into what was formally a large, attractive pool. But the torrid sun had drained its life, and what little water remained was stagnant green and covered in algae.

Garrison Hole was dry except for one shaded arm lying directly beneath bank- side trees, and two small pools separated by a limestone outcropping. Johnson Grass and volunteer oats sprouted in tenuous, scattered clumps from cracks in the stream bed. Otherwise, we didn't see as much as a turtle. An old, tri-colored cow stood up to her knees in the biggest pool. Her flanks were sunken, ribs plainly visible. She had the scours and a greenish discharge coated her hips and back legs. She stared blankly, tail lashing at the flies buzzing around her inflamed anus.

"Git on there!" David hollered, heaving a clod in her direction. "Git!"

Wild-eyed and bawling, the cow heaved herself out of the water and lumbered up the bank, slack udder swinging from side to side. She crashed through the undergrowth and disappeared.

"Siddown right 'ere." Dee ordered.

We dropped on our haunches in the middle of the dried-up pond. The ground was blistering hot and the place stunk of moldering plant and animal life. .

"You stay right 'ere, and don't you fuckin' move," he said, pointing upstream to David, who continued on in that direction until he was out of sight. Dee studied us for a long moment and started to say something, then changed his mind.

Nervous minutes passed. Resting against the bank and, importantly, in the shade, he continued to watch us, eyes half-shut. He was motionless and seemingly quite composed. We twisted and fidgeted, confused and miserable…two slabs of meat sizzling on a grill.

"These guys are really pissed off." Pete said.

"What was your first hint?"

"You think they'll let us go, or we gonna' hafta' fight our way out?"

I looked at him incredulously and shook my head. *Fight a gun?*

"My ass is cookin' an' I'm gettin' tired o' this." He complained through gritted teeth.

"Well, I'm havin' a wonderful time."

To add to our discomfort and my sincere concern that Pete might do something dumb and get us killed, swarms of gnats suddenly attacked in droves. They were so thick we were inhaling them, and close behind were squadrons of mosquitoes. We slapped and swatted. Dee laughed gleefully. They didn't seem to be bothering him.

"Stupid jerk," Pete whispered angrily.

I had a sudden inspiration. I grabbed my knees, pressed them against my chest and, as nonchalantly as I could, looked up in seeming admiration of the open expanse of blue sky. Under my breath I said, "Pretend you're enjoying this."

"What?"

"Don't let him think we're scared."

"How's that gonna' help?"

"Just don't let him know anything." There was a long pause. I knew Pete was trying to determine if I was still in full control of my faculties. Finally, he responded.

"Okay, I guess."

"He thinks he's got the upper hand." I whispered.

"Well, hell, he does!" He said too loudly. Whispering wasn't among Pete's acquired skills.

"Ssshhh," I cautioned. "I know that, but don't let him think we care. Him and his brother are both a few bricks short of a load. Maybe he'll get confused and make a mistake. Then maybe we can get out of this mess."

There was a pause while he digested my logic. "Sure." He said finally, obviously unconvinced.

As we lapsed into silence, something else very unexpected happened. A cloud drifted between the sun and us, and that hadn't happened in…days. It had been weeks since there was a cloud in the sky. I couldn't remember the last time. I also noticed that a sort of haze had formed, and there was a strange mugginess. The sun still pounded us relentlessly and the mosquitoes and gnats were only into their second course. But then something jolted me…something like music. At least it was almost like music; only it wasn't anything I could identify. And it was coming from Pete. It took me a moment to figure it out. He was humming something vaguely familiar. He was humming the "Hallelujah Chorus", but I didn't identify it immediately because he was humming the bass line. *The bass line.*

"What are you doin'?" I whispered.

"Throwin' him off guard," Pete answered, then continued.

"Would you…" Before I could say "quit", Dee jerked to his feet.

"What's 'at noise?" he shouted.

Pete kept it up.

"Whatever you're a' doin', shut up!"

174

Pete didn't miss a note.

"Goddamn you, you better shut 'at shit up!'"

"Cmon' Dee, it's just a little somethin' George wrote." Pete said.

"George who?"

"Why, George Freddie Handel." Pete's humming continued.

Dee walked toward us.

"You better shut the fuck up. I done tol' you, no noise, no talkin', no nothin'! You keep y' fuckin' mouth shut."

"What you got against ole George, Dee? He's purt' near popular as Webb Pierce."

Dee swung the pistol up and pointed it at Pete, who regarded him calmly but stopped humming. *Thank God!* I had trouble breathing again.

The three of us formed a very still tableau for a very long moment. Finally, Dee snorted, lowered the pistol, and returned to his spot in the shade. "An' I better not hear no more o' that Handle shit. You got 'at?"

Might as well gamble, I figured.

"Yeah…we got that!" I sang out to the opening chords of the mighty chorus. Pete laughed. Couldn't help it, I guess. Dee was only a few feet away.

If he's gonna' shoot, he's only got time for one round before we'll be on him.

"Reckon he's confused enough now?" Pete whispered.

I was tempted, but determined to keep my counsel a little longer.

"No!" I whispered savagely.

Hell! It's me that's confused.

What we were doing there and what he had in mind for us was a mystery. Yes, we'd bent their noses when we flew by on our bikes. But that was a joke, a prank. And yes, we'd screwed up his stupid trotline, but he had to know we hadn't meant to. That was a year ago anyway. This thing was headed somewhere, only I didn't know where. The Garrisons had placed themselves at terrible risk. They had to know that when our fathers learned what they'd done, the only place they'd be safe was in jail. Our dads would hunt them down and

175

find them, and when they did, the retribution they exacted would be savage and merciless… and nobody would lift a hand to stop them.

With us, the Garrison brothers had crossed the line. The joke had worn as thin as our pants' seats and, as far as I was concerned, they were into real criminal conduct. That is, unless they suddenly released us and had a big laugh at our expense. But, for some unexplained reason, I didn't think that was going to happen and, beneath our bravado and flippancy, Pete and I were very frightened. After all, despite our bluster, we were still, really, just showoff teenage boys.

For what seemed like hours we sat, sweating, swearing silently…and gradually wearing down. The sun was now directly overhead. In its relentless glare, we shriveled like Garrison Hole. Dee had placed us in the hottest possible place he could find, baked earth beneath us, blazing sun above. The heat was swiftly replacing Dee as our primary adversary. We were growing desperately thirsty. Since nothing else seemed to work, I uttered a silent prayer that God would rescue us… and that we'd have all the water we wanted.

Garrison had our canteens and was drinking from one of them, making a big show by running his tongue over his lips and sighing contentedly. My thirst was becoming unbearable and I knew Pete was probably in worse shape. On most of our creek trips, Pete always drank his canteen empty before we were through fishing, but he had few qualms about creek water. He drank it liberally and never experienced any problems. Considering the livestock and wildlife that watered and performed other unsanitary functions upstream, I wouldn't touch the stuff. But at that moment, even creek water would have been delicious. I looked at Dee. He caught my eye, took another long pull from the canteen…and laughed.

I tried to swallow but found that cotton didn't go down well. I tried clearing my throat, thinking I might bring up some moisture. Nothing there either. I was worse than parched. I was the Sahara. Pete was hacking uselessly. I nudged him with an elbow, made a face, and shook my head negatively. I knew his psychological makeup all too well. *Sometimes he just didn't think ahead.* He'd reach a point where he'd make a move, one that might get at least one of us shot. What we needed was a diversion… something that would allow us to make a quick, concerted effort. We had to get to Dee before he could trigger a round. But nothing that made any sense came to mind. He had positioned himself well and there was no ruse he wouldn't immediately recognize. He was in control of everything...except nature.

A great, blue flash signaled a simultaneous explosion... the loudest thing I'd ever heard. Rattled, we looked up to find ourselves enveloped in dark shade. A towering cumulus cloud was almost directly overhead, and the thing seemed to spread from horizon to horizon.

Where did that thing come from and how did it manage to sneak up on us like that?

A scant minute later there was another blue flash, and within seconds, the crash of thunder. The three of us sprang to our feet. "Deo Gloria!" Pete croaked.

Just like him to be disrespectful even in a crisis. No reverence for the Almighty, who obviously received my prayer and is, even now, responding to it.

I silently offered a little thank you and urged him to keep it up. Then I remembered Daddy's forecast. *How did he figure that out?* But then, Daddy was always figuring out things like the weather.

"Sit back down 'ere!" Garrison yelled. Now, I had more to worry about with Pete than with Garrison. He was mortally terrified of thunderstorms and didn't mind anyone knowing it. For Pete, all lightning was aimed at him and every thunder bolt targeted the exact spot he occupied.

"Think we oughtta' make a run for it?" he asked nervously, more concerned with the lightning than with Garrison.

"Think you can outrun a bullet?" came my immediate response.

Garrison waved the gun at us. "Shutup out 'ere. An' sit back down!"

Pete's fear of the storm was increasing. His eyes were growing wild and he was taking deep, tightly-bunched breaths. "Well...I know I cain't outrun lightin'," Pete whispered firmly. "An' I'll trade lightnin' for a two bit bullet any day."

"What was 'at?" Garrison rasped.

"It's lightnin', you idiot!" Pete snapped at the top of his fear-laced voice. "Whatta' you think it is?" He had misinterpreted the question. I nearly fainted.

Garrison's response was a shot just over our heads. I actually heard the supersonic pop of the bullet before I heard the report of the pistol.

That's it! We're dead now.

"Run yore fuckin' mouth one more time you little turd," Garrison snarled. Pete lapsed into sullen silence. I could hear his heart pounding through his t-shirt.

"What are you thinkin' about?" I whispered hoarsely.

"I'm thinkin' that's two shots an' he's got four left."

"I think we better shutup an' wait." I demurred. So we did, for several minutes.

A momentarily forgotten thirst returned, along with the gnats and mosquitoes. Just when our misery seemed unbearable, another blue flash came with a deafening CRAAAACK! followed by lingering rumbles into the vastness of a rapidly darkening sky.

Pete lurched up, now utterly heedless of Garrison, who also scrambled to his feet. I watched as Pete's fists clenched and unclenched.

He's right on the edge. He's losin' it!

But Garrison took no immediate notice of him.

"Goddamn!" Dee exclaimed. "That was close!"

"You better stay right there under that tree!" Pete suggested loudly.

Under any other circumstances I would have laughed out loud but, in Pete's sandpaper rasp, I caught undeniable signs of fury. His eyes were jet black now and fixed on Garrison with the coldness of a rattlesnake about to strike. Pete, terrified by the impending storm, was steeling himself to take Dee on. Which was almost as stupid as thinking he could whip hot lead. I grabbed his arm and shook him hard. I was the only person to whom he would respond when his emotions were running away. "Hey!" I snapped and shook him again. He finally turned to me with a wan smile.

"I'm okay," he said, breathing heavily, "but I ain't stayin' out here in the open."

"It's gonna' be alright." I encouraged. "We're gonna' get outta' this."

178

He had sounded desperate, but I thought I might keep him under control by staying positive. Pete had something else in mind.

"Throw me one o' them canteens, Garrison." Pete ordered, his face a mask of contempt.

I've got to stop him from challenging this fool. I know what he's tryin' to do, but he's
gonna' carry it too far.

"What'sa' matter? You boys gittin' hot out 'ere? Want some water? Want some o' this?" He teased, voice dripping with sarcasm. He raised the canteen to his lips and took a long swallow. "Ahhhhh, that's good!"

Damn you!

Garrison took another long pull from the canteen. And if the situation wasn't convoluted enough, Dee chose that moment to spring yet another surprise. David appeared around the bend, but he wasn't alone. A dejected figure stumbled beside him. I shook my head, not believing what I was seeing.

"Sonofabitch!" Pete exclaimed hoarsely… and I knew it wasn't just me. I wasn't seeing things.

This was no apparition.

"He's got Dawn."

A deafening BOOM! accompanied by a great white flash seemed to surround us.

Fuzzy followed our scent from the house to the trestle. There, he took a soak in one of the tepid pools. He lingered awhile then pulled himself out on the bank and shook vigorously. He smelled something attractive, chased it down, and found bits and scraps of a jackrabbit taken by a hawk the day before. Fuzzy ignored the ants, flopped onto his back, and rolled with blissful abandon in the doggie perfume offal of an advanced state of putrefaction. Momentarily satisfied, he sat and scratched at a tick gorging itself in the fold of his left ear. He was about to take a final roll in the reeking remains when a variant breeze brought him a whiff of something he recognized. Fuzzy's nose lifted and swung from side to side, homing in on the familiar scent. He whined, barked, and struck out in a lazy lope up the creek

179

THE TRAIL

The old man regained consciousness. He thought briefly about getting up but knew he couldn't. Movement was painful beyond comprehension. Even breathing was an adventure. At least he was in the shade; so he lay still and waited…

Dee Garrison had plenty of experience battering old men, and it had not gone to waste this fateful day. The old man was too weak to lift and point the heavy pistol and Dee Garrison had simply taken it from his aged, shaking hand. After slamming his head into the tree trunk, he beat him mercilessly, murderous kicks raising puffs of dust from the old man's coveralls.

"Whut now, Dee? We gonna' snatch up 'at calf?" David asked.

"Fuck 'at goddamn calf," Dee replied, breathing heavily and holding the gun aloft. "We got bizness to tend to."

"What about this ole fart?"

"Fuck him too," Dee said, taking a liberal gulp of whisky. "I dunno' if he's still alive even, but if he is, he won't last long in this heat."

They headed back toward their car, leaving in their wake an orphaned calf and a dying old man.

What the hell happened and how long's it been?

The old man tried to pull things together.

What am I doin' under this tree? An' why do I hurt all over?

He remembered the calf slipping from his grasp and running away, but nothing after that. He knew something was terribly wrong though; and he began to suspect the worst.

I'll be damned. Is it finally down to now? All that livin' finally caught up with me? Gonna' end it right here maybe? Why, that ain't so bad. If I go right here on my own ground and nobody a havin' to spend no money on me or tend to me, things could be a helluva' lot worse.

He lapsed into deep unconsciousness…a stillness broken only by the occasional fluttering of his wispy hair in the fitful breeze. When he awoke, the wind had changed and the sky had darkened.

How long I been here? Must be nigh onto dark the way it looks.

He thought he heard something approach, but his ears rang from the beating he didn't remember, and maybe he only sensed it. When he finally summoned the strength and will to open his eyes, he saw a large, dark, funny-looking, very familiar dog sitting next to him.

He knew that dog...knew the big red one it ran with and the two boys that they belonged to...the ones that treated his place like their own private park.

Good boys, them two, always close the gates and don't run the stock.

The dogs even visited him from time to time and weren't averse to sharing his dinner scraps. He smiled faintly, remembering their fierce growls as they argued over bones he'd toss their way. Fuzzy whined softly and lay down close to the old man. A pink tongue decorated with large black blotches tenderly licked at the blood crusted on the wrinkled face. With terrible effort, a gnarled hand found its way to a shaggy head, and the big dog snuggled even closer.

"What are you a doin' here, fella'?" the old man managed to croak softly.

Fuzzy cocked his head at the strange sound of his friend's voice. His keen senses told him something wasn't right. And there was something else...a scent...a scent he remembered as unfriendly...the scent of an enemy that once posed a threat...but ran from a challenge...

"You lost?" the old man asked.

Fuzzy whined and bent to lick his hand.

"I guess you ain't seen m' calf."

The old man tried to stand but halfway up, knew he wasn't going to make it. He eased himself down, breathing heavily. Fuzzy barked...loud, sharp, and questioning.

"You'd like t' hep me, wouldn't y'? Wal, go fetch them boys o' yours."

Fuzzy barked again. The old man smiled, too weak to laugh.

181

"Don't talk back to me, goddamn you! Go do somethin' useful."

He smiled again, amused that wit still flourished, even at what he was beginning to understand was the end of things. *I'll give it one more chance.* He knotted his fingers in Fuzzy's thick ruff. He'd try to use the dog's strength as a brace and make it up onto his knees. Maybe the dog could pull him up against the tree, and...maybe...he could regain his feet. He struggled valiantly, and Fuzzy seemed to be helping. But then the pain came; blinding, white-hot pain that lanced down his arm to cleave his chest like a sword. He coughed and it felt as if his ribs were exploding.

"Oh, Sweet Jesus!" he groaned, falling back against the tree trunk.

Fuzzy whined again, his tail wagging anxiously as he danced about. Finally, unable to understand, he lay down beside the old man.

His head was spinning. Through the foliage the old man saw brightness and shadow, leaves and sky...and in the far distance, a pinpoint of light. His body was paralyzed now, but he could still move his head, if only slightly. And the pain was still there...only it didn't mean much any more. A breeze stirred, sweet and refreshing. The pinpoint of light grew bright...brighter...a brilliance greater than he'd ever known. The breeze freshened and dry grasses rustled and whispered. Upwind, a stand of cottonwoods loosed fragile blossoms in pale, diaphanous drifts that rode the breeze like snowflakes on winter winds. A chill swept him and the light became a vast and endless tunnel. He found himself able to rise. A flash split the lowering sky, the crash of thunder immediate. Pain vanished. He knew now where he belonged, and the old man stood tall and strode confidently into the light. Fuzzy cringed in the face of his most terrifying enemy. Whimpering, he crept close to the old man, just as the first wolf, in a dim and distant epoch, sought the company and protection of humans.

I had read about rape. The crime itself, the act of rape, had its own special kind of fascination. We didn't know much about it; certainly couldn't understand the motivation for it. Knowing almost nothing of the subject we pondered, Pete and I calculated that at some point, nature would cause a woman being raped to become sexually aroused... after all she was engaging in the act of sex. We'd seen endless movie scenes where a woman struggled with a man intent upon taking a kiss only to relent, then relax, then fling her arms around him in a display of mounting passion. We figured rape worked pretty much the same way. We perceived rape as a venture into the darkest recesses of the human libido. Only later were we to learn that it was an act of rage... of an aggressor imposing his will by force. It was assault. It was little different than beating someone because you could. No matter what we made of it, we thought it was a swinish act.

THE STORM

I didn't want the girl that stumbled along in front of David to be Dawn, but I knew it was. Had to be her… couldn't be anyone else.

"'Bout time you got back," Dee said.

"Couldn't get 'em goddamn knots loose."

Dee shook his head in disgust.

Dawn didn't seem to recognize us. Her eyes were red and puffy, one side of her face was slightly swollen; and there was a variety of small cuts and scrapes…as if she'd been dragged by her feet. She seemed dull, dazed… like she'd taken a sleeping pill. A much too large cotton dress was ripped down one side from shoulder to waist, forcing her to clutch the fabric together to cover her breasts. Her auburn hair was wet and matted. Raw rope burns girdled both wrists; another had left a red welt on her neck. She staggered as sharp limestone flakes cut painfully into her feet. She was in terrible shape. I looked at Pete. He was stunned. We were both trying to accept what we were seeing.

Why is she here? And what have they done to her?

"Dawn!" I shouted, forgetting about the Garrisons.

At my voice she recoiled and cringed. For a brief moment I thought she looked at me, but she didn't seem to know me.

"Don't upset 'at bitch," Dee chuckled. "She's had herself a hard day."

If I had been in turmoil before, emotions were rolling over me now like great waves crashing on rocks.

"What's goin' on here?" I persisted.

Dee only smiled.

Damn! We're playin' into this. This is what he wants. He actually enjoys this.

Pete and I were on our feet and I knew what he was thinking.

Run over 'em.

We were both incredibly quick and I was even a little quicker than Pete. I could sense his thoughts:

184

*Let's take 'em RIGHT NOW, buddy. They got no fuckin'
chance against us. I got the big one, you take the crazy bastard. And
don't stop hittin' 'em till they're down an' bleedin' an' still.*

And it would have been heroic...and almost surely fatal. So we
didn't charge. We didn't overpower them. We did nothing. We were
silent and helpless as Dee enjoyed his little game with Dawn cowering
beside him.

Pete found his voice.

"You pretty brave, kickin' a girl around," he shouted, quivering
with frustration.

That wiped the grin off Dee's lumpy face. He walked toward
us, gun waving from side to side.

"Shutup and siddown, shitface," he threatened.

Pete, you're only playing into his hand!

Pete ignored him and continued. "What a pair o' scumbags!
How about you and me, assface? Straight up. Just the two of us. An' y'
shitbag brother kin watch while I stomp yore guts out.... like I done t'
him."

*Oh, God, he's crazy as Garrison. He's gonna' get us both
killed.*

Dee Garrison may have been an assface, and he most certainly
had a shitbag brother, but he also had a weapon...and he wasn't afraid
of Pete. He slammed the gun barrel into Pete's stomach. My heart
stopped, so sure I was that a bullet was next. I tensed for the shot as
Pete buckled and fell. He couldn't breathe and the veins in his neck
grew blue and bulging. Finally, he managed a great, gasping breath
...then lay still. I bent to help him up.

"You want some too, fuckface?" Garrison snapped, leveling the
pistol on my forehead. The hole in the barrel looked like I could stick
my thumb through it. But I didn't stop. Ever so slowly, I crouched next
to Pete. He gagged and brought up some yellow bile. There wasn't
much I could do for him.

"Awright," Garrison said, primarily to me, "now you little
sumbitches jist stay right 'ere. An' you better tell your buddy t' keep his
fuckin' mouth shut, or I'll shut 'im up for good. We gonna' talk some
bizness... that is, if y'all don't git y'selves shot."

Pete could only manage a grunt, obviously hurting pretty badly. Dee chuckled and walked back to the shaded bank where he sat, drank, and stared at nothing. While David guzzled from the other canteen, I stole a glance at Dawn and, for a fleeting second, detected a glimpse of recognition.

"You gonna' live?" I whispered to Pete.

"I'm gonna' live to kill that bastard." he grunted. "We gotta' do somethin'."

"I know." I responded, wishing I had a clue as to what that something might be.

My attention went back to Dawn. David had shoved her down and was pouring water over her head from one of the canteens. She endured the indignity with style and only lifted her face in an attempt to capture some of it in her mouth. Even in her disheveled state, Dawn was beautiful. She reminded me of a frightened and abused animal, waiting patiently for an opportunity to flee. Her eyes caught mine and I knew I was in love with her. Of course, I had no way of knowing if Pete had shared the same experience with her... and immediately felt guilty for even thinking about it. I had to do something though. The girl I loved was not going to endure a nightmare like this.

I figured she'd been kidnapped. That was certain because there was no way she was going anywhere with the Garrisons of her own free will. Indignities she had suffered I could only guess at, but rape seemed very likely. From the dullness of her eyes, I deduced that she'd had been raped by at least one of them and maybe both. A great compassion overwhelmed me. I loved her and would save her from all evil. The fact that she'd been violated changed nothing.

"They raped her," I whispered to Pete.

"What?"

"I said they raped her."

"How'd y' know?"

"I just do. We gotta' do something."

"How will us doin' somethin' change her from bein' raped? Besides, what difference does it make? If they raped her, it sure as hell wasn't her fault."

"That's not what I meant," I said, "It's just that...."

"I know what y' mean.. We're gonna' get her and us outta' here awright, but they gotta' screw somethin' up for us to have a chance."

Dee whirled and came toward us again.

"What're you two yappin' about?"

We were silent.

"I thought I tol' you keep yore fuckin' mouth shut!"

The silence continued.

"So what're y' yappin' about? Answer me goddamn you!"

"How can we answer and shutup at the same time, you fuckin' moron?" Pete roared back.

Neither of us saw it coming. The gun whipped up, then down, and there was a resounding crack as the barrel bounced off Pete's head. A deep cut in his scalp immediately yielded a steady flow of blood. Pete winced and his knees buckled, but he remained standing and said nothing as blood ran down his face.

"Hey!" I shouted. "What's the matter with you?"

"You want some too?"

I ignored the threat. "Lemme' see," I whispered, trying to examine the cut.

"Quit. You want him to hit you too?"

I didn't and Pete was obviously going to live. I quickly saw why. His fear of violent weather overrode even treatment as violent as he'd just endured. There was another flash with another earsplitting cataclysm of thunder. The sky had turned a dull purplish-black tinged with green; and it seemed like night was falling. From a distance came a noise we couldn't identify, a low, rumbling sound, like a passing train, accompanied by a much higher frequency hissing. It grew louder, there was a deadly stillness, day became night…and the strange noise grew into a mighty roar.

"Good Gawddamighty!" David bawled, pointing through a gap in the trees. "Lookit that!"

A quarter-mile away, a black, boiling cauldron spun in a giant circle at eye-blurring speed. A hundred feet above the cauldron, a grey-white spiral reached up…far up into a whirling mass of black cloud. The spiral adjusted its shape continuously, bending, straightening, even breaking off from the ground at one point, only to re-connect moments later. Beside the monstrous apparition, two smaller, snake-like shapes descended halfway to the ground. Continuous lightning streaked throughout the funnel At that moment, I knew primal fear for the first time.

Pete's hand descended heavily onto my shoulder, his fingertips penetrating to the bone. If it held steady, the tornado's path would take it across the creek a hundred yards away. We watched, fascinated and terrified, as it passed through the trees downstream, and were stung by debris blown out of the whirling mass. It moved into the adjoining pasture and continued perhaps three hundred yards, blowing apart a windmill and literally exploding a tin-roofed cattle feeder, before lifting back into the cloud, a passage marked by broken trees and a rain of leaves and scraps of vegetation. For a moment, we were all speechless. Then David began screeching like a banshee. "My Lawd, it's a omen, a omen I tell'ya! Yeeeeoooww! Yeeeeoooweee! Did'ya see that? That sonabitch! Yeeeeoooowww!"

"Shut that shit up!" Dee ordered. "Weren't no nuthin'! Fuckin' wind that's all."

"But, Dee…"

"I said shut up. Cause we gonna' go t' work." Dee grabbed Dawn's arm and jerked her off the ground.

"Dee, don't!" she pleaded, attempting to pull away.

She sounds like she knows him.

"Now don't go fightin' this, bitch." he intoned mildly, seemingly pleased with himself. "You prob'ly gonna' enjoy it!"

Dawn tripped and fell. He dragged her along, seeming not to notice. Rage swept over me and I tensed, but he had the gun and there was no chance of doing anything. What little nerve I had left was lost. I finally found my tongue, though. "What's the matter with you? Why don't you just leave her alone? You got us. Just Leave her alone!"

Dee laughed. "I got all'a ya!" he yelled defiantly, shoving the gun in his belt. "Now, lookit what you gonna' git!"

He spun Dawn around, grasped the top of her dress with both hands, and yanked down and out. The fabric fell away, leaving Dawn utterly and completely naked. I was slack-jawed at the sight. Dawn made no attempt to cover herself, though in retrospect, the effort would have been useless. Her brilliant auburn hair hung in a dull, wet tangle.

The ivory skin was smeared, streaked and blotched red in places from the rough treatment she'd received. And, despite the perfect symmetry of her body...rounded breasts, tiny waist, and exquisite conjunct of pelvis and thighs...I was drawn to her eyes. She was again a beautiful, frightened animal, terrified and confused. I experienced the overwhelming desire to protect her, moved by compassion and more than a little rage at her tormentors. Overcome with emotion, I cried out something that was without doubt senseless to anyone but me.

"Leave her alone!" I shouted.

He shrugged, and withdrew the pistol from his belt. Then he seized Dawn's hair with his free hand, and yanked her to her feet. She screamed.

"This what you want, shithead?" he shouted angrily. I had no clue how he expected me to respond. "Come on up here and git 'er then." he said flatly. "I got customers gonna' git her. So you come on. You be first, motherfucker!"

Silence, utter and complete. I was still totally confused.

"Wh..wh..what?" I sputtered.

"I said, come git her, you pitiful little puke." He dwelled lovingly on the quandary he had placed me in. His enjoyment in my humiliation was almost complete. But more than anything, he relished Dawn's mounting terror. "You want me to leave her alone, then, by God, you come git 'er."

Pete nudged me. "Get her. It's what he *wants*. Get her away from him."

"I'm not sure." I said, torment and ambivalence sweeping over me. I knew he didn't mean what he seemed to be saying...

Dawn stood impassive, eyes on the ground. A breeze kicked up, increasing in speed until it was stiff and noticeably chilly. The wind ruffled through her hair. She shivered, bracing against it, goosebumps forming on pale skin. There was a blue flash, and a peal of thunder rolled threateningly.

David finally spoke up. "You gonna' let her go?" He asked, obviously puzzled.

"She ain't a' goin' nowheres till one o' these little limpdicks here fucks 'er. Maybe both of 'em." Dee sneared.

189

David suddenly looked as confused as we were. Dee walked over to me and thrust the pistol in my stomach. "You ready fur this?" His breath smelled like rotten fish.

"Why come you gonna' make *them* fuck 'er?" David demanded, sullen and angry. "You never said nuthin' 'bout that!"

I suddenly comprehended at least part of what was happening.

Without warning, Garrison slapped his brother hard across the face. David reeled backward, tripped, and fell.

I sensed Pete tense beside me. Simultaneously, Dee raised the pistol and pointed it straight at us. "You gonna' draw straws or somethin'?" he asked. "Or I could jist *shoot* one of you," he continued amiably, "and the *other* one kin fuck 'er. Reckon *that's* what I'll do." Pete and I remained silent. David pulled himself up slowly. The wind howled down the creekbed. Dawn's shoulders shook, her wracking sobs lost in the wind and rumble of the rising storm.

Dee turned to Dawn and grabbed her hair again. She flinched, looking more frightened than ever. "Now let's git on with this. Which one fucks...or," he grinned, "gits hisself shot?" With a sweep of his arm, he threw Dawn toward us. She fell, like a stringless puppet, at our feet. Pete and I both reached to help her up.

"Enough of this crap!" Dee snarled, looking directly at me. "Now, git with it!" The hammer of his pistol snapped into the cocked position with a cold, metallic click. He leveled it at me. "You hear? What're you waitin' on? You queer or somethin'?"

"No," I said, breaking out in a cold sweat. "I just can't."

Dawn stood nervously between us.

"Cain't?" he boomed. "Cain't? What'sa' matter, you ain't never had no *pussy*?" There was nothing I could say that would make any sense. The only position I was in, could be in, with regard to Dawn, was that of protector. What I'd be doing by obeying, would be the same as rape. There was no way I could explain that to a cretin like Garrison. Hell, there was no way I could do it anyway. I had no idea how you went about it; and I had no intention of learning under *these* circumstances.

"That's it!" David screamed. "The little shit's a virgin!"

Dee grinned, then laughed out loud. "That right, boy? You a fuckin' virgin?"

190

I remained impassive. He was dead on. The stylized, semi-romantic, stone ache inducing passion-in-a-back-seat trysts, or even rudimentary feel-it-up sessions on a couch with parents uncomfortably nearby, were yet to come. It was a more innocent time and teenage virgins were the rule, not the exception. The only real passion I had ever experienced was in my dreams.

"Well fuck me to tears!" Dee said, laughing heartily. "We gonna' git to watch a cherry get busted!"

I had a breaking point. I hadn't known when it would occur, but I'd finally had all I could stand. Embarrassment, fear, rage and fatigue all roiled into one furious outburst. "Just leave us alone," I shouted at him, "just get outta' here and leave us alone! Now get outta here or you'll be sorry! You'll be sorry, you…you…Bastard!"

Near tears, I didn't really think about what I'd said; it just came out. I hadn't given any thought to how he'd respond either. He moved past his sibling and right up in front of me, close enough to be rubbing noses. God, how he stank! I had to wonder if he'd *ever* bathed. "Here's yore deal," he said coldly, "and this is the only deal you got, and it's the last time I'm tellin' ya'. You…got…ta'…*fuck* her! Then I'll leave ya' alone. You got that, shitface? After ya' screw 'er! And if ya don't…then we'll see who's sorry!"

He stepped back and waited. Nobody knew what to say. Of course, Garrison was lost in recurring waves of pleasure at our massive discomfort, which he interpreted as terror. He was the proverbial cat toying with the field mice. But, suddenly something did make sense – why he was forcing the issue. He wanted to mitigate his guilt by implicating us. If we *all* had sex with Dawn then…*Garrison was not as stupid as I'd thought.* The question of consent would be his word against ours. Of course, at the time, I was unaware of his plans for Dawn and of the attacks on Jane and the old man. That knowledge would have further complicated my analysis of the whole convoluted affair. It also would have heightened my fear. Dee Garrison was not only deadly serious…he was dangerously psychotic.

The silence went on. Finally, he raised the gun and leveled it, not at me, but at Pete's forehead. "Awright, shithead, have it *yore* way."

Pete stared straight at him. The trembling in his knees belied the fury he was feeling. I knew he wanted to rip Garrison apart. I felt the same way. But I also knew, like me, he was more than a little scared. Then he spoke, his voice shaky, but strong, "You're not a man, Garrison. You ain't got the guts." I shuddered. Now the fury was in Garrison's eyes. There was no way he was going to let that pass...but *he can't shoot him, not really, not murder.* And yet...

"Wait!" Dawn cried out. "Don't shoot him!" Her eyes grabbed mine. It was her turn now. She had to take command, because there was absolutely nothing Pete nor I could do.

Facing me, she said almost matter-of-factly, "We have to do what he wants."

I searched her face, trying to understand. I started to speak...but Garrison spoke first.

"Well now, ain't that sweet. The bitch wants it."

With no warning, Dawn whirled on him, "Shutup, Dee! Shutup you stupid fool!"

Completely taken aback, I glanced at Pete and then quickly back to Dawn. Something in her voice, an edge like steel, took us both by surprise. "We're gonna' do what you say, ya hear? We'll do it. You kin watch, watch 'n wonder 'cause that's all you *kin* do ain't it, Dee?" Then, turning to us, she said, "He wants to watch you do it...'cause he cain't! Oh, he can get it up," she continued, whirling on him, "he just cain't get it in!"

"You shutup!" Garrison screamed, advancing on her. "Shutup you worthless cunt! I warned 'ya, warned 'ya was gonna' pay!"

"I paid. I paid dear."

"Naw, ya ain't paid nuthin'!"

"I did, I did, I did..." she cried, again breaking into tears. Then, turning to us, "He's got this fool idea that he can make money by..."

"Ain't fool!" Dee interrupted. "I ain't no fool, bitch! It'll work! I'll make it work!"

"Never!" Dawn shrieked! "I won't be no whore!"

"That's enough! Dee screamed, "No more fuckin' talk!"

I was dumbfounded. A quick glance at Pete confirmed his shock. And, although we both wanted to say something, we were too stunned to speak. It may have been just as well, because Dee's previous rage had tripled. He stood sanguine, blood ready to pop out of his temples. His hand trembled, trigger-finger twitching dangerously. He

192

was ready to explode. Once again, Dawn took over. She was calm, her sobbing ceased. Looking directly at me, she repeated, "Let's do what he wants."

Slowly, Garrison lowered the gun. A faint smirk prowled across his face. Dawn threw her head back and lifted her arms to me. She was smiling as the tears welled up. I was in a trance, overcome, spellbound, oblivious. I blanked out the heat, the storm, Pete, the Garrisons...everything. There was no other world, only the two of us.

"Kiss me." she spoke softly.

"What?" I asked, my confusion mounting.

"Kiss me," she repeated. "Please."

I moved to her, tentatively, mesmerized. I remember trembling, visibly shaking. Then we kissed. Our lips *must* have touched. But it was not like I had dreamed because I was numb, unfeeling. My head was spinning. Peals of thunder rumbled overhead. The wind roared far too loudly. And I felt her hands slide to the snap on my jeans, felt the fabric slide down my legs... felt her soft, warm hands peeling down the elastic of my briefs...

There is a certain psychological excitement that builds with a storm. If you live in North Texas you expect thunderstorms. The gentle, all-day drizzles experienced back East or the soft showers on the Central Plateau rarely happen, especially in summer. Instead, these storms build rapidly, appearing from out of nowhere, mind boggling and violent; accompanied by head-splitting thunder and great white sheets of lightning. Shelter is an immediate objective and those caught "out in the open" are not to be envied. Getting thoroughly drenched is only part of the problem. And as this storm built, it was not only a part of our dilemma...but, quite possibly, the answer to it.

UNCATTLE

The Gradkin cut-off was a shortcut to Jane's Country Store and while it was rough and unpaved, it was not unusual to find a car using it every now and then. However, it was unusual to see a brand-new, shiny, '55 Chevrolet convertible streaking ahead of a billowing cloud of dust.

"Buddy, I don't know why I take these chances for you," Kara Lynn complained, behind the wheel of her father's latest toy.

"Aw, he won't mind." Buddy answered from the vinyl seat next to her, "Besides, we ain't gonna' tell him."

"He would definitely, definitely not like us comin' all the way out here."

"Oh come on! Ten Mile's not way out here. Besides, you said you wanted to stop by your Aunt Jane's place."

"Why do you just have to know if they're down at Bluehole?"

Buddy braced himself against the dash. "Damn! Be careful, Kara Lynn...you almost hit that turtle!"

"Do you mind? You know I cain't stand a foul mouth. And you promised! No more swearin!"

"Kara Lynn, either watch what you're doin', or let me drive."

"Let you drive? We're lucky *I'm* even gittin' to drive Daddy's new car! Besides you didn't bring your pillow so you can see over the dashboard."

"Hey!"

"I'm not makin' fun of you, Buddy Phillips and you know it. And you didn't bring it, did you? And you still haven't tol' me why you absolutely have to hang around Don and Pete. They think they're sooo smart, callin' everybody that don't agree with them cattle! That just makes me furious! They sure as heck better not try an'cattle me! What is all that cattle stuff, anyway?"

"Kara Lynn...I, uh, it's hard to explain. Please just take my word for it."

"Take your word for what?"

Buddy lapsed into a studied silence. What was the use anyway? Girls were just different than boys and there was much a guy just couldn't explain to them. If you played football together, you were part of a team, and not just on the football field. Teammates connected in ways guys could never connect with girls. And that was that. It was fun to be with a girl when she looked good or was stroking your ego. It was great in the back seat at the Jefferson Drive-In Theater getting all sweaty and heated up. Otherwise, being with a girl was a complete and utter bore. Besides having you as a possession to parade around, they seemed to take little joy in things; certainly not with the same exuberance with which a male faced life. And, there was the matter of temperament. If your buddy was in a foul mood, it might last an hour, then he was over it. With girls, foul moods lasted for days. Guys never had headaches. With girls, headaches always lurked nearby, ready to pounce when you least expected it, or whenever they found one useful. And men didn't leak. But every woman, every last one of 'em, was required to spend a small fortune on pads, and napkins, and God only knew what-all...because every last one of 'em leaked. And once a month, you were required to approach them with the degree of care you would accord a constipated wildcat.

But mostly, it was the informality, camaraderie and conviviality of your buddies that girls never seemed to understand, and always resented. And you didn't have to talk to communicate it. Girls talked incessantly, as naturally as breathing...even if there was nothing to talk about. There was no way Buddy could explain this to Kara Lynn. If he hadn't liked her so much, maybe he could have, but Buddy really liked Kara Lynn.

To be sure, his attraction to her was questioned often enough. Buddy was forced to simply shrug his shoulders in reply. Obviously, Kara Lynn returned his affection, but there was something about the way she nagged at him that was...well...neat. She made him do the right things, and Buddy figured that made him a better person. It mattered not at all to Buddy that his Kara Lynn looked like a shotputter in skirt and blouse, or that their doting togetherness in the halls guaranteed the subtle snickers of uncomprehending idiots. Kara Lynn understood Buddy. At least, she understood his faults, both real and imagined. Still, she was a girl; and girls would never understand that the premise of the cattle concept was a way of railing against the

195

trite, the cheap, and the commonplace. Comprehension was a male thing.

"Take your word for what, Buddy?" she repeated, unwilling to let the matter drop. Buddy thought it was a good time to change the subject.

"We might better put the top up, Kara Lynn."

"Why?"

"Looks like it's gonna' rain."

As a counterpoint, they heard the distant rumble of thunder over the noise of the car.

"Soon as we get to the store." Kara Lynn agreed.

They stopped, signaled, and turned onto Hidden Road. Jane's Store was just ahead.

"I been worried about Aunt Jane ever since it got so hot." Kara Lynn observed. "She could have a heat stroke in there and nobody'd ever know it. Mama's been tryin' to get her to move in town with us, you know, or with Uncle. She ain't got no business livin' way out here by herself."

Buddy was slamming the door behind him before Kara Lynn braked to a complete stop in front of the store. At first, she thought she'd said something that made him mad...but he wasn't going into the store. He was sprinting across the road to Jane's house.

"Come on!" he shouted back. For all her bulk, Kara Lynn swiftly caught up with Buddy, who knelt beside the crumpled little figure. Kara Lynn fell to her knees beside her great aunt. The old lady's face was pale; and when Kara Lynn placed a palm to her forehead, she felt unnaturally cold. Kara Lynn feared the worst.

"Aunt Jane... Aunt Jane?" she intoned, softly stroking her forehead. "What's the matter? Can you tell me what happened? Aunt Jane? Can you hear me?"

Buddy looked up. "There's a lotta' blood here on her dress."

Kara Lynn's hands flew to her mouth.

"What was she doin' with this?" Buddy asked, as he lifted a double-barrel shotgun from the ground.

Jane moaned as Kara Lynn lifted the old woman's head to cradle it in her lap.

Her eyes opened and she managed a faint smile as she recognized Kara Lynn. Her words came feebly: "Oh, baby…I's sorry you had to see this…"

"What happened?   Aunt Jane, can you tell us what happened?"

"It was them Garrison boys," the old lady whispered.

"Them two!" Buddy blurted.

Jane flinched, seeing Buddy standing above her.

"It's all right. It's just Buddy. He's with me. The Garrison boys are gone now."

"Kara Lynn," Buddy whispered anxiously, "we gotta' get her to the clinic."

"Aunt Jane. We have to get you up now. Can you tell me where you hurt?"

"Everwhur," the old lady slurred, "But I'll be allright. You gotta' tell somebody. They taken the little Ferguson girl with 'em."

"We can talk about that after we get you to the doctor."

"No!" The old lady gasped angrily. "Right now!"

"But you're hurt, Aunt Jane."

Buddy resolved the issue by picking up the old lady and starting toward the car. "First things first!" He stated flatly. Kara Lynn climbed into the back seat, and assisted Buddy in gently maneuvering Jane through the door. Buddy started the engine, pulled and turned a large, chrome plated "T" handle, and was rewarded with the sound of an electric motor and a ragtop rising slowly out of its stowage space. As he ensured that the locking lugs properly engaged the twin posts just above the windshield, he heard Jane and Kara Lynn.

"You're sure it was Dawn?"

"Positive. And they said somethin' about takin' her down to Ten Mile."

"Ten Mile Creek?" Kara Lynn wasn't exactly sure what that general description was meant to convey.

"You sure?" Buddy asked. "Sure they said Ten Mile?"

"That's what I heard."

"Hang on just a second," Buddy said, darting back across the road.

"Buddy, come on!" Kara Lynn protested. But he was already coming back with the shotgun. "Buddy, don't you even be thinkin' about doin' somethin' crazy!" She warned.

"Their old home place is somewhere down on Ten Mile," Buddy said.

The Chevy's rear tires were spinning in the loose gravel as a bulbous, black cloud blotted out the sun, and the first cold raindrops splattered onto the dusty road.

From his new perspective, the old man looked down at the inert figure and the big dog that lay beside it. A small disturbance raged around them, but it wasn't much, not much at all, really. "It's okay boy," he said, comforting the frightened dog. "Don't pay it no mind and it'll go away." Fuzzy whined and moved closer. Lightning terrified Fuzzy to the very depth of his being. He braced himself against the darkening sky and a howling wind that whipped the trees into frenzy, and gained security from the old man's presence. Thunder boomed again, and Fuzzy whined pitifully. The old man tried to stroke the dog's fears away, but the figure on the ground wouldn't move. "Leave the dog be!" he commanded, and Fuzzy responded by snuggling his cold nose under an ancient, gnarled hand. The wind lashed the earth, the sky turned midnight black and was rent by continuous lightning that produced massed barrages of thunder. And then the old man was far away; gone an incalculable distance into the consuming brilliance.

THE CLOUD

The wind died. Time seemed to stop. There was an absence of sound and motion. The vibrant cacophony of nature grew silent, replaced by an oppressive, sinister stillness. The very air around us seemed charged with electricity. I felt my hair rise; and Pete, the Garrisons, even Dawn, all were surrounded by a strange glow. There was a brilliant blue flash accompanied by an incredible, deafening explosion. Fifty yards away, a gigantic limb flew from an ancient oak as a fireball tumbled down the trunk and away into the creek bed. Large, wet drops began to spatter about haphazardly, only to be soaked up immediately by the parched earth. The storm had arrived.

The rain came. After endless weeks of drought, after days of parched earth and blistering heat, the rain came. Rain fell…fell heavy and hard, cascading in sheets. Soaking the dry land. And over the roar of the rain and the rumble of the thunder, we heard a low, keening wail far down the creek. The wail grew rapidly into a hideous shriek. We saw the tops of gigantic trees bend before the onrushing wind. We saw leaves, then twigs, then fallen branches kick up and surge toward us. The storm fell upon us, a howling monster that whipsawed and bludgeoned. A sky blacker than midnight spit fire in blinding flashes, and blasts of thunder rolled unceasingly. Broken and decaying vegetation became stinging, bruising missiles. A blue-orange flash rent asunder a nearby oak; the heavy jolt, felt in every joint, drove us to our knees. With it came the familiar odor generated by my dad's power tools, only thousands of times stronger. Terror seized us. A thing so powerful we could not comprehend it, so savage we could not countenance it, had searched us out and found us. We were in the maw of the beast. And as the elements split their seams, the bottom dropped out.

Fuzzy sensed the old man's passage. He barked urgently but there was no response. He nuzzled the old man's face and detected a familiar odor. He very well knew what that odor meant. It meant he was no longer of any use here. Fuzzy rose and padded nervously up and down. The storm screamed its fury and rain came in blinding sheets. Fuzzy sat one last time next to his old friend. Black muzzle raised to avenging sky, he gave vent to a deep, mournful howl. Far down the storm wind a big red dog stopped and perked his ears. Again came the dolorous baying that, although faint, Jeff instantly recognized as his brother. He loosed a booming, staccato response that was lost in the howling maelstrom. It made no difference that Fuzzy couldn't hear his answer; Jeff knew where he would find his friend. Fuzzy sprinted for the trestle. There was protection, cover and safety at the trestle. Fuzzy's powerful legs propelled him faster than he had ever run before.

THE CHASE

The equation was overloaded; it wouldn't balance. Up until now, the storm had been a frightening diversion from our dilemma; but now it exploded in a culmination of lightning, thunder, wind and rain. The wild fury of a fully-developed storm descended upon us. With the cold, driving rain came darkness exceeded only by that of moonless night. I couldn't see anything farther than a few feet in front of me. The wind whipped down the channel tearing at us, staggering us with its intensity. The lightning was continuous, the accompanying thunder unceasing... cracking explosions lost in those that immediately followed. The violence of the storm completely eclipsed our situation, us, everything...except the chance for which we'd waited so patiently. Like frightened rabbits, the Garrisons had huddled together, eyes fixed on the fury of the storm, completely overwhelmed by the elements. *Now...*I thought...*Now is the time...*

"Blindside!" I screamed. Pete didn't move, probably couldn't hear me, I figured, so I filled my lungs and bellowed again: "BLIIIIIINDSIIIIDE!!!"

I was wrong. He'd heard me because he was already charging the Garrisons. I charged from the opposite side, lowering my head in a bull-like rush. Then, as if orchestrated by the heavens, a gigantic clap of thunder smashed overhead at the precise moment Pete and I smashed into the brothers. Indeed, we hit them blindside. Pete drove into their backsides. I caught them chest-high. The double impact knocked them off their feet and their weapons flew through the air as they collided with the ground. Pete and I must have bumped heads because suddenly, there was a loud buzzing sound, and everything seemed to be happening somewhere else, to somebody else. I was dimly aware of choking on water I had inhaled. Then, I was being lifted and violently shaken.

"Let's go!" Pete shouted above the din. I still couldn't quite put things together. I coughed repeatedly, doing the best I could to take a deep breath and clear the cobwebs at the same time. "Let's GO, Don! STAND UP!" He shouted at me. Everything came back in a rush; and I knew I had to get up. My head was throbbing and I couldn't get my eyes to focus. There was two of everything.

201

"Wh..wh…What?" I managed to stutter, my legs buckling. Suddenly I was steadied by an arm around my waist.

"Can you make it?" Dawn asked.

My vision snapped back and, with that, my legs steadied somewhat. Looking through a curtain of deluge, I saw the Garrisons, still stunned, floundering on the ground, probably searching for their weapons. I grabbed Dawn's hand and we tore off toward the bridge. Sheets of rain were pelting us like nails, making it hard to keep our footing. We had to run with our heads down to keep from being blinded by the driving rain; but kept going as fast as we could, hellbent on putting as much distance as possible between us and the Garrisons. Suddenly, Dawn slipped out of my grasp.

Small depressions had filled with water and she had stepped into one, falling heavily, screeching in pain as the slick limestone tore into her flesh.

"Dawn," I cried. "You all right? Pete, wait up!"

She nodded, grabbed my arm and, grimacing, pulled herself up.

It was then I realized she was still naked. Quickly, I stripped off my shirt and handed it to her. It was sopping wet, but she managed to slip it over her head. She looked back over her shoulder, as if expecting to see her tormentors close behind us, which Pete and I fully expected too. I knew we had to keep moving. "Come on!" Pete yelled above the clamor. He was barely visible, though only a few feet away. The rain slashed and stung, filling my eyes, making the distant banks a blur. "Come on, run!" He repeated.

But, we couldn't run. Dawn was limping; worse yet, she was barefoot. I had to stay with her. She tripped again against the jagged edge of a submerged rock. I tried to catch her, to break her fall, only to distinctly hear something in my left shoulder snap, accompanied by sharp, stabbing pain. I moaned and turned to her as she sat up and clutched her foot.

"Let's see," I said, worried she might have broken something. Bending forward, I almost blacked out from pain that knifed through my shoulder. I tried to raise my arm, but couldn't. Barely able to see through the driving rain, I quickly examined her foot. Blood flowed from a nasty gash next to the little toe. She looked at me anxiously.

Suppressing the pain, I lied, "It's not bad, Dawn, but I doubt you can run on it."

"I've got to!" She protested, attempting to stand while grabbing my shoulder for balance. The pain flared wildly, and I howled. "I'm sorry," she exclaimed.

Pete had made it back to us. "What's goin' on?"

"Dawn's hurt," I yelled through gritted teeth, "and I've done somethin' to my shoulder."

Pete's lips compressed into a tight line, brows deeply knitted.

"Well, hurt or not, we still gotta' get outta' here!"

" I know that!"

"Can you walk?"

"Yeah, but I don't think she can. Dawn?"

"I'm okay, I'll make it!" She yelled, bravely limping forward. Again, my admiration soared. In addition to everything else, the girl had grit!

Suddenly and unexpectedly, Pete swept Dawn up in his arms and began carrying her. I watched dumfounded, anguishing over why I hadn't done that. He plunged ahead with her while I stood and watched, wallowing in regret and…yes…jealousy. God, I thought, what's the matter with me? Envy? Jealousy? I hated myself; finding little solace in the fact that I couldn't have carried her even if I had thought about it. A jagged flash of lightning jerked me back and I scurried to catch up.

"Where the hell are we?" Pete screamed, stopping and turning to me. "How much farther, you think?" I tripped in the downpour, awkwardly bumping into them. Another flash, and I could see that Pete still carried her securely. Her arms were circled around his neck, her face buried in the hollow of his shoulder. My heart sank as I noticed that she seemed very…content…to be right where she was. They didn't seem to even notice my inadvertent clumsiness. I had framed an "I don't know" response when lightning illuminated the bridge, only a few yards away.

"Straight ahead!" I shouted confidently.

"Thank God," Pete sighed, turning and splashing ahead.

"Amen," I concurred, relieved for more than one reason. A few more steps and we were at the incline leading up the bank to the bridge, our bikes, and the road to home and safety. Pete let Dawn down easily. Even through the blinding downpour, I took dark notice of how her arms lingered around him, even after she had firmly gained her footing. We moved to either side of her, to furnish as much support as we could during the climb. I wasn't certain how much help my crippled wing would provide, but I brushed that thought and the pain aside. It was then that we discovered the enormity of the problem that faced us.

The bank we now intended to climb, had to climb, was the same steep drop that Pete had tumbled down only a few hours earlier. Our first steps demonstrated just what a chore this was going to be. I was immediately in mud up to my ankles. The hard dirt of the trip down had become a slick, inhospitable quagmire for the trip up. My next step sank in even deeper. I could not help but note the anxiety on Dawn's face. She had begun to shiver, a combination of cold rain and burning tension. Pete was faring little better. The mud was so slick that gaining sufficient, if any, traction was impossible. He clambered up a few feet, only to lose his footing and slide back down.

It felt as if my feet were encased in wet cement. I had to pull so hard just to break a foot loose that I felt panic rising. But I fought to beat that back and managed to free first one foot, then the other, only to feel them sink back into the ooze. Actually, all I was managing to do was dig a trench of sorts. Finally, what little footing I had managed to secure gave way entirely; and I slipped, face down in the muck, awkwardly sprawling and clutching at an exposed tendril of tree root. The three of us wallowed in that stinking mire, vainly attempting to get up the bank to safety. When I looked up, I could see that we were attempting the impossible, at least, the way we were going at things. Holding fast to the root, I had the glimmer of an idea. We were trying to shove our way up with our feet. That was never going to work. We'd have to pull ourselves up, hand over hand. The problem was, I had only one useful hand and I didn't think Dawn had the strength.

"Here," I yelled, extending my good right hand to Pete and clutching the root with the crippled left one. His eyes told me that he immediately knew what I had in mind. We'd have to help each other up. But eventually, we just might make it. In any event, it was better than staying where we were. He reached for my hand. I pulled with all my strength. Surprisingly, while there was discomfort from my crippled shoulder, there was no unbearable pain. I had to be careful not to twist, though…"Push, Dawn, push!" I yelled as she shoved Pete from behind. We grunted, shoved, pulled, pushed, yelled…we had to get up that bank! Pete fought his way a little higher up, got a grip on another root, and reached back…

It was working. Pete was tall, and managed to move up the bank ahead of me to a fairly secure position. I held onto him with my bad arm, and pulled Dawn up next to me as Pete stabilized our combined weight. Our hopes rose with each foot of slow, but sure, ascent. "Come on, keep moving," Pete shouted, as he pulled Dawn up past me and next to him. The downpour came in thick sheets now, even heavier than before, but we could feel we were winning. Dawn managed to crawl a few feet higher, as Pete pulled me up to his level. I started to move up past Pete, reaching for her hand, when we heard the flat crack of Garrison's pistol.

We weren't even halfway up; and we weren't about to be shot on that bank like wingless flies impaled on a wall. "Back down!" Pete yelled.

Sliding back down to where we'd started, we were covered in mud, but partially concealed by the saturated Johnson Grass. We guessed that the Garrisons were close, maybe fifty yards away or less. The bank was useless to us now. We had to get down the creek. We turned and started running. I reached for Dawn's arm, but she waved me off. "I can make it!" she cried.

The rain pounded down in torrents as our feet pounded along the channel of a rapidly rising Ten Mile Creek. I looked over my shoulder and, under a burst of lightning, saw the Garrisons behind us. Perhaps it was my imagination but, through the lightning flashes, they looked wild, crazy…demonic.

Ignoring our injuries, we sped under the bridge and around the first bend. An atavistic urge for survival propelled us, oblivious to the elements and to pain. We could sense them closing. Fear continued to drive us, but exhaustion was taking its toll. Each step became an agony, a slow motion ballet of desperation. Pete stumbled, tried to recover, but stumbled again, finally sprawling headlong into the rising water. I splashed up beside him. "Come on, get goin'," I yelled, yanking him up. "Keep goin'," I shouted to Dawn.

"Where are they?" Pete grunted heavily. We couldn't see them, but we thought we could hear them sloshing rapidly after us, closing the gap every second we waited.

"Right behind us! This way!" We quickly caught up with Dawn, who was now limping badly. I saw a possible shortcut down a ledge that paralleled the creek, about halfway up the bank. "This way," I repeated, grabbing Dawn's hand.

Pete leaped ahead of us, but quickly balked. "Can't make it! It's too narrow!" Another pistol shot cracked, followed by the whine of a ricochet.

"We can make it, Pete. Go on!" I yelled.

"Too narrow!" He protested.

Dawn pushed past us and sped across the ledge.

"Let's GO!" I shouted, sprinting for the bank.

As we teetered, clambered, and clawed our way down the length of the ledge, a bullet smacked into the bank beside us, followed by the ominous report of the pistol. How Dawn had managed to race across was beyond belief. The ledge was not more than a foot or so wide. Her toe must have been a grisly mess by then, but fear was a powerful narcotic.

Another bullet whistled by, smacking solidly into a slender, bankside willow, not a foot from my head. "Don't slow down!" Pete shouted, "Keep on runnin!" And run we did, as fast as we could, over the rocks and mud, through the swirls of wind and rain; three frightened children racing down the creek toward Bluehole...

Fuzzy was running on sheer will alone, increasingly terrified as the storm intensified. He'd long ago exhausted everything but the adrenaline that surged through him with each lightning stroke. The outside of his heavy coat was soaked which added to the difficulty of his journey, and he could no longer see well enough to avoid the hazards and dangers that lay in his path. Ancient, deeply buried genes of his wolf ancestors screamed out for shelter and the safety of the pack; and the frightened dog raced through the storm with a single purpose. Somehow, his great heart and fierce courage would see him through to the trestle and hopefully, reunion with the only pack he knew... his big red brother and the boy gods he worshiped.

206

REVELATION

Kara Lynn was worried; not about her great aunt, the doc had assured her he had stopped the bleeding in time and that, given her disposition, Jane was sure to recover. She was worried because Buddy had taken off on a mission she barely understood, but feared might be dangerous.

Arriving at the clinic, they had barely gotten the old lady inside when Buddy yelled, "Keys!" and, despite concern over her Dad's certain objections, she relented and watched Buddy peel out of the driveway and down the street.

Her first assumption had been that he was off to find Constable Hastings, who was probably at Bab's Café, since the verbose raconteur could usually be found there holding court among a handful of cronies. The lawman was seldom at his office. However, her deduction modified when, ten minutes later Hastings had shown up at the clinic and listened intently to her story about Jane's accusations. Then, not changing his expression, Hastings had simply said, "Garrisons, huh?" and gone into the next room to interrogate her aunt.

Now, still in the ante room, Kara Lynn decided she had waited long enough; there was little more she could do for Jane and she needed to know Buddy's whereabouts. She was well aware of his impulsiveness and she remembered the shotgun. "If he's gone to find Pete 'n Don…" she mused angrily, crossing to the hallway fully intent on walking over to Barbara Dell's house and demanding her friend drive her out to Ten Mile Creek.

Suddenly, the front door flung open ushering in, not only a rush of wind and water, but the hulking figure of Bric Dodd.

"Coach Dodd!" Kara Lynn exclaimed, surprised at his appearance in a slicker and baseball cap.

"Hey, gal! What you doin' here, brain surgery?" He quipped, an outrageous grin covering his rain-splattered face. It was the day of his regular ear-fungus treatment.

"It's my Aunt Jane, Coach. She was stabbed."

"Stabbed?"

"Yeah, 'n robbed by the Garrisons."

Dodd's expression immediately moved from jovial to grim, as a dark countenance swept over his deeply-lined features. "Son...of...a..." he began, removing the cap and rubbing fiercely below his irritated ear.

"And I'm worried, Coach. I'm worried bad."

"Her condition's serious?"

"Not about Aunt Jane, Coach...about Buddy."

"Buddy? What's wrong with Buddy?"

"He's furious. And he took off after Don 'n Pete."

"What?"

"Yeah, and he's got a gun."

"What'a ya mean took off? Took off where?"

"Ten Mile Creek"

Bric Dodd rubbed harder...

Along the way, Fuzzy sought temporary shelter, pausing beneath a stand of willows when the rain blew like wind-driven darts, blinding even his acutely accurate sense of direction. But the terrifying flashes and earsplitting explosions drove him from that scant protection. An ear shattering blast shook the trees to their roots and sent the big dog scurrying along the high creek bank, eyes narrowed to slits against the stinging rain. He found himself scrambling madly back up a steep incline after almost falling into the rising water. Somehow he managed to keep his footing and skirted the slippery places. Then the trestle loomed up, huge and imposing, a buttress against the powerful forces that Fuzzy regarded with unreasoning fear.

BULL

The trestle was a haven. He knew of a cave of sorts, a deep burrow that generations of coyotes had dug beneath one of the great slabs of rip-rap lining the bank beneath the structure. It was in that burrow he would snuggle, safe and dry, until the tempest passed. He whined in anticipation as he started up the bank, but the wind changed suddenly and a familiar scent filled his sensitive nostrils. Huge figures loomed up in the darkness and Fuzzy found his way blocked. A massive, four-legged creature stood over the entrance of the burrow he so desperately sought. Anger welled up in the big dog. A deep growl issued from his throat, and the guard hairs of his wet ruff rose menacingly. He gave vent to a series of deep, chopping barks.

The great bull ignored Fuzzy's challenge and moved away from the herd huddled under the solid supports, stepping out to meet this adversary. Fuzzy snarled hideously, lips drawn back over ivory daggers, and the bull acknowledged his presence with a warning bellow. The standoff had begun.

The bull took a few more ponderous steps toward Fuzzy, extended his massive head and bawled a second warning. He would tolerate no wolf in his presence. Behind the bull, his harem milled uncertainly, the cows still rattled from the frantic stampede to the protection of the trestle. The bull snorted, pawed the damp ground, and bellowed another challenge. Jagged shafts of lightning raced across the black sky and thunder rumbled ominously. Snarling ferociously, Fuzzy stiff legged closer to the bull. There was an incandescent flash and blackness turned to brilliant, blue-white light. The ground shook at the instantaneous blast of thunder that rattled even the sturdy trestle supports. The terrified cows bolted away into the driving rain. The bull whirled at the flash, and ran a few yards after his harem, only to reverse himself, and issue another deafening trumpet of warning. Now his wide, splayed hoof raked up thick clumps of dirt and rocks. He raised his great head and a string of thick saliva drooled from his mouth. He shook his horns in a display of utter contempt for his puny, water-logged adversary. He took three quick, heavy steps toward Fuzzy, stopping with a great WHOOF! of expelled air. Fuzzy moved slowly forward in a low crouch, belly almost dragging the ground, answering the bull's challenge with hideous snarls and deep, rumbling growls. The bull lowered his head and charged. Fuzzy sprang ... and from out of the storm a big, rust-red streak appeared, landing squarely on the bull's wide shoulders.

Two inch daggers sank deep into the bull's flank and Jeff savagely ripped the tough hide. The bull bawled, and humped violently to rid himself of the unknown demon that tore at him. At the same time, the bull's sweeping horns barely missed Fuzzy as the invigorated dog slashed at his neck, leaving deep furrows that filled instantly with blood. Immediately his fangs found the target he wanted and sank deeply into the bull's tender nostrils. Jaws that could crack a ham bone closed in a vice-like grip. The bull skidded to a stop, wild-eyed at the torture inflicted by Fuzzy's merciless lock on a most sensitive feature of his anatomy. He lurched frantically as Jeff's fangs savaged a fold of skin at his throat then left that to seek a more substantial grip. Still enraged, but feeling the onset of fear, the brute bellowed and began a frantic series of whirling jumps to rid him of his tormentors. The bull's great bulk prevailed, flinging the canines aside and rolling in the soaked turf.

As Fuzzy and Jeff gathered themselves the rain continued to pound them. The bull snorted, puzzled by these wolves that confronted him, wolves that only the day before he had sent scampering with only a half-hearted charge. Now, with blood oozing from the wounds they'd inflicted, they seemed more than a match for him. Breathing heavily, he stood his ground, watchful and unsure...

Jeff had followed Fuzzy's trail halfway to the creek when the storm hit. As he neared the trestle, the storm reached its full fury and, like Fuzzy, he sought the protection of the coyote den. Coming upwind, he heard Fuzzy's attack barks and the bull's reply; and broke into a collie's long, flowing stride. He circled a group of panicked cows galloping clumsily away from the bridge when a bright flash illuminated the combatants. Jeff didn't have to consider his actions; the genes of his ancestors took care of that. He leaped onto the bull from the rear, managing to inflict a lot of pain, but little real damage. The bull quickly bucked him off. But when Fuzzy managed to focus the bull's unwavering attention by securing a grip on its nose, Jeff was free to attack elsewhere, and what had begun as a one-sided fight suddenly became a contest of equals. As the storm reached its maximum intensity, the combatants squared off, with only the law of wild things to govern the outcome. Deguello…no quarter asked, none given. The bull lifted his bloodied head, blinking against the sharp onslaught of wind and rain, bellowing his fury to a relentless and vengeful sky. Every fiber of his being urged him to charge, to trample his tormentors into scraps of grease, blood, and hair beneath hooves the size of dinner plates. But the charge never came because something in the dim recesses of the bull's instincts cautioned against it. He hesitated, bawled, and pawed the ground…but didn't charge.

For the combatants, the world was frozen into an irresolvable confrontation, neither side willing to concede an iota of impetus. Then, heedless nature intervened with a great blast of condensed energy that filled the sky with light, fire, and smoke. Lightning struck one of the steel rails that crossed the trestle. At the point of the bolt's impact, the metal turned cherry red. Heavily oiled and creosoted crossties ignited instantly, only to be reduced by the driving rain to wisps of smoke that vanished instantly in the shrieking wind. So powerful was the strike that the enemies became statues, each finding in the eyes of their antagonists the substance of their fear. But it was enough. The symphony of death ended unresolved. The bull bolted after his harem; Fuzzy and Jeff took refuge in the abandoned coyote den.

FAR ENOUGH

It lay in plain sight at the water's edge, next to my foot. The size of a baseball, it was a simple composite of quartz and schist bound together with mud long ago petrified into rock itself. Formed in astronomical numbers by glacial movement... the product of eons... these chunks of rock were broken down by freezing and thawing then tumbled and rounded by countless raging floods. Finally, a single conglomerate... my conglomerate...a solid, symmetrical ball with tiny quartz crystals gleaming on its otherwise dull surface... an object that traced its beginnings to an unknown glacial moraine in a past so distant no human knowledge of it remained, came to rest in the bed of Ten Mile Creek... and waited patiently for me to find it.

Abruptly, the storm abated. It was still raining, but the turbulence was moving away, intervals between lightning flashes steadily increasing. We stopped, uncertain what to do next. We had laid some distance between ourselves and the Garrisons; but we knew they'd still be coming and that they wouldn't be far behind. Gradually, the sky began to lighten. Here and there, a ray of sun burst forth revealing a rapidly rising Ten Mile Creek. The water level in the primary channel was up to the our shoelaces; and it would quickly rise even further as runoff cascaded in hundreds of tiny waterfalls over banks that we knew would now be impossible to scale.

"Well, whaddaya' think?" Pete asked, studying one of the inclines.

I didn't have an answer, but our experience near the bridge had dampened any aspirations we might have about climbing. It was no time to be stuck in the muck. Pete started to say something else, but stopped short at the sound of voices just around the near bend. No time to contemplate...

We were off again, sloshing our way ahead; avoiding drop-offs and holes we couldn't see, but knew were ahead of us, while staying ahead of the danger we couldn't see, but knew was behind us. We were nearing the limits of our energy as we rounded the last great abutment. Passing the jagged rock cliff, we entered the wide, flat stretch of limestone leading to the waterfall that now roared into the depths of Bluehole. My initial impression was how different it seemed from earlier in the day.

During the long dry spell, an abundance of debris had accumulated in the drainage of the creek. With the downpour, downed trees, broken limbs, and a mountain of smaller detritus found an inevitable way down the smaller streams and draws that fed the main channel. We were already beginning to see the dramatic effects of the deluge, as we watched sticks, leaves, clumps of weeds and even a small uprooted pecan tree, ball-root intact, disappear over the falls.

"Maybe they gave it up," Pete stated hopefully, looking back.

Don't bet on it, I thought, regarding Dawn, resplendent in wet T shirt and nothing else. She had fallen to her hands and knees in the water; having reached the point of complete exhaustion. Kneeling beside her, the sight of heavy, swaying breasts were clearly outlined by the soaked fabric. My fascination with her was unflagging, even under dire circumstances. Entranced and empathetic, I smiled encouragement. Almost simultaneously, her eyes swung and held mine for a long moment...

She is deliciously deliberate, I exult. At last, there can be no doubt! It's me! She's mine! As I reach for her, slender arms lift to me. I speak her name softly, almost reverently...Dawn...

"What did you say?" Pete was yelling.

"What?" I responded.

"I said, what did you say?"

My answer was preempted by the arrival of the Garrisons. Before we even saw them, we heard the younger one's nasal bray, "Gotta' be down here somewheres!" Then, like apparitions, they rounded the bend, no more than fifty yards away. They saw us as quickly as we saw them. "There they are!" David shouted. "They's trapped. We got 'em!"

He was partly right. We *were* trapped and almost out of options. The water level had risen so high that Bluehole was as swollen as an over-ripe cherry. The rock ledges that encased the pool were too high to go around, the banks too muddy and slick to climb. We couldn't go up, we couldn't go around, and we certainly couldn't go back. All paths were blocked...save one; which meant they didn't

213

"have us", not yet. For a brief moment, we stood near the edge of the raging falls...contemplating...then...

"Let's go," I yelled, yanking Dawn to her feet. Pete shot me a glance, nodded, and I knew he understood what I had in mind. The three of us leaped into the churning, muddy, tumult that was now Bluehole. Though it wasn't a deep drop, we hit the water hard and immediately plunged into the murky depths.

Below the surface, we entered a turbulent, surreal world. Away from the falls, the water was reasonably clear; under the falls was just the opposite. Pete and I had been swimming in Bluehole many times. It was too big to traverse underwater; so I knew we'd stay submerged as long as we could, surface, then go back underwater again. Underwater! Damn! I didn't even know if Dawn could swim! The impact had separated us and, although the water was a murky mess, I thought I should be able to locate her quickly enough. I twisted and looked, but couldn't find her. *Where are you, Dawn...where are you?*

I pushed down sharply, away from the roiling surface. Keenly aware of debris, I dove as deeply as possible toward the smooth bottom. To my right, I saw a moving shadow. It was Pete, swimming for the far side. I looked to my left. Still, no Dawn. Where was she? A few more strokes and suddenly I discerned another shadowy figure silhouetted against the faint light. I stroked and kicked toward it. If it was her she *could* swim, because whatever I saw was swimming. Then I noticed something wrong, something in the clumsy, spastic way she was flailing, twitching and twisting spasmodically, as if pulling awkwardly against some invisible force. My senses heightened. If she was in trouble...

I had taken only a few strokes when the shadow became more distinct. To my amazement, it was the Monster, the King, The Very Brim of Very Brim...still hooked and battling, pulling the cane pole down, then losing the battle as it floated back toward the surface. Of all the ironies! The fish and the fisherman, both trapped, both attempting to escape, both battling terrible odds. Then, as suddenly as it had appeared, the shadow vanished into the translucent depths. But where was Dawn? I whirled about and, miraculously, she was there.

Immediately I saw she was having problems. She seemed to be performing an underwater ballet, suspended vertically, just below the surface. I breast-stroked closer and my assumption was confirmed. It *was* Dawn! Only she was sweeping around and around in some kind of circle, with her arms and legs flailing about, trying to escape something. Suddenly, it dawned. That something was the vortex. That perilous whirlpool in the center of Bluehole held her like a steel trap. The rushing waters had magnified its force. It still wasn't strong enough to endanger a strong swimmer, but Dawn? I knew I had to pull her away, but my air was gone. First, I had to surface. I had to have air!

Quickly, I clawed my way upwards, toward the light, breaking the surface with an enormous gasp. I had enough presence to take three deep breaths, holding the last. Then, just as I started to dive, Dawn's head broke the surface a few yards away. She was fighting being sucked under again, but hadn't reached the point of panic yet. Instead, she fought desperately, but intently, like a trapped animal. I picked a point just a little upstream of her to allow for drift, and churned toward her.

At the same time, I heard the Garrisons yelling something. A quick glance over my shoulder revealed that they had reached the edge of Bluehole. I knew we'd have to deal with them, but for the moment, yanking Dawn away from the whirlpool would take everything I could muster.

The problem with even a small whirlpool is much the same as that of a riptide. The current doesn't seem like much at first; but all your energy is required just to keep from being sucked out, or down. You've nothing left over to break free of the rip or from the circulation of the whirlpool. Treading water furiously, I reached for Dawn and caught her wrist. Immediately, I kicked off, clutching her slippery arm. For a moment, nothing happened. We didn't move. *My God*, I thought, *I've no strength left. We're not going to make it.* Then Dawn kicked hard and...suddenly...we broke free. I hung onto her for a second or two, until I was sure she was strong enough to swim for the other side.

"Can you make it?" I screamed. She nodded and we took off. Ignoring the angry shouts we could only faintly hear above the roaring falls, one thought drove us as we stroked for the far side…*Get The Hell Away From There!*

After a minute or so, I felt the rocky bottom coming up steeply. Breaking out into the shallows, I was literally sobbing for breath, unbelievably tired. It would be so easy to just lie here. The storm was over, the water was comfortable enough…and what a wonderful place…alone with a virtually naked Dawn, girl of my dreams. But instead, I stood, dragging her up with me. I wasn't sure how much longer she could last. From her looks, she'd about had it. I managed a final, lingering look at her pale perfection, then curtailed my prurient thoughts with a sharp command, "Dawn! Come ON!!"

She grabbed my hand and we were off again, splashing over the hard, firm surface we had found in the shallows. The stream raced a foot deep over rough limestone, making our forward progress tenuous. I could still hear the Garrisons on the other side yelling in the wind. They'd have to swim across to get to us and, by then, I had every intention of being long gone. I didn't even bother to look back.

Having managed to get us out of harm's way, and now in a desperate hurry, I yanked Dawn along, practically dragging her up to a chalk-rock shelf paralleling the creek. As soon as Pete showed up, we could truly be out of a mess we'd never wanted in the first place. As soon as Pete showed up…and that…Pete showing up, that is…was the rub. Dawn gasped and grabbed my arm. "Look!" she exhorted, pointing toward the center of the pool.

I shuddered in disbelief, yet almost too exhausted to care anymore. Maybe what I was seeing was another mirage. I wiped my hand across my face, not fully comprehending what I thought was there, but hoped wasn't. Dawn screamed, "DO something! You have to DO something, Don!"

Do what? I hurt everywhere. A stiffening pain raged through my left arm and shoulder; a pain I had stifled until then. Sucking it up, through gritted teeth, I ordered Dawn back behind the ledge. She didn't move. She only stood and stared at me, eyes clothed in disbelief; the same look I had seen that night behind the bleachers. *Why are you standing there? Do something!* My heart withered. I stared to speak, but was interrupted by the raucous laughing of the

Garrisons. Now, gazing across the pool, I saw why they were laughing. I knew the mirage was real.

Just off the far shore, the devil brothers stood on a limestone shelf, bracing themselves against the ankle-deep current. Dee was grinning sardonically, arms loose at his sides, pistol still in his hand. David was laughing hysterically, splashing about in circles, waving the knife above his head. They were both watching Pete, who was treading water in the middle of Bluehole, futilely attempting to clear himself from a huge tangle of tree roots in which he had become ensnared. Pete was in one hell of a fix and the Garrisons were enjoying it immensely.

The younger one continued his impromptu war-dance while warbling his usual garble and inanely crying out, "Hey! Motherfucker! You done fucked up!" he screamed, pointing at Pete, jumping up and down. Dee watched in silence, his arrogant, satisfied grin intact.

I still didn't know what to do. My shoulder had seized up, I had no energy left, and Garrison had a gun. So momentarily, I simply stood there staring, puzzling over the absolute unbelievability of these events…at this whole, incredible day. Once again, as I had been so often in the past, I was inert.

Pete must have sensed my thoughts and, as he continued to struggle, started yelling at me, "Damnit, do somethin'! Don't just stand there!"

Without warning, Dee pulled off a shot in our direction. As the bullet whizzed overhead, I ducked behind the ledge, pulling Dawn down with me. Suddenly Pete shouted, "That's SIX, Don. He's outta' shells. Go git some help!" *What*, I thought, *he's been keepin' count?* "Go git some help!" He repeated. "Go git some help!"

Maybe that would have been the best thing to do. After all, there was Dawn to consider. She was hurt and bleeding, though, for the moment, relatively safe behind the rock shelf. I knew Pete well enough to know he wasn't going to drown. And I didn't think the Garrisons were going to risk the whirlpool or the snag in some silly attempt to attack him in the middle of Bluehole. But still, the equation didn't balance. I knew I couldn't leave and that I was going to do something…but, what that was…what in the hell that was…I hadn't the foggiest…

"Shoot him," shrieked the younger Garrison. "Shoot that sonofabitch!"

His older brother smirked and slowly raised the gun. I could only hope Pete had counted down accurately. Accurate or not, he did the best he could to make himself a small target, squeezing down behind the roots. He looked at me again and yelled,

"Get OUTTA' here, Don! You ain't helpin' anything just standin' there!"

Paralyzed with indecision, I most assuredly was not helping anything. Surely he won't shoot, I thought. He won't do anything that stupid. We're witnesses. *This has to be a bluff.*

From across Bluehole, a short eternity away, Garrison looked at me. "Shoot him! Shoot that cocksucker!" the younger brother kept screaming. In Dee's eyes I saw the personification of evil; I knew, at that instant, that he indeed would shoot, that he was capable of murder. My spine turned to jelly; my insides degraded to mush. Still, I could not move. Dee turned back to Pete, gripped the pistol with both hands, and aimed carefully. The roar of the water ceased. I looked down and away…and only then did I see the conglomerate…

THE BATTLE

With the fading storm, Fuzzy and Jeff emerged from their warm, dry den. By the time they were a hundred yards down the road, the rain had stopped. A shaft of golden sunlight broke through the rapidly evaporating cloud mass. Very shortly, steam would begin rising from the black pavement, forcing the dogs into the roadside mud. They trotted casually, in their mile-eating, sideways gait, coats now dry and glossy, the violence of the storm quickly forgotten. Jeff struck a familiar scent that no downpour could dissolve. He whined happily, moving quickly, nose to ground in ever expanding circles. Fuzzy joined him and they both barked thunderously as the scent straightened. Their sideways trot became an easy lope. From time to time they paused to check the scent, whining in anticipation. They were following their masters, headed straight for Ten Mile Creek. Beneath the trestle, the abandoned calf bawled insistently.

I could throw a football fifty yards and place it in the hands of a running teammate. On occasion, I could hit a bounding rabbit with a rock. I could throw hard, very hard, harder than any of the other guys, and remain dead on target. So, hitting something that was standing still, maybe thirty yards away, was no great feat.

In one fluid, uninterrupted motion the conglomerate was in my hand and on its way. Before Garrison could squeeze off what Pete figured was an empty chamber, the concentrated weight of the rock found its mark, striking him squarely in the ribcage just below his outstretched arms. There was a dull thud, and the pistol fell into the water. Strangely, he sank silently to his knees, hand pressed against his side. I knew I'd hurt him, but I couldn't really tell how badly. I hoped I'd at least broken a rib. From my chance discovery of the projectile, which was shaped perfectly for throwing, until the moment of impact, no more than five seconds could have elapsed. How quickly the tide of war can change.

His brother was still imploring him to shoot, not aware of what had just happened. He turned to see his sibling floundering in the shallows. "What'sa' matter with you? Get up! Stop foolin' around!" He yelled. At the same time, Pete managed to slip free of his T-shirt, untangling himself from the roots. I plunged into the pool and swam out to help him. The water had risen considerably and we quickly made it back to a rock shelf that, before the storm, had been dry land. We pulled ourselves up and, instead of running, turned to face the Garrisons.

Simultaneously, a large tree limb floated by. Briefly, I followed it as it bumped along, stopping and starting, then gliding majestically out of the pool and downstream, finally disappearing around a distant bend. As I watched, I felt something profound...but whatever it might have been faded with the muddy current.

Pete, breathing deeply, was bent over with his hands on his knees. "Thanks," he gasped. "Where's Dawn?" *Good question*, I thought, looking around. I hoped she had hightailed it out of there. Or, at least, was still hiding behind the rock ledge. I started to call out for her, but was stopped short by yelling from the far bank.

"You sonsabitches!" David Garrison shouted, kneeling beside his brother. "Sonsabitches!" he screamed again, just before he leapt into the current and began to swim toward us.

"Lookit that goofy fucker!" Pete exclaimed. "He must think he's Tarzan with that knife in his mouth."

"He's gonna' drown himself."

"Nah," Pete responded, "He's gonna' cut his hand off."

"Where's Dawn?"

"Don't know. Maybe she took off."

"Dawn!" I shouted, scanning the area.

"Well, I ain't runnin' another foot." Pete said, abruptly moving to the edge of the limestone outcropping. Obviously, he intended to provide a welcome of sorts to the younger Garrison, who was still thrashing toward us.

"Okay," I agreed reluctantly and sat down beside him. We were dead tired, we had overcome enormous odds, and we simply were in no mood to keep running. So we sat, analytically detached, observing David Garrison's labored progress. As he approached the shallows, we stood. He lurched awkwardly to his feet, still up to his knees in water. In a dramatic gesture, he withdrew the knife from between his clenched teeth. *Shoulda' kept it*, I thought idly, again mentally kicking myself.

"Where's 'at bitch?" he demanded, waving the blade tip at us.

"None of your damn business," I snorted.

"You hurt, Dee, motherfucker."

"Good." Pete said, flatly. Neither of us moved.

Knife poised aggressively in his right hand, Garrison took a cautious, soggy step toward us, then…another. We stood impassively as he moved forward, one hesitating step at a time. Six feet away, he stopped, dark eyes darting from Pete to me, then back to Pete. His face was flushed; but it was hard to tell whether it was from anger or fatigue. Either way, he was not in much of a position to challenge us, knife or not. Still, there was something else I saw in his eyes. I was certain Pete saw it too. A weird light shone, a vacancy sign, flashing brightly. If he'd been goofy before, he was now completely, totally crazy. He turned to his brother, still crippled on the far bank.

"Hey!" he yelled, "I got 'em! Bring the gun! I got 'em!"

Pete's response was a lot more to the point. "You got a lot more'n you want, shithead." The crazed brother grinned madly, and slopped through the remaining few feet of water, straight
at us, waving the knife wildly about.

Instinctively, we separated and moved to either side of him. He faced Pete first and I picked up a fair sized chunk of limestone and side-armed it at his backside. Again, on target! He staggered at the impact, then whirled to face me. Pete stopped and snatched up a gnarled, wrist-thick section of broken limb. Garrison raised the knife, but didn't have time to step toward me before Pete swung the limb down hard. There was a loud crack as it bounced off the boy's head and flew out of Pete's slick, muddy grasp. Garrison's knees buckled; but he didn't go down, which surprised me, because I knew Pete had spared no effort. A primal scream erupted from Garrison's throat and he turned to lunge at Pete, knife slicing the air between them. Pete must have experienced deja vu as he side-stepped, easily avoiding the knife while driving home a straight right to his jaw. Garrison reeled, stumbled backwards, and toppled headfirst into the water with a resounding splash. Pete immediately clutched his fist to his chest. I looked at him questioningly. "You hurt?" I asked.

There was a long pause before he finally grunted, "All the way up to my elbow."

Garrison was still face down in the water, starting to float away down-current. I stepped quickly into the water, grabbed the back of his collar and pulled his head up. "Help me get him outta' here," I shouted to Pete.

"Screw him!" Pete snapped through clinched teeth.

"Get in here and help me get him out!" I roared back. I wasn't going to stand by and watch somebody drown, regardless of the trouble he'd caused us. Pete delivered a string of four-letter-laced invectives, but got up and splashed into the shallows with me. Crippled as we were, we managed to pull Garrison out onto the bank. I couldn't tell if he was breathing or not; but right then, that didn't make a lot of difference. I didn't even know why I'd cared enough to drag him out of the water in the first place. It just seemed like the right thing to do.

Pete sat on the shelf again, nursing his hand, while I recovered Garrison's knife; which had fallen into the shallows. I picked it up and studied the long, shiny blade, which clearly reflected my features in miniature. I was more than a little vain about my looks; and I sure didn't look very good right then. That's when my lights went out…everything turned black.

I don't know how long I was out, probably no more than a minute or two. I was vaguely aware that the right side of my face was in a shallow pool, but I could feel a strong, cold current from my waist down. I was having a difficult time making sense of things; and just then, it seemed easier to drift back into the comfort of the blackness than to try to do anything else so, I surrendered to it…

"Get over here, Pukeface!" an all too familiar voice wheezed. Suddenly, I was back. I raised my head, the effort nauseating me. I was still confused and disoriented, wondering why I would be lying in a pool of pink water. The voice seemed to be coming from behind me so, very slowly, I made a huge effort to roll that direction. The haze began to lift…

A few feet away, Dee Garrison was raging at Pete. He was bent severely to one side, one hand pressed against his ribs, the other holding a pistol. Things started coming back… Slowly, but surely, I began a return to the land of the living. The Garrisons! We'd been fighting them

222

all day, but I thought we'd finally managed to escape. I faintly remembered that the older one was about to shoot Pete, and I'd…It was all coming back quicker than I could process it, but we were still in trouble. I knew that much. Gingerly, I moved my hand around over my head. It didn't take long to find something that hurt. There was a large knot on my scalp, just above my ear. When I looked at my hand, it was smeared with slime…and blood. I remembered hitting him squarely with the conglomerate…remembered the gun dropping into the creek. *How in the world had he retrieved the pistol and gotten across Bluehole?* Had to solve that later; because, at that moment, Pete faced a forty-five caliber problem.

"Get over here, Pukehead." Garrison repeated.

"Look," Pete countered, "why don't you just let us go?"

"Cain't do that…least not no more." Garrison answered, suddenly whirling on his brother. "Hey, where's the bitch?" He demanded.

At this point I decided his attention was diverted enough to try and get up. I was wrong.

"Sonofabitch!" He yelled, rushing over and violently kicking me in the side.

"Crap!" I groaned, clutching at the pain in my ribs as I rolled into a fetus-ball, moaning in misery.

"Now, we're even, farthead!"

Not by a long shot, I thought, gasping for breath and bracing for another kick.

But instead, he turned back to his brother, "Well?"

"That was good! Kick'em again."

"No, moron…where is she, the bitch?"

"How should I know?"

"Well, go find her, idiot!"

"But…"

"You wanta' end up in TDC gittin' butt-fucked by some big, buck nigger?"

"Huh?"

"You been yellin' fer me ta shoot'em all day. I cain't jest shoot these two!"

"Yeah, but…" Suddenly the light broke. "Oh, now wait a minute…ya mean?"

"I mean."

At that moment a simultaneous dawning struck. I struggled to clear my head, to regain my senses. Pain raged below my armpit, but I managed a semi-raised position. I shot Pete a glance and, from his expression, I could tell that he realized, as I did, that Garrison had deduced that leaving any of us alive wouldn't very smart. And, from his perspective, it made sense. His past criminal record, combined with this day's rampage would leave him facing the maximum penalty when caught – if caught. And, in his twisted mind, we were the key to his capture. Forsaking his Dawn-for-hire scheme, he'd come to a deadly decision. With us gone who was left to testify against him? His brother, on the other hand, hadn't quite put it all together.

"Now, wait a minute," David stammered, "I jest thought ta hurt'em some…not to…"

"Stop thinkin'! Ya ain't got whut it takes ta think! 'Sides, idjet, you put us here! Now, jest go find the bitch!"

"But…"

"Now!"

Shrugging, the younger Garrison turned, but had not taken two steps when Pete, for some inexplicable reason, shouted, "Fuck you, Garrisons! Fuck you both! Fuck you!"

David, who had recovered his knife, turned back. Dee simply stared at Pete as if he'd lost his mind; which, in my way of thinking, he had. Otherwise, why would he purposely aggravate someone who literally had our lives in his pistol hand? But before I had time to contemplate, Dee shouted at Pete, "Didn't I tell ya ta get over here?"

Despite the rage in Garrison's voice, Pete didn't budge.

"Did you hear?"

"I heard y', butthead!" Pete yelled, defiantly. Suddenly another dawning; Pete was buying time, time not only for Dawn to get away, if she hadn't done so already, but time for me to clear my head, suppress my pain, and be of some use in what had become a life-or-death situation. He understood Garrison's character better than most. Stripped of every other facade, Garrison was still, at heart, a bully; Coach Dodd had proven that last fall. And bullies usually responded only to bigger bullies, or at least someone willing to stand up to them. That's what Pete was doing... standing up to him. If the truth be known, he was also trying to apply the advice I had offered earlier...confuse him. And it seemed to be working, because Garrison looked confused. But he was also determined.

"If you ain't over here by the time I count ta' three, yore a dead man.." He continued obdurately, voice labored with pain, which I was happy to have inflicted

Pete will probably get himself shot. I thought, shaking my head, somehow trying to force myself back into alertness. *Pete thinks I'm helpless...which isn't all bad because Garrison has to think the same thing.* Pete and I had tried contacting each other through mental telepathy ever since we'd had a seventh grade teacher who firmly believed that it was entirely possible. Now, I concentrated every fiber, neuron and nerve cell of my thoroughly addled brain, trying to get a message to Pete that I was okay.

Just stall him until I can get things together! Just stall him. And, for heaven's sake, don't enrage him any more than he is already!

He got the wrong message.

"Garrison, you are a useless bag of shit. You and your idiot brother. I don't give a fuck what you do."

Even though I agonized silently, I could have predicted Pete's response. He'd read one too many Tarzan novels, and had been radically impressed by the ape-man's penchant for facing certain death with the icy calm of an English Lord. Only there had been nothing calm nor English about his insults, and this crazy sonofabitch was about to gun him down! Couldn't he see that? *Damn you!* I raged impotently. *Has fatigue addled you? Has your good sense floated down the creek with that tree limb?*

"One," Garrison croaked, so furious he was barely able to get the sound out.

I had to do something. But what? Pete faced him with the stoicism of a zombie. I rejected the thought of trying to tackle him. If the gun went off accidentally, Pete was in the direct line of fire. But wait, wasn't he out of bullets? *Can't take that chance...*

"Two," Garrison rasped. His back was to me. If I could make it to him, I might be able to do something...anything. Maybe if I distracted him, Pete could take him out before he'd be able to turn and shoot me. As silently as I could, and with no little effort, I made it up to my knees. I was on the verge of lunging for him when…

"Three!"…and a number of things happened more or less simultaneously.

A loud, deep "BOOM!" reverberated down the limestone banks and, a foot in front of Garrison, a spray of water erupted from hundreds of tiny impacts in a small circle. Stunned, Garrison stopped in his tracks and looked up at the bank. Following suit, we could not have been greeted by a happier sight. To our amazement, and for the last time he ever would, Buddy Phillips towered above us on the near bank, sturdy legs in a shooter's stance, a smoking double-barrel shotgun cradled against his shoulder. "The next one's for you, Garrison!" he yelled.

"Buddy!" Pete shouted, flabbergasted and grinning like Christmas.

Buddy ignored Pete's greeting. "Now drop that…that pistol!" he yelled, his voice quavering. "I said drop it!" Buddy repeated. To one side, David appeared confused, twisting the knife aimlessly. He looked over at Dee, who remained impassive.

"Shoot the sonofabitch, Buddy!" Pete yelled. I was sure he was kidding.

"I will." replied Buddy, waving the tip of the gun around. "I'll shoot ya'."

"The fuck you will!" Dee said in a rock-firm voice.

"Pull the trigger, Buddy! Shoot him!" Pete yelled insistently.

"I…I will." Buddy answered, sounding very hesitant.

"Yeah, Buddy, you go on and shoot! Why don't you *shoot,* you stupid little fuck?" Garrison challenged sarcastically, acutely aware of Buddy's anxiety.

"You…you…you better believe I will."

"I believe you a lyin', scared little boy! That's what I believe, you little fuck!"

"Goddamn Buddy! Stop foolin' around and shoot that piece of shit!"

"Shutup, Pete!" I barked, sensing the sudden departure of Buddy's former resolve.

"But he needs to…"

"He needs to stay calm and keep that gun on these guys."

"Stay calm's *ass!*" Pete erupted, obviously enraged at my interference. Now I had a hothead and a faintheart to contend with, as well as the Garrisons. With each passing moment, Buddy's nerves were turning to clabber. *My, God,* I thought, *he's shaking...visibly shaking.*

I knew something had to be done quickly, and was on the verge of doing it when, without warning, Garrison turned to his brother and said, "Get up there and get that little fucker."

"Me? Why do I have to?" David replied.

"Fuck you then! I'll do it myself!" Dee roared, starting up the embankment.

Both Pete and I sensed what was about to happen. "Watch it Buddy! Watch it!" Pete yelled. But it was too late...

Buddy panicked! He leveled the shotgun, cocked the hammer and closed his eyes; and I'm certain he intended to pull the trigger. But then, the sure-footed little halfback shuffled his feet and slipped on the wet grass of the upper bank. With a loud BOOM! the gun discharged into the wild blue yonder as a flailing Buddy tumbled down the embankment, slamming into Garrison, whose too-late attempt to get out of the way left him squarely in the path of the flip-flopping marksman. At the same time, the shotgun and the pistol flew from respective grasps, cartwheeled lazily into the air and splattered into the muck at the bottom of the incline. Garrison and Buddy flopped closely behind, rolling into an unceremonious heap at our feet.

Almost instantly, my wits returned and I yelled, "Now!"

Pete charged the hapless younger brother, who had been standing stunned, watching the Jack 'n Jill routine on the bank. Pete wrapped his arm around David's neck and pulled him back toward the water. I lunged at Dee as Buddy scrambled to one side. I rammed into him and drove him into the mud. I cocked my fist but, as I raised my arm, pain radiated through my shoulder and slowed the strike. Dee saw it coming and blocked it easily.

Dee outweighed me by nearly fifty pounds and easily reversed our positions; grabbing my hurt arm, jerking me over and slamming me into the muck. He rolled on top of me, pinning my arms with his knees, and was about to smash me in the face when Buddy leaped on his back and wrapped his arms around his head. For a moment, the larger man struggled with our diminutive friend, but then simply ripped his arms loose and flung him aside. I saw the opening and, with my good arm, clubbed a solid shot into Garrison's injured ribs. It was his turn to scream, and scream he did, clutching his side. He careened to one side and I got up quickly and kicked him clumsily, but to good effect, in the same spot. As he roared in pain, I stole a quick glance at Pete.

He had dragged David well into the stream and had one arm locked in an upward position with his own forearm securely pressing against the back of his neck so that his face was underwater. It was plain to me that Pete intended to drown him, but David used his free hand to jab the knife over his shoulder at Pete. Pete had to concentrate on keeping away from the knife and David managed to get his head back above water. In the meantime, I had to return to my own problems.

Garrison had retrieved the empty shotgun from the mud and, swinging it by the barrels, took a series of pretty healthy cuts at me. He finally clipped me on the shoulder and knocked me off balance, but Buddy charged him from the opposite side only to be whacked in the ribs… which had to hurt. My war became kind of jumbled after that… fights are disorienting anyway. I found myself struggling with Garrison for control of the weapon and, although I was certainly mobile and strong for my age, he had the bulk advantage, and it was all muscle. He took the shotgun away from me like I was last year's prom queen. But he was looking past me…. at something else. He dropped the shotgun and strode by me, shoving me out of the way as if I was completely inconsequential, which I guess I pretty much was by that time. He walked a few feet, bent, and retrieved the pistol; just jerked it up out of the mud and started laughing. My heart sank.

David Garrison still had his knife, for all the good it was doing him. He was no knife fighter and Pete wasn't even moving much to dodge his clumsy, slashing attempts. Nonetheless, we could not seem to maintain an advantage. David had the knife and Dee had a pistol we weren't sure was loaded, but couldn't risk finding out the hard way. Nonetheless, they were armed and we weren't.

Dee Garrison was aiming the pistol at Pete. But physically, he was spent and was having a hard time getting the heavy sidearm steadied. Finally, he raised his shooting hand and extended it to level, grasping his shooting wrist with his off hand. I knew he'd shoot as soon as the sight came even with Pete. There was nothing to lose, so I planted a foot to charge him… which I knew, in all likelihood, would be futile. Then fortune's tide turned again…

With a savage roar, a four-legged, eighty pound devil in black launched himself over the edge of the bank and landed squarely on Dee's chest, knocking him flat on his back, gleaming fangs driving deep into the hollow of his shoulder. The big dog's head jerked back and forth, the flesh rending with each yank.

Right behind him a red blur charged across the rock shelf to land on David, ivory scimitars scissoring through his forearm to grind against bone. The knife clattered away harmlessly. One hundred sixty pounds of black and red fury had finally located their deities and they would kill *anything* that threatened them. They were far too quick, savage, and efficient for any man to defend against. Dee knew only that something horrible was happening to him. Shrieking in horror, he attempted to crawl under a ledge. Fuzzy shifted his grip, went for his groin and was rewarded with a more yielding target than a shoulder. Dee screamed with frightening intensity as Fuzzy savaged his scrotum.

The younger brother did what most people do when attacked by a fury they cannot comprehend. He turned away. And, as he did, Jeff released the grip on his arm, seeking deeper purchase in an exposed backside, driving fangs that could kill into his flank just above the hip. David turned, howling with pain and fear. Dragged relentlessly down by the red demon, he tripped and fell over his prostrate brother. With their targets rendered *hors de combat,* the dogs closed for the kill, executing the process like their wolf forbearers… with merciless efficiency. Luckily, my conscience was working. We'd seen them kill more than one dog. We knew what they were like at a kill… and, at that moment, that was their intent.

With nowhere to run, no place to hide, no help in sight, the brothers kicked frantically at apparitions that ripped, tore, and flayed… that were everywhere and nowhere at the same time. Their savagery was chilling to Buddy, whose expression bore the grim realization that Fuzzy and Jeff would finish the job if we didn't intervene. Pete and I watched with fascination, and more than a little vengeance, as they carried the day. I wasn't worried; I knew we could call them off. And the Garrisons weren't long in figuring out that their salvation lay with us.

"Git 'em offa' me! Git 'em offa' me! Git 'em off!" Ohhhhh Hep me! Lord God…git 'em off!" The bawling and blubbering ran together and we couldn't tell which of them was howling the loudest. Pete stood nearby, arms folded. I believe to this day that he was enjoying the carnage.

"Pete!" I yelled. "That's enough!" I stepped forward and seized Fuzzy's ruff, "Fuzzy, that's enough, boy…that's enough. Pete, damnit…get Jeff offa' him!

Pete regarded me with obvious displeasure then shrugged and reached for Jeff's collar. "Awright Jeff, c'mere." But he did it half-heartedly, barely pulling Jeff off a pleading David, Jeff's front feet off the ground, legs stiff, eyes wild, thick saliva drooling. Most people can find the point when they're "even", but that was something of a problem with Pete. He was never fully satisfied that "even", as a status, had been achieved. In a fight, he would always hit, or kick…or bite his adversary one last time. Now, he feigned Jeff's collar slipping out of his hand. Pete was a terrible actor… never managed to fool me. Roaring in to finish things, the big dog savaged David's calf, splitting the skin from knee to ankle exposing and tearing the thick, underlying muscle. "Pete!" I yelled, horrified. He shrugged, but pulled Jeff firmly away.

We held them at bay, their short, chopping barks echoing down an otherwise silent creek. We petted and "good dogged" them until they began to relax. But there was no doubt of their intentions as fearsome growls issued from both at the brothers' slightest movement.

"Oh, God hep'! God hep' us! Them dogs gonna' kill us, Dee! Oh, Hep me! Oh God, hep' us!" David wailed, his hands up to shield him against a murderous fury restrained only by whatever mercy we were willing to demonstrate. I tired of his whining.

"Oh God *SHUT UP!*" I snapped in disgust. Pete made a deprecatory gesture.

"An' there they are….. the big, brave Garrison brothers. Get a load o' this shit! How 'bout it now Dee? You ain't afraid of 'em? Huh? Whatsa' matter Dee? You runnin' y' big mouth earlier. Whatta' y' got to say now?"

But Dee didn't respond to Pete. He had only one thing in mind.

"We do anything you want," he begged, "jist keep 'em dogs away from us. Don't let 'em at us no more. They kill us you don't keep 'em off. We done had enough".

I didn't trust Dee. He was too mean to ever give up. I figured he had another trick up his sleeve; but Pete entertained no such thoughts. He cleared his sinuses and spat on him, in what for Pete was - almost - the ultimate gesture of contempt. He would have urinated on him, had he the slightest idea that I would have countenanced it.

Dee might have been devious, but David was howling and blubbering in great, heaving sobs. Both of them were torn, ripped, and bloodied from more slashes and punctures than we could count. Fuzzy had torn a deep gouge in the side of Dee's neck, from which there was a considerable flow of blood. I motioned for Pete to look at it.

"Don't ask me t' do that, Don," he complained, "I don't care if that half wit bleeds to death." But I knew he'd do what I asked him. He finally grabbed a handful of greasy hair, and gently enough to satisfy being humane - which truly surprised me - inspected the upper extremity he had most recently been doing his best to hold underwater until its owner expired. "It ain't spurtin', so he ain't gonna' die," he observed, and spat on him as well. The Garrisons were no longer menacing. They were just whipped.

Maintaining a rein on my fine furry friend, I bent over and picked up the knife which, ironically, lay at my feet. I didn't let the glistening blade enthrall me again. Instead, I started to throw the weapon down the creek. Then I remembered doing that before and paying a fearful price for my carelessness. I looked at Pete, kneeling and stroking a still rumbling Jeff, grinned, and flipped the gleaming blade squarely into the middle of the whirlpool.

Groaning in pain, the Garrison boys helped each other up. Dee placed an arm around his younger brother's shoulders, still shaken, but once more glaring defiantly at us. "You fuckheads ain't shit without them mutts." He growled. And, for a moment, I fully expected him to abandon his fear and charge…but, if he did entertain such thoughts, they were quickly deterred by a voice booming from above…

"Garrison, you think you're some sorta bad? You ain't so bad!" Immediately, all eyes shot to the top of the incline.

231

It was Bric Dodd, looming above us, furiously rubbing his ear, words reverberating like the voice of God. Shocked, we stood, eyes wide, mouths agape.

"Coach Dodd!" Buddy yelled.

The Garrisons took off.. No signal, no warning, no cue. They simply turned and splashed awkwardly downstream, their courage left somewhere in the rapidly receding waters of Ten Mile Creek. The fierce Garrisons, braver than the brave when armed to the hilt, tucked tail and ran away.

Instinctively, Pete and I started to release the dogs, but once again, as it had done so often on the football field and in the classroom, Dodd's voice stopped us. "Hold them dogs, boys!" he yelled matter-of-factly. Immediately we restrained Fuzzy and Jeff, stifling their efforts to run the Garrisons down.

"But, Coach…" Pete started to object.

"They'll be runnin' into Constable Hastings at the Sixty-Seven Bridge." Dodd interrupted. "He'll handle 'em."

"Coach they…"

"I know, Robbins." He again interrupted. "I know. By God, boy, you did learn how to hit someone."

We weren't sure how long Coach Dodd had been there or how much he had witnessed but, at the moment, he seemed the seat of all knowledge, the purveyor of all instruction, the omnipotent distributor of all we ever hoped or dreamed. Still, I felt compelled to speak…"But, Coach they…"

"And remember, Shook," he continued, this time interrupting me as if I wasn't there, "this fall I don't want you ever callin' a "T" play inside the ten yard line. That's not what I want from my varsity quarterback."

Immediately, a surge of adrenaline shot through me and, I swear, sunlight exploded all around us and every bird on Ten Mile Creek sang in harmony.

"By, God," Dodd said, turning and starting off, "I got me some of my Tough Twenty right here…Yeah, I'll get that cage 'n wagon 'n we'll…" his banter faded as he walked away, voice melding into the rain-soaked undergrowth. God had come and gone.

232

There was a moment of silence, then we all turned and looked at each other. Finally, Buddy broke the silence, "What'a ya think he meant by..."

"Buddy..." I snapped.

Pete finished my sentence, "...don't be cattle."

Then, to our great surprise, Dawn stepped from behind the rock shelf. "Hey, you guys."

"My God, Dawn!" I blurted out, moving to her and receiving a lingering hug. "We thought you had..." Before I could finish, she disengaged to hug Pete, while Buddy patiently waited for his chance.

"Guys, can we just go home?" She said, almost pleadingly, offering no explanation as to where she had been the last twenty minutes. But we didn't care. We were just overjoyed to see her.

"You bet." I answered.

So it seemed our saga ended as quickly as the storm. I knelt in front of my beautiful ugly dog and praised him mightily. "Good dog, Fuzzy. Good dog," I kept repeating, hugging him as fat, salty tears ran down my cheeks. He, of course, like any good dog, expressed his feelings with licks, whines and rough paws to my bruised body. Pete sat on the outcropping stroking Jeff's head, lavishing "Good Boys" on the great red dog as he cradled his hurt hand to his side.

"Reckon they'll ever mess with us again?" he asked.

Gingerly rubbing the knot on my head, I walked over and sat beside him, Fuzzy dogging my steps. "Not a chance."

"Well, then. That's that."

"That's what?"

He looked at me cynically, "Dummy." he sighed.

I grinned and we both laughed quietly, petting our dogs and staring blankly into space for several silent moments.

Finally, Pete broke the tranquility, "How did they know where to find us? How in the hell did they know?"

"The dogs?"

"No, the Garrisons, stupid. Of course, the dogs."

"They're just smart animals."

"Yeah, but trailin' us through all that storm, and showing up at just the right time?"

I sighed and scratched the big black head resting on my knee, with the placid eyes looking up at me as if ready to answer. I then looked over at Jeff, sitting beside Pete, his mud-caked fur drying in the warming sun. I looked at Pete and then straight ahead before saying, "Well, you know collies." We were too tired to laugh again.

I suddenly turned my attention to our other two companions. "You two ready?"

Before answering, Dawn kneeled in the shallows and began splashing water on her face.

"I cain't wait to get home 'n cleanup."

"Yeah," Buddy said, following suit, "and get some real clothes on, I bet."

That blindsided *us*. For the first time since the storm had begun we were suddenly aware of Dawn's dilemma. My dirty T-shirt barely covered her privates and, quite honestly, she was so battered and bruised that she resembled anything but our high-school heartthrob. She'd been fine until Buddy mentioned it, but made so immediately aware of her attire, she blushed…but I'm not sure it was due to embarrassment. She'd revealed much more that day than anyone expected. Watching her, dripping wet and disheveled, yet still glowing with subdued radiance, my heart went into a series of flip-flops. However, I thought it best to change the subject. "Buddy, what a surprise you showin' up. You saved our butts."

"Yeah," Pete jumped in, "and where'd you get that gun 'n how'd you find us?"

"Well," Buddy, still quite shaken by the experience, replied, "the shotgun belongs to Kara Lynn's aunt."

"Jane?"

"Yeah, we went by her place earlier, before the storm hit, 'n found her in pretty bad shape."

"Bad shape? Then she's not…" Dawn asked, not really sure what to think.

"Yep, them Garrisons robbed her 'n cut her pretty bad."

"She's gonna' be all right?"

"She's tough. Kara Lynn 'n me got her to the clinic, then I drove on down to the bridge. I braked too hard and put her dad's car in a ditch. I seen ya'lls bikes down there where you told me you hide 'em, then I heard gunshots...so I just put two 'n two together..."

"...and got here just in time." Pete said, finishing Buddy's sentence.

"Buddy," I interrupted, moving to him and patting his shoulder, "you were really somethin' today."

It was the diminutive half-back's time to be embarrassed. "Aw, Geewhiz you guys...I..."

Dawn suddenly broke into tears. I immediately shot a glance at Pete, who bit his lip and looked back helplessly. Dawn rose and turned her back to the rest of us, reluctant to share whatever she was feeling, continuing to sob. Pete motioned to me. I walked over and put my arms around her. She turned, not looking up, just burying her head in my shoulder. She managed to find the hurt one. I flinched, but held fast, realizing my physical pain didn't compare with the flood of emotional torture breaking loose inside her. I started to speak, but stopped...knowing nothing I could say would suffice. Then I began to cry, tears streaming down my cheeks to fall onto her matted auburn mane. I glanced over my shoulder and saw that Pete was staring at us through reddened eyes. He coughed and turned away. We weren't going to see him cry. Finally, I broke away saying..."Hey, let's go home."

With the others falling in behind, I started upstream. We hadn't taken a dozen sloshy steps when we all stopped at the sound of splashing behind us. Turning and looking in the direction of the noise, we saw a fierce struggle going on in the shallows. Something was tearing up the surface, something was fighting to...then I recognized it! Flopping half-in-and-half-out of the water was the Monster, the Birm Of Brim valiantly fighting for the depths, still hooked and, lacking the strength to pull the cane pole any further, battling for its life in the shallows.

"My God, it's the Monster!" I yelled, suddenly realizing what was going on.

"The Monster?" Buddy yelled back, waiting for a reply that never came because Pete and I, Fuzzy and Jeff on our heels, were too busy splashing through shallows.

The King was going nuts, thrashing and swirling about, desperately trying to break away. Quickly, I waded into the deeper water and seized the line above the lead weight near the Monster's head and lifted the fish up out of the water. There was still plenty of fight in him as, even suspended helplessly in the air, he fought to shake free of the hook.

"Get back dogs!" I yelled, holding the King high above my head. He, like us, was battered and bruised. The dorsal fin was shredded and a multitude of scales were missing. The tail was tattered and, all in all, the mighty warrior looked as though he had been through the wars. Still, considering the length of time he'd been hooked and the enormous stress of the struggle, he was far from being counted out…tough little fish, those brim.

For a moment I held him squirming in the air, the sunlight glimmering off the wet, muscular body. As the dogs kept leaping up attempting to reach the Monster, I glanced over at Pete and could read his parallel thoughts. Anyone in their right mind would take the prize to the nearest taxidermist. The fish was a giant of his kind, a record, weighing at least two, maybe three, pounds. Mounted on a den wall, he would inspire countless "Oooohhhss" and "Aaaahhhss" from all those who knew anything about brim fishin'. But…it had not been a day for right minds and I knew the inspiration of the moment was enough to last a lifetime.

"Poor fish, it's so pretty." Dawn said, almost sadly

That did it. I carefully removed the hook from his torn lower lip and gently placed the Monster in the shallows at our feet. "Get away, Fuzzy," I barked, shoving his muzzle aside. He and Jeff had the curiosity of cats. "Move Jeff, bad dog!" I couldn't admonish one and not the other. Whining protests, they backed off. For an endless few seconds the fish remained motionless, a shadow caught between the worlds of fear and freedom. Was he too exhausted to make it? Then, the fins moved slightly, a bit faster, the gills expanded fractionally, then fanned back and forth, and, with a flick of his tail, he was gone…a brilliant shadow shot into the violet depths of freedom.

Fuzzy and Jeff could control themselves no longer as they splashed to the spot where the King had been. They pawed the water, sniffed about and then, deciding there were better things to do, ran around play-fighting in the water, getting thoroughly re-drenched.

I cupped my hands over my face and inhaled deeply, breathing in the pungent smell, absorbing the memory of the passing of the King.

"I didn't know brims grew that big." Buddy remarked.

"They don't."

"Boy, he was a whopper," Pete added, still quite impressed.

"He was the King," I responded, feeling a little depressed.

"Think he'll ever bite again?"

"Would you?" I asked sharply.

"Not after what he went through."

I looked at him thoughtfully, wondering if I looked as haggard as he did. Then I surveyed Dawn standing a few feet away basking in the warmth and security of the sunlight. She too looked like a battlefield casualty, but was recovering splendidly. In fact, she almost seemed to glow. The experience of the day flashed before me; and I reviewed it detached, uninvolved, as though it were a book I had read or a picture I'd seen. The whole thing seemed so unreal, like a dream turned nightmare and back. But we were waking up. Hadn't we jumped on our bikes and started down the hill only a few moments ago? "He'll bite." I said. "They always do."

The day had turned a brilliant yellow, with golden streams of sunlight sifting through the treetops. The merciless heat had been tempered by the deluge, and the humidity had lifted. A refreshing breeze puffed its way down the creek. Somewhere downstream, Bluejays scolded pesky sparrows as they competed for footing beside a freshly formed pool. A red squirrel darted up a glistening elm, unhindered by wet bark or dripping leaves. Soon, a multitude of frogs began harmonizing with countless crickets in a chorus of joy over the land's newfound wetness. Insects that had folded their wings and hunkered down, leaped back to activity - buzzing, flying and humming in ecstasy engendered by the recent rain. Above, the sky shone clear bright and baby blue, freshly scrubbed and stretching out to dry.

TO KILL A FAT PIG

We worked our way back up the creek, gathering our scattered gear as we went. Fuzzy and Jeff ran ahead, splashing like pups in the stream then tearing after something... or each other... through the undergrowth. "Well, at last I got to meet Fuzzy 'n Jeff," Dawn observed wryly.

After the storm, the pools along the way were much deeper, and the stream, which usually washed clear and sparkling over the limestone bottom, ran muddy. Overhead, the huge trees glistened in a riotous hue of greens. Bright sunlight filtered through, and we trudged wearily through oddly patterned shadows. The world felt crisp, fresh, and cleansed by the storm. Finally, we sloshed past the stand of willows and the bridge hove in sight.

I felt a tug on my arm. "Look, there's people up on the bridge," Pete said.

My heart rate quickened, thinking that by some possible quirk of circumstances the Garrison boys had regrouped and were waiting for us. Then I saw the white car, then the lights on the roof, then the big man in a suit standing at its rear. He was standing next to someone I couldn't quite make out; but Dawn was off and running.

"Mama!" she screamed as she raced ahead. At that moment I was reminded, despite all she had been through, that she really was just a teenage girl...not a sex object, mysterious vixen, or alluring temptress. That would, without doubt, change the second I was able to regard her in tight white shorts and halter top, with her hair brushed, shining, and scented faintly of roses. But right now, she was just a little girl seeking the comfort of her mother's arms. Fuzzy and Jeff bounded after and then ahead of her, scaling the muddy embankment with ease, tail-wagging up to Mrs. Ferguson. They barked back at us to hurry up.

"Funny, ain't it," Pete observed, "how they know who our friends are."

"Yes," I responded, "and who they aren't."

We found our bikes still tucked away in our hiding place, and moved them up onto the road. Dawn was wrapped in her mother's arms. We acknowledged Mrs. Ferguson with a nod.

The big man turned to us...

"I'm Sheriff Bill Decker. Me an' about twenty o' my deputies an' about half this town's been lookin' for all three o' you kids, and I sure am glad you're alright." Bill Decker was the longtime Sheriff of Dallas County and a famous lawman. He didn't show up at every crime scene, but the reported kidnap of a high school girl would bring him running. Pete and I didn't know what to say, but Buddy was at no loss for words.

"It was them Garrisons, Sheriff Decker. They uh, they…stabbed old Miss Jane down at her store…done stabbed her…uh… 'n robbed her too, then they… they…"

"Now settle down, young man. I know all about them Garrisons. What I wanta' know now, is what's been goin' on down here. "

"Well for starters, they tried to kill us." Pete said.

"Well, everything's okay now, boys. They was picked up down to the Highway Sixty-Seven bridge. They in custody now."

Unable to contain himself, Buddy continued, "Sheriff Decker! I… uh… I shot at 'em Sheriff Decker! Shot at 'em with this here shotgun!"

"Better let me have that, Buddy." Decker responded, extending a big hand for the weapon, which Buddy dutifully handed over.

"Those Garrisons are crazy," I said, wanting to get my two-cents worth in, and suddenly we were all talking at the same time, trying to tell as much as we could about the experience.

In only a few seconds, Decker had heard enough. "Boys… boys… it's okay. We'll all go down to the fire station an' you can tell me everything. Right now, I got anxious mothers and a couple o' vigilante dads to deal with. How 'bout ya'll, Miz Ferguson? That little girl alright?"

"I just need to git her home," she grunted.

"Sheriff Decker?" Dawn interjected, "You know anything about Miss Jane?"

"Well, her niece was at the doctor's office and said the old lady was doin' as good as could be expected. The doc stitched her up and she was sayin' she wanted to go home. So I wouldn't worry all that much. Now, you two git in the car here, and we gonna' git you home." He opened the door for Dawn and her mother. Just before Dawn got in,

239

she turned to me. Our eyes met and locked in instant understanding, sentences without words. She smiled and mouthed, "Thank you."

"You boys think we can get them bikes in the trunk?" Decker asked.

"We'll ride 'em home if it's okay, Sheriff. It's not that far." I answered. "Buddy's gonna' need a lift though." I continued, glancing across at the road at the disabled Chevrolet.

"Yeah," Pete chirped, " 'Cause I ain't gonna' pump him."

I laughed, adding, "Anyway, he deserves a ride after what he did."

Decker grinned briefly. "Well then climb on in up here with me."

The big Sheriff paused a moment and his level gaze penetrated to our bones. "Have your folks bring you down to the fire station after you get cleaned up and the doc looks you over." He paused, sighed, and looked away for a moment. "An' one thing I gotta' know. How'd you boys manage to get the best of somebody mean as them two?"

Pete stared at the ground.

"Collies." I answered quickly.

"Collies?" Decker pushed his fedora back and scratched his forehead.

"Yes sir." I said. "Best dogs ever were."

Decker took off his hat, shot Fuzzy and Jeff a questioning look, got into the car and started the engine.

Dawn turned and looked out the rear window. Her eyes met mine, and I knew that this time I had not disappointed her. I also knew, as the car ground through the gears and gradually faded out of sight, that I would never forget her.

"It is soooo sweet the way she looks at me." Pete said abruptly.

"Looks at who?" I snapped. He shook his head ruefully, as if I was a total idiot and he had to explain everything to me. *From the top of the trestle, it's almost fifty feet down.* The thought was refreshingly delightful.

"And did you feel the tip of that sweet little pink tongue when you kissed her… like I did?" he continued with a knowing leer.

"Shutup!" I snapped, knowing he was dead on the mark. Obviously, he had taken advantage and stolen a kiss while carrying her.

I was furious, but too exhausted to do anything about it. "And don't you start anything. Let's just get outta here, I'm starvin'." Pete was already standing on his pedals and pumping hard. As I pulled beside him, I had a thought, "You know," I said, "I'm glad I got witnesses, 'cause nobody would ever believe I caught the Monster."

"Witnesses?" Pete asked, staring straight ahead.

"Sure, you, Buddy 'n Dawn."

"What're you talkin' about?

"You all saw me catch it."

"Ain't nobody seen you catch nothin'."

"Sure you did!"

"Ain't seen you catch nothin'," he repeated.

"What? You know I caught the Monster!"

"There you go…dreamin' again." Pete said, pumping hard and moving ahead of me.

"Jerk!" I spat.

"Dummy!"

"Cattle!"

"Cain't cattle a King Cattler!"

"You *are* cattle!"

And so the banter continued as we pedaled away from Ten Mile Creek. Except for the ditched new convertible, everything seemed back to normal. The sun returned to its duties, birds chirped and flitted, gnats swarmed, and horseflies buzzed to the attack. And we knew tomorrow the wily, watchful brim would be waiting for us as usual.

241

POSTLUDE

The Garrison boys were convicted of assault, battery, attempted murder, kidnapping, and several other offenses, but not rape. The younger one was committed to the state institution in Terrell, and died there many years later. The older one pleaded out, and was duly incarcerated in the Texas prison system. He got out on parole after a few years, only to be quickly caught in a two-bit burglary, committed again, paroled, convicted of indecency with a minor and sent away for a very long stretch. The last I heard, he was still serving time.

Fuzzy died a year after our adventure. On one of his cross-country journeys he was badly torn up, and a subsequent infection required us to have him put down. My beautiful, ugly dog enjoyed life to the hilt. Jeff lived on for many years, the object of much affection, always a friend and protector, and no doubt missing his buddy. He died in 1967, at the age of fourteen. Pete chiseled out a deep grave for him in the limestone bedrock of his back yard.

Dawn didn't return to school the next year. We rode by her house several times, but it was empty. The only thing that moved was a tattered screen door banging open and closed in the hot, fitful Texas wind. Many stories circulated concerning her whereabouts, but none ever panned out. I never saw her again. She simply disappeared…fading into memory like the beautiful dream she was.

Pete and I remain fast friends. Although we live several hundred miles apart, we stay in touch. He's married, has kids, and continues to regard most people as Cattle. On occasion, he can still be an opinionated ass; and now, as then, I relish telling him so. The years have exacted their due and we've slipped a little…probably more than we'd care to admit. But show us a nicely shaded hole of water in a gently flowing creek, put cane poles and a pack of salt pork in our hands, and we'll show you a heavy stringer of brim. We often laugh about our experiences at Ten Mile Creek.

Bluehole no longer exists. Civilization and residential zoning took its toll, reducing the once mysterious body of water to a wide spot in a polluted creek. Some of the trees remain, but the wildlife and the brim have been replaced by houses, people, and manicured lawns. You would never recognize it as a once lovely fishin' hole. That seems a shame, because I'm certain somewhere among those houses and people... are two teenage boys who'd love to be after the Monster at Bluehole.

THE END

Made in the USA